TH

MOON IN

THE WEIR

A NOVEL

Brian Carter

Illustrated by the author

Best Wishes,
Brian Carter

Torbay Books
7 Torquay Road   Paignton   Devon TQ3 3DU

By the same author

A Black Fox Running
In The Long Dark
Yesterday's Harvest
South Devon Inn Outings

Carter Country
Jack
Lundy's War
Nightworld
Walking in the Wild
Where the Dream Begins

First published 1984 J. M. Dent Ltd.
Republished 2011 Torbay Books
Copyright © 2011 Text and illustrations: Brian Carter

Torbay Books
7 Torquay Road, Paignton, Devon TQ3 3DU

Printed and bound by CPI Antony Rowe, Eastbourne

The otter

The dog otter came bounding up the coombe through the wild daffodils, reeds and flags to the well-head of the River Hems. Moonlight slashed across the departing shower and stampeded the landscape out of darkness. It was a countryside of round hills, small fields, copses and narrow lanes. The wind roaring down from the north east had brought snow to the tors of Dartmoor and sleet and rain to South Devon. Barbed wire and grass quivered with restless energy, exciting the otter who was keenly aware of everything around him.

The moon blazed then faded and another squall buffeted the coombe only to race on leaving a silvery wetness behind it. The otter's leaps were heavy. He thumped down his front feet, humped his back and flung his hindfeet forward, moving in undulations that were characteristic of most of the weasel family to which he belonged. Since his birth two years previously he had hunted the head-waters of the rivers Teign, Exe and Okement, searching for a mate. But no bitch had answered his whistling and he had become a wanderer.

From nose to the tip of his tail he measured a little less than four feet. Rain winked on his umber-coloured coat and his broad, flat head, and tiny drops beaded the tips of his whiskers. Bits of goose-grass clung to the pale hairs of his throat and chest. Although he had left the Teign soon after dusk the showers had failed to wash away the brackish smell of mud from his coat. He stopped suddenly and shook himself. Almost at once the sleekness vanished and his fur became darker and spiky. Arching his neck he sniffed the air, pricking his small ears and mirroring the moon in round, black eyes. Then once more the rain roared down, louder than the stream but not as noisy as the wind in the oaks on the slopes of Sladesdown. Earlier that night the otter had taken eels from the Teign and eaten crayfish and frogs among the cressbeds of the Kester Brook. But the mating hunger hollowing his belly persisted and at times he felt as taut as the barbed wire that was singing between the fenceposts.

Leaving the Hems he lolloped on past Parkfield, Bulland and Baddaford to Five Lanes where his instinct betrayed him. The wind had risen to gale force and was scattering the blackthorn blossom from the hedgetops and opening a rift in the clouds to let the stars in with a rush. It pushed him across two fields and down a wooded slope to the M5. The motorway glinted black like a wide, frozen river. Under the trees the otter hesitated. The strong smell of petrol and carbonized oil mystified him for it conjured up no image of creature or thing in his mind.

A blur of noise and light opened the darkness, crescendoed and was gone. The otter slithered down the bank onto the grass verge and bounded across the slow lane. He was half-way into the middle lane when another glaring stream of light burst around him and sudden thunder had him hissing with terror. He laid back his ears and crouched before the sunburst that roared out of the night. Fear dribbled from the scent glands at the base of his tail and wreathed him in musk. But the driver of the articulated lorry had glimpsed something dark and long-tailed in his headlamp beams.

'Christ', he grated, and his knuckles whitened on the steering wheel.

Then the lorry was swerving into the fast lane and the windblast made the otter stagger. He sneezed and bolted back to the trees where the noises and smells were familiar.

By the time he had reached the River Dart half an hour later and stood sniffing the water opposite Buckfastleigh railway station he had forgotten the incident. The river in spate, thundering across the weir, was something he could understand. The moon sailed out of the clouds and the torrent blazed with silver fire. He mounted a rock and deposited a pile of small, glossy, black spraints. The rumbling turmoil

mesmerized him, and the rain intensified the water-smell. He
trod through his instincts and entered the cold swift flow. Ears
and nostrils closed automatically as he submerged and glided
over each arm of the weir to become a swirl in the current.

Before he had met the lorry the dog otter was travelling in a
wide westward loop that would have brought him up the Dart
and across the watersheds of the rivers Tavy, Cowsic and
Walkham to farmland beyond the moors. Now he was letting
fortune carry him over the shallows under Austin's Bridge and
on through the woods where the night was as loud as the
rapids.

He remained underwater for no longer than a minute then
rose for air and sank again. But in the boulder-strewn narrows
he bobbed along on the surface using his tail as a rudder and his
webbed feet dog-paddling when the pace of the river slackened.
Every so often he turned sideways to the current and let it roll
him over and over. His grunting 'hah!' of pleasure was lost in
the din of the spate. The thrill of being one with the water
eclipsed all other emotions and needs. Dimly through the
spray and the thrashing treetops he saw clouds blot the moon
and sail on to leave the sky pale and starry above South Devon.

Brimful of rain the Dart swept him past Derry's Copse into
the lazy S bend that ended at Riverford Bridge and another
weir. Then he was riding a deeper run down to the little island
in front of Staverton Bridge. Here he hauled out, shook himself
and sprainted on the heaped roots of an alder. A car crossed the
bridge as the rain fell hard, dimpling the black polythene
shimmer of the water. Presently the thunder of the long weirs
below the village engulfed him and he swam through clouds of
fizzing bubbles, loving the way the water shuddered around his
body and threw him about. The flux sent its messages along the
whiskers rooted in the nerve pads of his muzzle. He thrust his
nose from the spume and saw the stars flaring and the sky
scribbled over with twigs. Lidding his eyes he tried to bite the
water as he would bite the back of a bitch otter's neck.

The night smelled of something fresh and enigmatic, the
kind of nameless scent of the outdoors a cat carries in its fur
when it comes in from the garden. The otter gave another of
his flat, grunting cries and flew weightlessly on through the
stars and the moonlight which were illusions. He was a
shadow like all the creatures before him that had swum the

Dart since the first dawn. But the river was deathless. It wore the seasons as it wore the moonlight.

Sometimes he encountered large fish swimming upstream but these were full-grown Atlantic salmon on their spring run to the spawning beds and they were too fast for him. When they leapt the silver scales flashed on their flanks. Cobbled with light the river swung through the parkland of Dartington under stands of oaks, spilling into the corners of the meadows but flowing silently now to the final high weir and its tidal waters whose limits were the ancient borough of Totnes. Pushing his pugface out of a storm debris of twigs and grasses the otter saw the new Brutus Bridge looming above him and felt the current surrendering its strength to the flood tide. He paddled through a fresh shower and after it had died the rooftops of the town were gleaming and the three arches of the old bridge framed the stars.

He was among dinghies and motorboats riding at their moorings, and the water tasted briny and was tainted with diesel. The otter swam in midstream. Reeves' timber yard was on his right and the mast of a cargo ship ticked rhythmically against the sky. The night was quieter now but the street lights and the long drawn-out snarl of a motorbike alarmed him. He dipped his head, arched his back and uncoiled in a dive that took him just below the surface. Flexing his body and tail he undulated through the tide.

Aldebaran burnt between cloud banks and in the otter's eyes. He raced down to Fleet Mill Reach and hauled out to rest on the old quay above the hulk of a sand barge. And he rolled in the grass to dry off and lay awhile by the shine of Fleet Mill Pool where mullet were feeding. The otter was hungry and the fish were making rings on the water which was cloudy but not opaque. He loped down the beach of shillet, pebbles and rocks and sank noiselessly through his own reflection.

The mullet flicked to and fro for they had smelled the otter and felt his presence. Then they heard him but could not see him. Wise to their ways he came at the shoal from below, knowing this was their blind spot. They scattered but with one bite he killed the fish of his choice. Returning to the beach he squatted among the driftwood holding the small mullet between his forepaws and cocking his head to eat it, from the nose down, pushing it into the side of his mouth and chewing with his molars until only a few scales remained. After the wind had dropped he heard a tawny owl cry from the farm above the pool.

The moon hung over the trees of Sharpham Point and brightness filled the little wind-sculpted hollows on the river's surface all along the Gut. The otter raised his head from the water and whistled half a dozen times. Each high-pitched note like a birdcall floated away unanswered. And the ache in his stomach hollowed to emptiness. He swam Sharpham and Ham Reaches. The Dart looped broad and deep along the navigation channel to Duncannon. Rising for air he whistled again but caught his breath at the sight of lamps and torches flashing on the shore. The Stoke Gabriel salmon fishermen were shooting their seine nets off the point and four skiffs were strung out close to the banks.

A swirl in midstream marked the place where the otter's tail had broken the surface. He dived and twisted obliquely to the right, using his body as though it were boneless. Broadside to the current he swam, flexing and uncoiling like a porpoise while the choppy ceiling above him fractured the moonlight.

Chance, which is the only law governing a wild creature's existence, brought him to the estuary of the Aishbourne River and Hay Creek. The tide was just right and there were little flatfish which Devonians call flukes in the sand and gravel of the gut. Swimming along the bottom he caught several and carried them one by one to the shallows and fed lying amongst the bladderwrack. The steel stays of yachts vibrated against alloy masts and the metal sang with a high-pitched whine.

The otter ate the last fluke and splashed through the ooze until the water deepened and covered him. He swam lazily beneath the pines of Gibbetfield where the shadows writhed like living creatures. But the tide was turning now and the tops of mudbanks each side of the creek were emerging and gleaming. The reek of seaweed mingled with the fainter smells of the farmland. From a shed somewhere close at hand the barking of a dog was muffled by the wind that shook raindrops out of the trees.

Nosing up the Aishbourne beyond the reach of the tide the otter felt weariness hanging on his limbs and suddenly he wanted no more than a dry place to rest in. He dog-paddled up the shallows, loving the white fangs of water smacking against his chin.

The hamlet of Hay ended at a bow bridge and the river became a narrow, swift-flowing trout stream meandering through meadows and spinneys of oak and dead elms. The night had settled into a hush for the wind had dropped and the water made a pebbly music. Then the moon vanished and rain fell and he climbed onto the bank and shook himself. Several dark shapes rose from the grass and lumbered towards him. And the moon came out again, twinkling on the tips of horns and in dark, solemn eyes. The otter whistled and one of the Friesians lowered her head to sniff the strange creature. Rain streamed off the cow's temples and dripped from her nose. The otter hissed and raised his voice in a yakkering cry that made the Friesian walk backwards to regard him anxiously. Dropping his head he chested the reeds and crossed a ditch full of rushes, reedgrass and water-plantain. He was cold and grumpy but still alert. Presently he found a disused chicken coop under some cider apple trees and crawled inside. An old meal bag made a comfortable couch and the roof kept out the rain which beat across the West Country into the small hours.

His sleep was dreamless. He surfaced from it, yawned and stretched. Through the broken slats of the coop the night was numb with silence and the clouds were gone. The otter returned to the Aishbourne and voided his spraints on a willow stump before taking to the water. A crow began to rasp from one of the many dead elms. Gulls cackled and wailed, and a wren sang behind the harts tongue ferns of the field hedge. The moon had paled and the stark contrast of light and dark was blurring. He pushed on, running through shallow water over shillet and stones, and dog-paddling whenever there was enough depth. Wild brown trout skimmed away and hung in the shadows. Beyond a derelict mill bands of mist lay across the leat. The otter could smell primroses and ramson crushed by the hooves of cattle. Then a reach of deep water persuaded him to swim through cloudy shafts of moonlight, the air bubbles dribbling from his fur.

Under Aishford bridge he encountered a pair of mink crouching on the sill eating an eel. The water weasels stared at him from blank, round eyes and hissed. Their coats of scorched chocolate brown were long-haired like the fur of polecats and ferrets. But the animals were half the size of the otter and shrank from him when he opened his mouth and showed his strong, canine teeth.

The steeple of Aishford church was silhouetted against a sky whose palor held a faint luminosity. Rooks cawed, a blackbird sang. Above the village the river clattered and gurgled over stones and grit or curled silently around spits and banks of flood-moulded silt. Elms, slaughtered by Dutch Elm disease, lined the left bank and there were goat willows in catkin and mounds of blackthorn blossom.

The dog otter plashed through the meadow grass until the woods closed in and forced him back to the water. He ghosted under Whidden Bridge while the geese penned in the nearby orchard bugled their alarm. Smudged gold had crept into the east and birds were on the move. Farm buildings were materializing from what had recently been a misty lake of darkness broken here and there by patches of moonlight.

Once more the river was too narrow for comfort and jumbles of fallen trees blocked the way. He passed beneath another bridge, pausing to spraint on a boulder. Then he took to the fields, skirting the Horridge Inn and the timber yard and cantering along the cattle-creeps under eared sallows and hazels. Longtailed tits and chaffinchs mistook him for a tom cat and began to scold. Now the countryside rang with birdsong, and mallard burst from the water-crowfoot as he crashed over a hedge of gorse and brambles, ducking to avoid the barbed wire. The gold flowers of marsh marigold choked the banks, and the leaves of fool's watercress and wood sorrel were catching some of the sky's brightness on clustered raindrops.

The otter lolloped over boggy ground that had been pockmarked by bullocks' hooves and braided with cowpats. Fields were slowly retrieving their greenness and in the corner of one he found a pool under a dam of flood debris and washed the mud off his paws. A bullock coughed, sheep bleated and a yellow hammer began to sing. He cut through the swirls of coffee-coloured water beside a copse of willows, scrub-oak, alders and ash. Here the trout-swims were four feet deep and the Aishbourne was curving around a marooned alder to scour a pothole from the grit. Every so often he found barbed wire strung across the water but he paddled on until a fallen sallow forced him into the pasture again.

His chin brushed the stiff young reeds and his body furrowed the grass and celandines. A herd of calves stampeded down the hillside to inspect him but he took a badger path over the hedge and leapt the drainage gut. To his right was a larch plantation halfway up a hillside yellowed here and there with gorse. The conifers were dwarfed by the tall oaks of Churchland Woods. Sailing high over the trees the buzzards, who were called coneyhawks by Devon countrymen, dropped their mewling catcalls onto the rabbit runs of Aishwell Common. The otter heard them and stood upright on his hindlegs, bracing himself with his tail. Sunrise touched the ragged wings angled to the thermal and glazed the tops of the trees. Then a shotgun clapped bringing woodpigeons rattling out of the larches. Five swift bounds carried him to the waters edge and his crash-dive sent the trout scurrying for cover. A water shrew hunting the margins of the pool nearly died of shock but escaped by drifting downstream like a ball of brown moss.

Rising among the roots of ash the otter lay in shadow showing only his nostrils. The two coneyhawks had gutted a young rabbit before he ventured from his hiding place and squirmed into the freshet feeding the pool. A hazel branch bobbed up and down as the race plucked at its tip, dragging it six inches and releasing it only to endlessly repeat the act. He trailed his nose along the polished bark feeling secure and invisible under banks of blackthorn and alder scrub. A little islet of mud and reeds had grown up against a half-drowned ash and the water poured each side of it, dirty brown and deep enough to cover a sheep. But the edges were translucent amber and crayfish lay under stones in the silt drifts. He dived and let his whiskers decode the ciphers of the flow, and coming up for air saw the hedges of Drang Cottages to the left. A smallholding of hen houses, runs, a cold frame and several ramshackle huts reached almost to the river.

The farmworkers' cottages were of grey stone and royal blue paintwork. Washing hung on the clothes line and a cock crowed. The otter wrinkled his nose as he caught the smell of pigs and soiled straw wafting from the shed whose front wall incorporated part of the parapet of Woodburn Bridge. Kicking his hindlegs he paddled under the nearer of the two small granite arches. On the sill were mink scats which he sniffed disdainfully before launching himself upstream into a coombe that had remained undisturbed for half a century.

_____ Foxcroft _____

Funnily enough the A49 sweeping Paul Revilious out of Stretford Lacey to the south took him past the place he loathed above all others – Cavendish Towers Preparatory School. For twenty-five years he had taught English Literature and History there to the sons of parents who struggled to find the fees. Everything about the school proclaimed a lack of funds. It was seedy and third rate but managed to squeeze boys into some of the less distinguished public schools which, until the advent of the comprehensive, had sailed perilously close to financial disaster.

In many ways Revilious was the stereotype middle-aged prep schoolmaster. Fate seemed to have stage-managed the down-at-heel gentility that went so well with his badly paid, dull post. And he might still have been, as he put it, 'casting pearls before weaners' if the old lady hadn't died on the eve of her seventy-fifth birthday, leaving him London property, a lot of money and a country house in Devon.

Revilious had read the solicitor's letter three times while the feeling went out of his knees. He hadn't given Aunt Victoria a thought since his mother's funeral in 1957, and he certainly had no idea he was the old lady's heir. 'Heir and sole surviving member of the family,' the solicitor told him over the phone. 'Selling the London property will take care of the death duties.'

Walking to the headmaster's study it had occurred to him that he was as free as the blackbird singing from the top of the cedar tree. But the irony of the situation amused him. It was his last term at Cavendish Towers. A fortnight before the arrival of the astonishing news Major Shackle, the headmaster, had told him they would have to let him go at Easter. The governers had demanded staff cuts and Revilious was expendable although he had politely drawn attention to his long and loyal service.

'Times unfortunately change,' Major Shackle had smiled, lifting his palms heavenwards, hinting perhaps that he was merely the agent of some divine scheme.

Revilious had no contract and was not inclined to make a fuss. But I should have asked him what sort of future I could look forward to, he thought. Forty-eight years old, homeless, unemployed, without friends and relatives, and absolutely no job prospects.

'You can't be serious,' the headmaster had said, after a brief glance at the letter of resignation. 'Your departure a week before term finishes would cause all sorts of administration problems. Surely another seven days won't interfere with your plans?'

'I'm sorry, sir,' Revilious had replied quietly. 'On the other hand some people might feel I've been rather shabbily treated after twenty-five years at Cavendish.'

'You sound like a retired railwayman cheated of his gold watch.'

Revilious had shrugged and smiled, and departed.

That afternoon of late March was cold and windy. He gunned the Fiat down the M5 watching the soil in the ploughed fields change from chocolate brown and sepia to red. At Totnes he collected the keys to Foxcroft and consulted the ordnance survey map. But branching off the Kingsbridge Road things began to reassemble in his memory: a high-hedged lane darkening under cloud shadow, an oak at a crossroads, a farm entrance, fields gliding up into the sky. The landscape registered like a forgotten piece of music suddenly brought to mind in a most unexpected way. Then he was cruising through Aishwell and dropping down a gear to climb the hill out of the village to the wooded brow.

The wind shook the catkins and showered the windscreen with raindrops. Revilious cut the engine, wound down the side window and stared through the hazels and scrub oak into the coombe. The river below was the Aishbourne – his stretch of it. And all at once he recalled childhood fishing expeditions on other rivers of the South Hams, summer afternoons of thundery heat, and his parents quarrelling. But happy memories prevailed as he drove down to Woodburn Bridge. He should have had a second look at the map he reflected, easing the car onto the verge and walking the fifty yards of muddy lane to the cottages. 'Should' belonged to Cavendish Towers. Revilious was a man of independent means with the world at his feet. The realization left him lightheaded. Later he promised himself he would crack a bottle of Taittinger and smoke a good cigar.

Pigs were rooting in the river bank mud where the Aishbourne cut a deep bend from the grit and silt. Revilious laid his forearms on the parapet and gazed into the water. It was full of light. Veins of bronze and ochre gushed over silver speckled sand and grit. The shadowy scurry of trout ruffled the deep, looping swim.

'Even Isaak Walton couldn catch they little devils,' said a voice, and a young man joined Revilious. The stranger was belted into an old trench coat. His beard was inoffensive and well-trimmed, more naval than hippy.

'Not that you'll ever have the chance,' he continues. 'Foxcroft is a no-go area for human beings.'

'How do I get to the house?' Revilious asked.

'Go back up the hill and down the other side till you'm nearly in the village and turn left. Then tis first left again. There's no one there, though. It's been empty since the old lady died. Up Aishwell they say it's haunted.'

'I'm the new owner,' Revilious said shyly, extending his hand, ' – Paul Revilious.'

'Ted Healey,' the young man responded, and his clasp was warm and confident. 'I'm your neighbour, sir. I live over there – No. 2 Drang Cottages.'

He gestured at the grey buildings beyond the pig house and added: 'Tidn a patch on Foxcroft.'

It was a kind of disguised apology for having next to nothing, and Revilious recalled his own willingness to say sorry at the drop of a hat.

Aloud he said, 'Are those your pigs, Mr Healey?'

The young man coloured and nodded.

'They'm on a little bit of your land, sir.'

'They're welcome to it,' Revilious smiled.

Settling once more in the car and adjusting the seat belt he glanced into the driving mirror. God, I feel ancient, he thought. The wind had laid thin bands of grey hair across a forehead heavily cross-hatched with lines. He looked nearer sixty than fifty, and the drooping grey moustache did not help. It made his face which was long and narrow look permanently morose. The large brown eyes returning his gaze were about as lively as a couple of sultanas. Yet he had a good mind and strangers seeing his face for the first time might have considered it more sad than glum. Revilious sighed. He wore the boredom of his Cavendish Tower years like a tortoise shell. Putting the Fiat into reverse he turned and set off up the hill under Churchland Wood.

On the wooden arm of the signpost was the name Bullenford. He drove unhurriedly and the rain slanting down brought a glitter to the countryside. For no reason at all he pulled into a gateway and regarded the shower tail away. A farm labourer on a tractor was going slowly and interminably up and down the field. Revilious did not envy him.

The Fiat bumped and swayed down the long, twisting drive under apple boughs waiting to blossom and on through an oak wood in bud to the weedy gravel beside his new home. The housekeeper was expecting him the next day so he had the place to himself. In the blond light of late afternoon he sat on the bonnet of the car and sank his hands in his jacket pockets. The sky above Foxcroft was wallpapered with rooks and he had a peculiar notion of being surrounded by birds keeping their bargain with birth. At Cavendish Towers he always had to be on his guard against the ragging. In times of stress he would retreat behind a smile of resignation and close his ears to the jibes. But the past was dying in the margins of Foxcroft's solitude. A twenty-five year long nightmare! he thought. God!

–what an admission! What had the man said about killing time and damaging eternity? Revilious shook his head. To court mediocrity was an unpardonable sin. The meanest life of hard physical toil had more dignity than his erstwhile spiritual stagnation. He wondered if some disillusioned Afghan was standing in the courtyard of a house in Kabul questioning his existence. What sort of birds were flying across the mountain cwms of Afghanistan? Were human eyes lifting and noting the stoop of a falcon or the slow circling rise of gulls above the dust of Russian tanks?

Foxcroft was a square, late-Georgian house of pale honey stucco hiding behind a virginia creeper that was beginning to leaf again. The brass fox head on the front door and the elegant windows captured pieces of the sky in gleams. The bedroom windows on the north side had wrought-iron balconies – a gauche touch, Revilious thought, starting to unload the car. But after his cramped quarters in Cavendish Towers Foxcroft offered the kind of privacy and comfort he associated with pools wins or successful bank raids. Smiling to himself he began to ferry the cases and cardboard boxes of books into the hall.

'Good old Victoria,' he chuckled, but the sound of his voice in the empty house was disturbing.

Aunt Victoria was his mother's sister but the Foxcroft girls had never been close. Victoria had inherited everything when Paul's mother had run off with the poor and unaccomplished Edward Revilious much to her father's disgust. Almost immediately after Revilious senior died of influenza in 1936 Lord Foxcroft had a fatal heart attack. Paul's mother had received a small allowance from Devon but was not encouraged to visit her elder sister or correspond. For Mrs Revilious life turned into a game of compromise, of keeping the bailiff happy at the expense of the tradesmen. Victoria remained unmarried and became a nomadic recluse shuttling between a rented villa in Florence and the late spring and summer at Foxcroft.

'As far as we know,' Bertish the solicitor confided, 'she enjoyed her own company. Sometimes she bought paintings and Foxcroft has an extensive library. But your aunt did not contribute to charities or sit on committees, and she certainly did not entertain. The estate was also neglected.'

A selfish life, Revilious reflected, recalling with a pang of heartache his mother's struggle and the down-and-outs in Hereford's shop doorways on Saturday nights. Big, gilt-framed, highland landscapes by Brianski hung in a hall of burgundy coloured walls and dull green carpet. Revilious slouched through Foxcroft, stooping as he had since adolescence in a vain attempt to disguise his height and sparse build, and half-expecting to encounter the old lady everytime he opened a door. Despite the solicitor's letters, the will and his meeting with Bertish he was waiting to be told it was all an elaborate hoax. Things that began pleasantly at Cavendish Towers had a way of ending in confusion and jeering laughter. 'Bilious Revilious had been caught again!' But the stiff-legged Sheraton furniture lending a touch of Jane Austen to the diningroom really did belong to him. The blue and gold Crown Derby cups and saucers, the white fluted Dresden tea service, hand-painted with convolvulus and daisies, could be picked up and used whenever he wished. But Jane Austen would not have approved of the fireplace. It was wide and deep, more farmhouse perennial than Georgian.

The Honorable Victoria Foxcroft had crammed the diningroom with things plundered from those periods of English history she considered attractive – Regency chairs, huge silver candelabra, silver cigar boxes, Georgian table silver, massive and depressingly sombre oils depicting domestic scenes from Victorian middleclass life. Only the kitchen belonged to the second half of the twentieth century and here the old lady's influence was missing.

After depositing his things in one of the small, north facing bedrooms overlooking the pond, Revilious went out onto the lawn. Rooks were cawing and beyond the garden wall the Aishbourne rushed over a weir that was purely ornamental. Standing with his jacket collar turned up against the wind Revilious thought he had gatecrashed someone else's dream. He ambled into a little gone-wild orchard of cider apple trees and came to the pond. Its dark green calm mirrored some of the evening glow and trout were rising. In the centre of the pond was an island thick with scrub willow, alders, reeds and brambles. The margins of blue-green sedges, reeds and hemlock had not seen a grass-hook for decades. On the far side, oaks stood tall and a rookery of half a dozen nests was just visible through the massed branches. The pond was full of fish but there were no wildfowl. Three days later he discovered why.

Mrs Butcher, the so-called housekeeper who was no more than a glorified daily help and cook, told him about the mink. 'They'm just big water rats,' she said. 'And they'm everywhere on the Aishbourne. Her ladyship didn care, though. Her didn care about anything. Her lived like a nun and her wouldn have no one on the estate – not the hunt or the anglers or them mazed ramblers. That's why Foxcroft is so over-growed. Her ladyship kept to herself.'

'But she loved the wildlife, Mrs Butcher. If I were a buzzard or a fox I'd think this little valley was paradise.'

'Her ladyship liked her books, paintings and furniture – nort else. As far as she was concerned nature kept folk from dropping in. You wouldn know Foxcroft was here. That's why its never been burgled. Your auntie wadn too keen on trees and flowers and things.'

Mrs Butcher lasted a couple of days. She hated the way Revilious stamped his own personality on the house. He pushed the chairs back from the hearth and filled the drawingroom with woodsmoke after having the gas fire removed. Revilious could not forget the two-burner gas fire in his Cavendish Towers bed-sitter. Gas fires made him angry. There was nothing like the crackle of ash logs and pine cones to cheer up a room at night.

He and the 'housekeeper' parted amicably. Mrs Butcher could not come to terms with good manners and humility after three decades of self-punitive servitude. And Revilious admitted to himself he was rather set in his ways. Then the master of Foxcroft trimmed his moustache and walked his mile of river and began to catalogue the bits and pieces of the Devon spring. Sheltering under the brim of the panama bequeathed to him by his father he came to realize that his long innings at Cavendish Towers hadn't been utterly futile. He had located the nests of seven different kinds of songbird in the school grounds, watched badgers on the headmaster's lawn and seen a dog fox courting a vixen in the bicycle shed. His natural history diary had provided comfort on winter evenings when the classical music, rasping and clicking from the old gramaphone, had lifted him out of himself.

Occasionally, whilst sitting among the daffodils on the island below the Home Weir, he felt a little sad and alone. He was the last of his stock, the last human being on earth carrying the blood of Revilious and Foxcroft. Of course it wasn't important, he conceded, but at times it blighted his pleasure. With his sense of history he believed the only sort of immortality outside the creation of great works of art lay in the survival of the family name. He loved the thought of generations reaching back through the ages and the newborn standing at the frontier of the future like astronauts poised to explore the unknown.

Before the end of his first week Revilious was passionately in love with Foxcroft. Rising at dawn he explored the small meadows and copses that clothed the coombe. In Aunt Victoria's escritoire he discovered a hand-drawn map of the estate with every field, clump of trees and orchard, the pools and islands carefully named. It inspired him to put on his waders and follow the Aishbourne from Woodburn Bridge upstream to Woodburn Barton Farm. He saw mink in Lord's Pool, Wotton's and Bowden Pools, and found the trout swims from Orchard Island to the weir full of fish. A vixen had her earth in Venn Copse in the north of the coombe and the western fields, bounded by tall wild hedges of ash, oak, hazel and thorn were pitted and scarred with rabbit burrows and runs.

Three brooks fed the Aishbourne and six orchards of old neglected cider apple trees lured the redstart and the nightingale. The whole coombe was a natural wildlife park haunted by almost every animal from brown hares to badgers. And Revilious began to tick off the wild flowers as they came into season: celandine, stitchwort, red campion, marsh marigold. The chilly start to the spring did not seem to have affected the blackthorn. White blossom and mists of green leaves added a special West Country beauty to Foxcroft. Close to the river and in the boggy corners of the copses, willows and sallows were covered in fluffy yellow catkins.

Revilious waited impatiently for the first cuckoo to call across the coombe, and searched the sky each morning for the return of the swallows. Now his long face had a bit of colour in it and the hang-dog look had vanished. When dusk fell he settled on the balcony of his bedroom, well-wrapped up against the blueing air, and turned his binoculars on the pond and the wooded hills. After dark he came to the fireside and switched on his new stereo. While the jacket potatoes filled the kitchen with their aroma it was pleasant to crouch over the flames sipping Chivas Regal and listening to Brahms's Alto Rhapsody. As soon as he had got to know his way around Aishwell and the surrounding countryside he promised himself he would buy in some authentic farm cider.

Later, between records, he heard the barn owls crying from the western boundaries of Foxcroft and settled on the hearthrug with his *The Wild Flowers of Britain and Northern Europe*. But Aunt Victoria's map continued to absorb him and his visits to little secret places made it more meaningful. He loved the names – Westerland, Furze Acre, Hazard Copse, Old Bethlehem, Zion Spinney, Tucker's Orchard, Yeo Field, Dunwell, Brookhill Field, Forders. The landscape had become a blood thing and he was part of it. Sitting before the yellow flames, catching the whisper of rain on the windows, he felt he had a destiny after all. Foxcroft would remain wild and true to itself for at least his lifetime. It wouldn't be difficult to pursue a personal sort of Taoism and continue his aunt's policy of non-interference with nature. He would have no dogs or cats in the coombe. Nothing would be allowed to disturb the animals and birds. What had come into being through the selfishness of an old recluse would be left to develop as it chose.

After a sunny day he stood on the balcony and watched the green waters of the pond darken to mahogany, and listened to the gurgle of the sluice. Every so often trout and dace leapt and ringed the glassy calm, and shoals of young chub flickered through the lilies. A little below the surface a giant pike glided into the weed, but the mink that generally swam and dived under the willow and alder branches were absent. Perhaps the pike has eaten them, Revilious thought. It looked big enough to swallow a child. He shuddered. Then something as dark as the pond pushed through the tangled undergrowth of the island. Revilious slowly lifted his binoculars and the dog otter paused and sniffed a bramble stem where a wagtail had shot its mutes. Revilious held the fierce pug face perfectly in focus. The otter stretched out its neck and placed its nose to the water and drifted through the surface. 'More of a melting than a sinking,' Revilious wrote that night in his diary. Bubbles broke from the otter's guard hairs and streamed away, and Revilious had a superb view of the creature swimming beneath the arrowhead of its own bow wave. The finding of an eel jolted it into a display of aquabatics. The eel was carried to the bank and devoured. Revilious stood like a statue although the cold was eating into him and making him shiver.

When night fell and the moon came up the pond lay invisible under shadow, and the dog otter's whistle seemed to echo the man's loneliness. The barn owls leaving Hazard Linhay added their own poignant cries to the hush. Revilious retreated and hurried down to the drawingroom where the fire was roaring up the chimney.

Whisky helped bring a glow back to his body but he did not need the music. He switched off the light and the fire drowned the room in shifting gold, dancing on the walls as reflected sunlight dances on the boles of riverside trees.

Magpie in the lane

He remembered standing at the window before climbing into bed, and listening to the nightingales in the trees across the pond. When the wind dropped they sang to lure the females as they arrived from Africa. And he went to sleep thinking of Tennyson and Cavendish Towers where nightingales sang from the sycamores, unheard and unacclaimed. But he was awake not long after dawn and hurriedly knotted his dressing gown. It would have been a mistake to have opened the french windows although the birdsong possessed the haunting beauty of medieval church music. Revilious wiped the condensation off the glass with his sleeve and peered into the morning.

The dog otter was returning from hunting the River Avon between the hamlets of Beneknowle and Diptford. He had crossed many small fields and found the Aishbourne at Forders Bridge under Woodburn Barton Farm. He was drowsy but his belly was full of elvers, frogs and salmon parr. A sheep coughed and a pair of crows flapped out of the branches of a solitary ash. The wind blew hard and kept the tree dancing, and the otter turned his muzzle to the sky before entering the river. His pads were sore and gorse spines were stuck in his tail and in the webbing between his toes.

He swam down an open reach until deeper water sent him sailing under alders and oaks. The right-hand stream carried him past the island where naked alders held a crow's nest and the drey of a grey squirrel. The deep undercut banks of ash roots were good holt places and did not go unnoticed. Then the otter came up against a jam of fallen trees and clambered over them to drop into Bowden's Pool which was a large, flood-excavated bend.

By now morning light was spilling from the palest and coldest of blue skies. The river was shining like the burst entrails of a great salmon, running with streamers of pink, black, gold and white. He drifted through the sudden lights and shades in a trance of well-being until he reached the sluice and slid over the flood-gate into the pond. Immediately the pike broke cover and skimmed across the muddy bottom and the otter went after it. But his efforts were playful and all the underwater corkscrewing and somersaulting sprang from an enjoyment of his own body. Swift and cunning the pike had no difficulty finding sanctuary among the branches of a drowned oak.

On the island the dog otter rolled and shook himself until he was spiky and neither of the land or the water. He curled up on his couch of reeds and ran his teeth like clippers along his tail, nipping out the grit and gorse spines. His ears twitched at the sound of a thrush cracking a snail on a stone somewhere nearby. Satisfied, he flopped back and groomed his chest. The shrill lay of starling nestlings under Foxcroft's guttering filled the little silences behind each gust of wind. Then the hiss of reeds chased him into sleep.

Revilious smiled and turned away. His new tenant would have to have a name, he thought. Something short and watery. Brookwise, Pebble – Lord! Pebble! Walt Disney might approve but no self-respecting otter would carry such a tag. Eventually, as he buttoned his corduroys, he decided on Skerry. Yes, he congratulated himself – a neat swirl of a name.

Downstairs he boiled a kettle and made coffee. Last night's fire still had some warmth and he sat with his feet in the hearth gently twirling the mug so that the Nescafe creamed. Otters were mysterious creatures. He knew a little about them but his books only gave a general picture and he was eager for details. Somehow it was an omen – the otter on his pond in the first spring he had really lived through, moment by moment, since childhood.

Revilious drove into the village just before noon and had a bar snack at The Plough. The pub had probably been splendid a couple of decades ago, he reflected, before Big Brewery doctored it. Still, the hideous fruit machine was muted compared to the one in the Royal George, Stretford Lacey, that went off like a machine gun whenever it paid out. Seated in a corner under the phony mullioned window Revilious felt contented. The chicken was greasy and the chips hard and tasteless but the pub had a certain West Country atmosphere which the two loud Brummies at the bar could only ruffle. They were firing jokes at each other and dragging the landlord into the smut whenever he chanced their way. The old man at the other end of the counter was hunched over his newspaper, showing the back of his navy-blue gaberdine to the rest of the world. Maybe he's deaf, Revilious thought.

The taller of the Brummies wore a black tracksuit top, jeans and a cynical smile. His thin blond moustache added a touch of cruelty to a set of hard features. The moustache bore testament to long, narcissistic grooming. Revilious peered into his glass of best bitter. The macho image made him cringe. Whenever he saw a man looking like a refugee from one of those awful American TV private-eye series he suspected mediocrity. The characters even had macho names: P. J. Hawser, Danny Hard, Hook. And they were either karate black belts or Vietnam veterans, miraculous athletes (despite the paunch), irresistible to women and poorly educated. Cadogan fancied himself as one of those boorish soap opera heroes, Revilious recalled, right down to the Brut aftershave and moustache. He shook his head and smiled. Cadogan had been the worst games master in the history of Cavendish Towers but he knew how to persecute lesser mortals. Somehow he had uncovered Revilious's two dark secrets: his failure to get a degree at Trinity College, Dublin, and the medical board turning him down for National Service.

'Mr Revilious has flat feet,' Cadogan boomed to an assembly of first years. 'Should have gone in the police – hey, Rev old man? An ave rare.' On the cricket field Cadogan was the swashbuckling clown but behind the staff room door he preyed on the weak.

Revilious finished his beer. Poor loud Cadogan. The faulty electric kettle had caused some concern among the more timid members of staff but Cadogan had played rugby for Surrey, or so he said, and had held a short service RAF commission. Revilious recalled the incident with the minutiae of detail generally reserved for nightmare. One moment Cadogan was standing there laughing, then he laid his hand on the kettle and five minutes later he had stopped twitching and breathing.

After the string of cool, showery days the morning was gloriously sunwashed. It was a mile or so up the lane to the Totnes Road junction. Revilious drove with the side window down and slow enough to catch snatches of birdsong and the scent of primroses. A magpie was tucked against the far hedge quarrying into a dead rabbit. The bird's black and white plumage was set against the massed green leaves and grasses. Revilious braked gently and the magpie pressed tighter to the hedge, and the dark blue Ford Estate cornering at fifty took man and bird by surprise. It tore out of a fine cloud of mud and water, clipping Revilious's side-mirror. Then it swerved to the left and brushed along the hedge before accelerating away. Revilious got out and wiped the dirt off his face. The magpie was fluttering in the middle of the lane.

'Oh God no,' he groaned, breaking into a run.

He stooped over the mutilated bird and gathered it up. It was jerking about but not of its own free will, and the light in its eyes was going out. A single drop of blood swelled from the tip of the black beak and the bird shuddered and lay still. The nictitating membrane sealed the eyes which a moment or two before had gleamed as brightly as the Aishbourne.

He laid the magpie high in the hedge and drove off. His hands were shaking. Yes, he thought, yes, whoever it was at the wheel of the Estate knew what he was doing. He aimed that car as if it were a gun. A lorry loaded with nets of swedes was trying to pass and the driver was leaning on the horn. Revilious waved him on.

In the Totnes offices of Messrs Bertish, Hockey and Cole he wondered how old Aubrey Bertish would react to a diatribe on mediocrity. His anger surprised him but did not surface during the business chat over tea and documents. Revilious bought second-hand books at Parnell's and strolled up the street to the market. He could not shake off the image of the magpie fluttering in the lane like a dirty bundle of rags. Walking among the stalls he thought it might have been rewarding to have shared pre-literate man's relationship with the living world.

The day was beginning to cloud over from the west and motoring up the hill out of town he met the rain. It was most unseasonable weather, Revilious thought, switching on the windscreen wipers. Under the hedge fifty yards beyond the turn-off to Tristford, and in obvious distress, was the old man in the navy-blue raincoat he had seen at The Plough. Revilious pulled up, opened the passenger door and said: 'I'm going through Aishwell.'

'Good of you to stop, sir,' the old man said. He limped across the road and flopped awkwardly into the car.

'Danged knee keeps givin' out,' he explained. 'I'll have to stop kickin' the cat.'

Revilious introduced himself and found his companion was Reg Yelland a retired farm foreman who lived alone in Aishwell. He was a cheerful old fellow grinning from a dark, wrinkled face, which would have looked gaunt without the humorous mouth. His grey-streaked ginger hair was greased to his skull. Unused to car travel he sat bolt upright, hands folded in his lap and that nervous grin revealing National Health teeth so big they might have been prised out of the mouth of a horse. But instead of dropping platitudes he seemed to find silence sufficient until a flurry of rain hit the windscreen and provoked comment.

'I don't mind spring rain,' he said softly. 'Not yer, not in Aishwell. It makes things grow. But I like all the seasons, Mr Revilious, though spring's a bit special.'

'Very special, Mr Yelland.'

The village was assembling on either side and the shower rushing on left behind it the medicinal scent of bluebells and drenched earth.

'This'll do, sir,' Yelland grunted. 'I live round the corner in Pump Lane. Next time you'm in The Plough I'll buy'ee a drink.'

'Farm cider, Mr Yelland?'

'They don't sell it at The Plough. But I know where you can get the best.'

He searched for the door handle but had to be shown where it was and how to operate it. Then the blue Estate crept out of a terrace of small, lime-washed houses and furrowed the bullock manure lying on the road, and sizzled away.

'I've seen that car before,' Revilious said.

'It's Charlie Gutteridge's,' Yelland grimaced. 'His brothers were up The Plough when you were there lunchtime. I don't go much on 'em. They'm a funny lot and I'm danged if Charlie idn the prize ornament. Us have got half Birmingham livin in Debn now.'

Revilious read for most of the afternoon and as soon as he had finished dinner came to the balcony. The pond lifted and scattered under the wind. Dusk brought out the owls but not Skerry. The otter was running through the meadows of Woodburn Barton Farm to the grounds of Huxton Manor. He came up the long low weir to the bridge with its four tiny arches and stonework covered in periwinkles, ivy and moss. He tried for trout in the shallows but had to settle for crayfish. Leaving the river he cantered along the borders of a covert and sniffed out a woodpigeon that had been shot at twilight and had flown half a mile before tumbling from the sky.

Skerry ate the bird and the trees swished and roared, shaking scraps of darkness across the starlit grass. Returning to the Aishbourne he whistled for the mate the water and his instincts kept promising. But the river became lonelier and smaller the further he travelled until it vanished in the sog of Aishbourne Head on Dartmoor.

The day after the magpie incident Revilious received a letter from the Master of the South Hams Mink Hunt asking permission to try the Aishbourne at Foxcroft. His terse refusal was in effect a declaration of war against blood sports, and before long most of the neighbourhood knew they had another crank in residence.

Farmhouse rough

By inclination he was not religious although many of his happiest moments at Cavendish Towers had been spent in the chapel. But the deathless poetry of the Old Testament helped bring him through patches of loneliness at dusk before the whisky and the fireside received him. It was sheer heaven to read what he liked when he chose. The penance of marking prep, of wading through badly spelt, hopelessly dull compositions, was done. Perhaps Christian really has crossed the Slough of Despond, Revilious thought with a wry smile.

But his research into the otter was not comforting. He found it hard to understand how people could live on an island with so many wild creatures and yet remain ignorant of their lifestyles and needs. He crossed the river above Home Weir and wandered downstream through fields of thick green grass and wild flowers. The day softened into something approaching Robert Browning's vision of April. Between the buds and tiny new leaves were glimpses of king cups, bluebells and alkanet beside the water. Staring across the dance of light at the flowers he saw the vixen come down to the Aishbourne and drink. Her ears and nose took whatever the breeze offered but he was downwind, leaning against the ivy-clad bole of an alder, and remained undetected. Then she sensed him there and looked directly at him for an instant and was gone. Revilious loved the silence of animals. Often he had stood mute before nature, recognizing in the perfection of a landscape or the song of a blackbird something that made words redundant.

Before long he reached a particularly beautiful stretch of the Aishbourne. At some time ten mossy rocks had been dumped in the river as stepping stones. He sat on the largest, dangling his wellington-booted feet in the water. Bullheads and sticklebacks were darting about and amongst the weir moss the silvery grey eels swam. Revilious tugged the brim of his panama down a couple of inches on his forehead and tried to read. It was depressing to unfold the tragedy of the otter's decline and at the same time plumb new depths of human cruelty and stupidity.

Things began to go wrong towards the end of the fifties. Farming went mad and sold out to chemicals. The organochlorine pesticides found their way into the rivers and down the otters' food-chain producing infertile bitches and a crash in the breeding population. The decline was so dramatic it brought the animal to the brink of extinction, but the hunts continued visiting the rivers each summer adding to the animals' problems. Throughout the sixties and seventies rivers were 'tidied-up' by water authorities and farmers. They were dredged and widened; reedbeds, marshes, wild field corners, riverside copses and small islands vanished before the drive to sanitize the British landscape. Intensive agriculture, which meant taking out a lot and putting in as little as possible, may please the economist, Revilious thought, but what is it doing to the countryside and the wildlife? According to the books too many waterways were being taken over for recreation like water-skiing, canoeing and angling. And otters hated noise. Human disturbance and pollution plus the loss of holt habitat meant that only a lucky handful could breed successfully each season. The more remote the region the better the chance.

The second half of the twentieth century was dominated by the slogan: If it makes money it's OK. A society which had so little self-regard couldn't be expected to care about mere animals, plants and birds. A government which took revenues from the sale of cigarettes wouldn't be too concerned about a non-political issue like the plight of the otter. If all the otters in the world perished overnight it wouldn't affect the dole queue or inflation. Nothing of interest to man would change but another piece of creation's jigsaw would be lost forever.

We have broken faith so often with the living world, he reflected sadly. Above the babble of the river he could hear cries of misery and terror rising from all the animals Man had exploited, tortured and killed since he discovered godhood in himself. Tears filled his eyes. Godhood! He gritted his teeth and stood up. Beyond the avarice which condoned almost everything that made money was the axiom of species self-ishness. It was a kind of crucible where base human emotion was melted down – racism, blind patriotism, extreme political ideology, religious prejudice, tyranny over all other life. Out of this stew came napalm, nuclear weapons, chemical weapons, factory farming and vivisection.

Recalling the terrible occasion when he had tried to voice his fears to a classroom full of bored thirteen-year-olds, Revilious blushed. His hands were shaking. The boys weren't accustomed to emotional outbursts but the giggling might have died away if Portman hadn't blown one of his notoriously loud raspberries while Revilious was in full song about hare-coursing. The uproar and Major Shackle's intervention confirmed the popular belief that old Bilious was potty.

'Stiff upper lip, Revilious,' Cadogan quipped ' – not trembling lower lip. In the end the parents call the tune. At Cavendish it's not the three Rs. It's the three Bs: Bulldog spirit, Bourgeois breeding and Blood-sports.'

On the terrace above the rockery and lawn he was out of the wind. Across the way the side of the coombe was visible through swaying branches. Birds constantly passed against the sky, and the song of the river and the song of the greenfinch were most soothing.

For a while he read some of the verses of W. H. Davies which were as simple and moving as children's prayers. Now the collar doves were crooning on the roof of Foxcroft and sparrows squabbled in the creeper. A bee bounced slowly along the garden wall and drilled up into the sunshine.

Skerry seemed to have abandoned the pond. Revilious's dusk vigils produced little save heartache and glimpses of the pike patrolling under the marbled surface. Seated in the armchair which he always drew up to the very edge of the hearth, he worried about the otter. And much later when the moon rose in its second quarter he selected a walking stick, put on his fell boots, buttoned himself into an overcoat and trudged up the coombe.

The cool night air sluiced the whisky muzziness from his head and by the time he had reached Huxton Manor he was enjoying himself. A cart track led to Yetson Bridge and on the sill his torch revealed spraints which were no more than a few days old. He remained on the treeless side of the river and the cattle path brought him to another bridge and the B3210. The night smelled like a newborn animal.

It was one of the few adventures Revilious had deliberately courted, although pushing further up the Aishbourne opened windows on past events he had forgotten. One May weekend during his last year at Trinity he had done the Snowdon Horseshoe by moonlight. He and West and Trailer had slept in the cowhouse at Hafod tan y Craig. Three of the best days of my life, he thought. Plenty of exercise and fresh air, beer at the Pen y Gwryd and something actually approaching comradeship. What had become of West and Trailer? He would start tracing them tomorrow, he decided while the gut-warmth swelled. Why had he stopped going to the mountains? Where had those friendships ended? – if they ever had been friendships and not just temporary pacts of convenience. Where am I going? What am I doing? Revilious groaned inwardly. The countryside was rising black and hilly before him and he had no desire to stray into it. Skerry wasn't there. Things came and went, and finally all that remained was the ache for what never happened.

He was no longer elated. He was cold and tired and needed his bed. Skerry had slipped out of his life but Foxcroft stood as solidly as ever in the darkness. He turned back, marvelling at the far-flung play of the stars.

*   *   *

One morning Yelland phoned and proposed a trip to buy cider from the mill at Yalberton near Stoke Gabriel. He was wearing his soiled gabardine and George Formby grin when Revilious collected him.

'You know the way, Mr Revilious?'

'It's the other side of the Dart, isn't it, Mr Yelland?'

Yelland nodded and assumed his rigid position, eyes front, as though he were willing the car to do what he wanted it to do – but diffidently. Revilious smiled. The flat, grey morning stood at the threshold of sunshine. Roads and hedges glittered after a night of heavy showers. They climbed out of Totnes and sped on to Longcombe Cross and the Stoke Gabriel turn-off. Every gap in the hedge revealed flashes of ravishing farmland, and towards Stoke Gabriel the sun at last broke through.

They purchased four gallons each of rough cider from Churchwards Farm, loaded the plastic containers and took the road to Kingswear. Revilious warmed to the old man's chat, steering the Fiat down the long, winding hill to the Dart Estuary. There was the inevitable stop for ale at Dittisham before Yelland navigated a sentimental journey through Cornworthy, Hay, Aishford and home past the Horridge Inn.

'I've never done that trip before,' Yelland said, ' – not in one piece. I can't drive, Mr Revilious, and none of my mates had cars when I was young. I did some of those places on Sunday mystery tours. The chara used to rattle round the lanes and always finish up at Stoke. No further. All my life I've wanted to go down the river from Stoke, cross over on the ferry and come back to Aishwell through the lanes. It isn exactly a big ambition. Ulysses would have laughed at me I s'pose.'

'Ulysses!'

'The Greek bloke.'

Dipping sharply the hill levelled out at Drang Cottages. The dark blue Ford Estate was parked by Woodburn Bridge on the wrong side of the road and there was no room to pass. Revilious pulled in beside the piggery and got out with some misgivings. Intuitively he knew his best course was to climb back into the car and find another route to Foxcroft but even as the warning registered he was walking onto the bridge. Three alsations were locked in the rear of the Ford, imitating a wolfpack.

'Small minded men like big dogs,' Reg Yelland observed. 'Ulysses had an old hound.'

'But Ulysses wasn't small minded,' smiled Revilious.

'He was an exceptional man, Mr Revilious. Those ancient Greeks! Exceptional.'

Charlie Gutteridge was on the bank peering into the pool. Revilious stared down at him from the parapet with a growing sense of helplessness. Despite the warm stink of the pigs he caught the odour of Yelland's raincoat. It was the mustiness of old age and neglect.

'Charlie likes his fishing,' Yelland said.

'Dry or wet fly?'

'Worms,' Yelland grinned. 'The Gutteridges expect their money's worth.'

Healey came out of his cottage with a cup of coffee. He gave the men on the bridge a friendly good-day and Gutteridge looked up. Revilious had never seen such an arrogant wedge of a face. The hooded eyes and thin acquiline nose, high cheekbones and sallow complexion were more Cairo than Aston. Gutteridge's fair hair was thin on top and brushed back to hang far too long over his shirt collar, and his sideboards would have been admired in Mecca ballrooms of the late fifties. He was tall and fleshy and he moved with a wary swagger which the waders and his long arms exaggerated almost to caricature. For a thirty-five-year-old he was in good condition.

Introductions were made without enthusiasm or ceremony and Gutteridge's lids lifted to reveal the stony eyes of a tortoise. He fixed them on Revilious while Yelland spoke about the river, and the water rushed under the arches. On the fingers of his left hand were three gold sovereigns set in heavy gold rings. Revilious turned away and leaned on the parapet, praying Yelland would shut up.

'Do you fish?' Gutteridge asked, in the Midland twang that turns 'you' into 'yow'.

Revilious shook his head but did not raise his eyes. 'Used to when I was a boy. Can't say I've had the inclination to pick up a rod since then.'

'O yes, I forgot,' Gutteridge smiled sarcastically. 'You're one of those anti-bloodsport blokes.'

'Fraid so,' Revilious said, colouring. 'I don't like killing for pleasure.'

Gutteridge sniffed and extracted a cigar from his breast pocket.

'The mink are a bloody nuisance,' he said. 'They kill the trout and the ducks so I kill them. I'd put down gin traps if it wasn't for my dogs. Bloody mink!'

Revilious thought an instant and said: 'They didn't ask to be brought here from America and exploited, Mr Gutteridge. If they're a problem we created it.'

'My fish don't care why they're here – they're here and they're pests. The Ministry of Agriculture pays a bounty for their pelts and I'm going to blast every little sod on my water. But,' he added lighting his cigar, 'it ain't no good me cleaning up this bit of the river if they keep coming down from Foxcroft. So suddenly my fish are your problem, Revilious. What you going to do about it?'

Revilious's hands were trembling again. He stuffed them in his pockets and said – 'The mink don't take many brown trout. They're not quick enough.'

'Are you calling me a liar?' Gutteridge said softly.

Revilious felt the tortoise eyes settle on him but continued to gaze down the river wondering how he managed to get into such sticky situations.

'Of c-course not,' he stammered. 'The mink—'

'The mink my ass! Any animal that comes on my land will have to take its chance. Any animal – fox, mink, cat, dog, bloody lion.'

Revilious's knees were turning to mush. He could hear Cadogan's booming laugh and scenes from the staff room swam up from his discomfort.

Gutteridge was smiling; Revilious knew without looking.

'Please don't come after them on my land,' he whispered.

'I can see you're goin' to be an awkward customer, Revilious. The old lady was an awkward customer. Foxcroft is crawlin' with vermin. The mink come under this bridge and use my bit of water as a take-away. From now on I'm going to hold you responsible.'

Revilious sighed. 'That is prepostrous. But whatever you do, stay off my land.'

'Or you'll do what? – smack my wrists?'

The colour drained from Revilious's face but he still refused to meet Gutteridge's stare.

'There idn no need for that sort of talk, Charlie,' Yelland said. 'Move your car and us'll be going. Mr Revilious don't want no trouble.'

'Good for a pint, is he, Reg?' Gutteridge sneered, climbing into the Estate and turning the ignition. From the side window he fired instructions at Healey above the barking of the dogs. Then the Ford took off and vanished up the hill.

'Nasty bit of work, idn he?' Yelland grinned.

Revilious was quivering but spots of colour had returned to his cheeks. He felt a little sick and his left arm hurt.

'The mink can be a nuisance, Mr Revilious,' Healey said. 'They've taken fowls from the back of my house. Us have to shoot 'em. Tidn none of my business, sir, but Charlie don't like to be crossed. I'd stay out of his way if I was you.'

Driving back to Aishwell Revilious regained his composure but did not mention Skerry. The otter's departure was probably for the best with a moron like Gutteridge camped on the edge of paradise.

'Here,' Yelland said kindly. 'He's really upset you hasn't he, Mr Revilious. Best forget un. No one likes the bugger but he's a big spender and some folk would drink with Hitler if he kept buying. Tez human nature.'

'Human nature,' Revilious echoed with faint irony.

'You won't see much of Charlie for all his lip. He's got a posh place over at Rattlecombe and only comes yer for the fishin' and the rugby.'

'Rugby?'

'He plays for Aishwell. They say he idn a lot of cop but he talks a good game.'

Revilious smiled and said, 'Why don't you come over to Foxcroft tonight, Mr Yelland, and drink some of this cider and a glass or two of scotch.'

'Thursday night is crib night. I usually plays with my old mate Bob Maunder up The Plough.'

Revilious's face dropped.

'But,' Yelland grinned, 'Bob wouldn't say no to a tot of whisky – especially if twas free.'

'Then bring him along, Mr Yelland. Anytime after seven.'

Maunder was a tall, ex-policeman in his late sixties. Revilious envied his air of confidence and well-being. The broad, open face belonged to someone used to riding life's punches. It creased into a smile as Maunder occupied one of the armchairs Revilious had bought in Totnes to replace the elegant but uncomfortable Regency furniture. The fire, the Chivas Regal and the cider met with his approval.

Apparently the two old men had gone to school together and their rapport amused Revilious. Conversation flowed across familiar social terrain – gardening, the weather, village gossip – to Gutteridge. Bob Maunder did not like the Brummie.

'Him and his brothers are swines,' he declared. 'Folk round here are easily conned but the Gutteridges don't pull the wool over my eyes. Charlie is an uncaring, grasping, vain forgery of a man, constantly after attention and approval.'

'Where does their money come from, Mr Maunder?' said Revilious.

'Betting shops, video films, rubbish food take-aways – that sort of muck.'

'Ah! – that's where I've seen the name,' Revilious said. 'Gutteridges, the bookmakers.'

'In my business,' said Maunder, 'gambling was trouble. Betting shops may be necessary – like brothels, but they are there first and foremost to cash in on people's weakness and misery.'

The ash logs blazed and crumbled into crusts of scarlet and grey. Maunder held his glass of whisky to the fire so that it flashed like a jewel.

'Gutteridge tried to buy Foxcroft from your aunt,' he continued. 'He wants to turn it into a restaurant and high class holiday village-cum-health farm, with Scandinavian-type chalets all over the coombe. At Aishwell the scheme was lapped up. It would bring a lot of work and money to the community.'

And the loss of all this, Revilious thought miserably.

As the evening progressed and the cider loosened their tongues he spoke of his ambitions for Foxcroft, and both his companions approved. Yelland was an uncomplicated, honest old boy but Maunder was deeper and more thoughtful. He sat in his flannels and hand-knitted cardigan and drank without haste.

'You're not married, Mr Revilious?' he enquired during a lull in the chat.

'A confirmed bachelor,' Revilious smiled. 'It's not for the want of trying, only I've never been exactly a prize catch or a great lover or anything like that. I was serious about a girl once – God! it seems ages ago – but she married someone else. I was always the fellow ladies chucked for other men.'

'I'm sorry,' Maunder said.

'Don't be, Mr Maunder. I couldn't have coped. I can hardly run my own life let alone organize and maintain a family set-up. I must confess it's working out fine at the moment – Foxcroft, Devon, freedom.'

Yelland, it turned out, was a widower who did not seem to miss his wife, but Maunder was divorced and although it had happened nearly twenty years ago the memory still hurt.

'Broken marriages are the occupational hazard of CID life,' he explained. 'The hours are anti-social, the work's demanding and unpleasant. It can turn the men who do it into zombies. So Joan ran off with a brickie, ten years her junior and about as reliable as an Irish watch. Eighteen months later she was dead. Cancer of the liver. I visited her in hospital but she didn't want to know. It was him all the time, even then.

'They buried her on a winter's morning. It was snowing and I stood by myself back from the small crowd of her relatives and his friends – like a stranger. He was at the graveside crying, really sobbing his heart out. Then I realized he loved her too and somehow that made the whole business unbearable. Unbearable.'

Fortunately Yelland brought them out of gloom with a colourful account of his own marriage which was all dog-fights and strained silences.

'I take it you don't pine for Elaine,' Maunder chuckled.

'Oh, I do, Bob, like I pine for toothache. Dang me! but the maid had a sharp tongue. I must have been drunk when I proposed. The little passion us shared went out of the proceedings as quick as heat leaves a cup of tea.'

It was nearly midnight when the old men got up to take their leave. After they had gone Revilious put on Vaughan Williams's Serenade to Music and fell asleep in the armchair too drunk to care about anything.

Owl light

He was watching the river above Home Weir when gunshots lifted the rooks and filled the sky with cawing birds. The gun banged again from the direction of Forders, and Revilious remembered the little vixen of Venn Copse and began to run. Three more shots rattled down the coombe. The fox had cubs and would be very vulnerable. God, don't let it be true, he prayed. Just this time make everything all right.

The brambles, nettles and cow parsley made the going difficult and once or twice he had to pull fallen timber out of the way. Crossing Lower Bowcombe Orchard he felt a tightening of the chest and was suddenly unable to breathe. One moment he was running, then he was on his hands and knees fighting for air and struggling to shake off the giddiness and nausea. He rolled onto his back and the sweat broke from his body, but the sky was still there between the lichened boughs and he focused on it as panic welled. The pain surged round his heart and spread across his ribs and faded. Slowly his head cleared and the birdsong returned in a rush of scent and colour. It really is a lovely day, he thought absently. He lay perfectly still, waiting for the pain and sickness to return. I've had a heart attack. The realization was chilling. No, he decided, gritting his teeth and gasping, that was absurd. He could count the branches overhead and the small white clouds sailing by were the property of a greater consciousness than his own. He closed his eyes and when he opened them again the sun was rising above Big Wood.

Nothing had happened to the vixen. Overcoming his fear of another seizure Revilious went out at dusk and walked slowly to the field above Zenn Copse with his binoculars, expecting to collapse at any moment. Before the light faded the fox appeared and trotted down to the river. Revilious took this for a sign and from that moment half-believed God had at last come over to see what he was doing.

*   *   *

The woodpigeon was courting his mate on the roof of the linhay, offering her slow, deep bows. From Redcleave Brakes to Glascombe Ball and beyond, the larks sang. Skerry pushed his nose through a whispering ceiling of grasses and sniffed the breeze. He had crossed the streams under Brent Moor and followed the Glaze Brook down to Bullhornstone Farm. In the stream under Corringdon Wood he had killed a sick swan. The swan had swallowed lead shot on the banks of the Dart where anglers often lost trace and weights. Skerry did not eat the bird but feasted on frogs which he teased as a cat tortures mice and ate whole after the screaming had stopped. His sleep had left him refreshed and although the sun had been up an hour he was eager to be on the move again.

He cantered past Owley and Lady's Wood Nature Reserve, crossed the railway embankment and came on to dash unobserved across the A38. Leaving the thickly wooded coombe east of Higher Turtley he climbed a hill with the panorama of fields, copses and streams falling away on all sides to dim horizons. He found the Avon above Bickham Bridge and was unwilling to lie-up despite the steady advance of morning. The sun shining from a cloudless sky seemed to be drawing the grass up to meet it, so potent was the life-force.

The otter's eyesight was not good but the weather thrilled him and he felt part of all that was happening around him. A golden sea of celandines covered the riverside pastures down to Garaland Copse. Skerry ploughed through it and entered the water and glided under Gara Bridge into a steep-sided valley of

oaks and larches. Below Weekmoor he sprainted on a boulder
at the junction of the river and a stream, and squirted a little
musk fluid before departing in the grip of the trout swim.
Birdsong and river-song were instantly cut off as he dived and
nosed along the pebbles and shillets.

Towards Bedlime Wood the mud was poaching in the sun
that gleamed on the shallows and the otter's guard hairs.
Skerry left a perfect set of seals on the shore as he bounded
from the water and ran along the disused railway to plunge into
the river again at Titcombe. His whistling sailed before him
and was answered by a querulous tomcat screech. Standing
upright on the sward against the blackthorns and hemlock was
a large dog otter. Skerry, like all mustelids, did not lack courage but he recognized in the stranger a hostility bordering on
madness. He dived, turning upstream under water and swimming hard into the current. The stranger had recently parted
company with a bitch at Slapton Ley for she had given birth to
cubs and no longer wanted him. He wore his lust like a goad
and would have pursued Skerry if a man had not appeared on
the railway bridge.

Where Bedlime Wood ended Skerry hauled out and shook
himself and rolled in the grass. He was close to a road and
heard voices. A gang of council workmen were resurfacing the
bend. Skerry bounded along the hedge and in the field corner,
half buried under elderberry and woodbine, came upon the
rusting shell of a Ford Anglia. He made this his kennel and
slept on the backseat until sunset.

Dusk was masking the farmland and one by one the birds
stopped singing. Skerry's ears twitched backwards and for-
wards. The hen robin whose nest was in the cavity where the
dashboard had been, scolded him and a blackbird added its own
manic complaint to the din. The otter left the Anglia and
pushed through the hedge. Almost under his nose on the other
side was the warm little body of a dead goldfinch that had been
struck by a car. Skerry ignored it and listened to the horses
snuffling and sighing from the nearby paddock.

The lanes ran purposefully from one farm and small community to another but the otter received his compass bearings
from instinct. He lolloped under Moreleigh Hill Brakes with
night swallowing the South Hams. Half a moon shone from a
clear, starry sky and he could smell cattle, sheep and naked

soil. Now the countryside belonged to his kind and to the
badgers and foxes, hares, rabbits and owls. He threaded through
cadences of silence by Moreleigh Parks and across the fields of
Stanborough. And his running brought death to three young
rabbits. The grating shrieks of barn owls quartering the
pastures between Halwell and Moreleigh celebrated the passing of life to life.

In the owl-light that he had known and loved since birth the
otter came down the long wooded coombe and raked a few
frogs out of Boreston Brook. At Chittlesford Bridge a poacher's
mongrel caught his scent and started to growl. Glimpsing
something black and catlike undulating along the bank of the
River Wash the poacher saluted it with both barrels. A solitary
pellet struck Skerry on the base of his tail and he turned and
snarled before splashing through the stream and vanishing into
the darkness. The mongrel refused to give chase.

The poacher was an unemployed TV aerial rigger named
Wharton who enjoyed the dole queue because it meant the
freedom to get out into the fields with gun and dog. 'A gentleman's life', he called it. Ever since his wife had gone back to
her mother he had been sharing his Aishford council house
with a teenage hairdresser. The girl kept telling him he was
Dean Martin's double – 'young Dean Martin, of course,' she
would laugh.

Revilious sat opposite Wharton in the doctor's waiting room
the next morning, separated from the young man by a low table
and a shaft of sunlight. A fat woman sporting surgical
stockings on both legs, waddled to the table and flicked
through the pile of Woman's Realms, Country Lifes and
Sunday colour supplements. In the end she returned to her
chair empty-handed and made a great show of examining her
fingernails.

Like a connoisseur evaluating postage stamps, Revilious
thought. Wharton was talking to someone elderly who
coughed every few seconds and tapped his open mouth with a
fist. Snatches of their conversation filtered through Revilious's
day-dreaming. Then he heard Wharton say 'otter'. The word
was dropped casually but it roused him.

'. . . scared the arse off my dog,' Wharton went on. 'I was on the bridge and it was running like hell down Boreston Brook – on dry land, like a big black cat. I haven't seen an otter since I was a boy.

'I've never seen one,' said his companion.

'I gave un both barrels,' Wharton added and Revilious clenched his fists and sucked in his breath.

'But the sod went through the Wash and up over like a bat out of hell.'

When Revilious's turn came he bounced into the surgery far too briskly for a sick man, and the doctor smiled. He was still smiling after giving his patient a thorough check-up.

'I don't doubt you, Mr Revilious,' he said. 'Stress is a killer and nature may be warning you to slow down. But,' and he sighed, 'I can find nothing wrong with your heart or your lungs, and your blood pressure is normal. If you don't enter any marathons or take up boxing you'll probably live to a ripe old age. So relax and stop worrying.'

'But the pain and the black-out were real enough.'

The doctor nodded and said: 'Stress. Slow down. Take a long holiday in the sun.'

Doctors always nod knowingly, Revilious thought, as if all their patients are simpletons and medicine is a mysterious occult thing.

He returned to the sunshine and the scent of cottage gardens. It was a little after ten o'clock when he drove back to Foxcroft by way of the Horridge Inn and Drang. Unbeknown to him the mink hounds were streaming out of their van at Whiddon Bridge and the field was preparing to move off down the water.

The mink hounds

It was the Master's intention to hunt the Aishbourne to Hay Creek and walk up the River Wash for a couple of miles. With the river so narrow good sport would be hard to come by but at least the mink would be harassed and parts of the Aishbourne below Whiddon belonged to prominent hunt subscribers. Captain Courtenay, who bred Jack Russells at his kennels between Aishford and Hay, lamented the ban on otter hunting. The captain had picked up a limp during the last war but still rode to hounds and made himself disagreeable at local conservative party meetings.

'Comes to something,' he grumbled. 'When an Englishman can't do as he damned well pleases in his own damned country. Otters were worth hunting, Fisk,' he went on, addressing the Master. 'Fine creatures full of guts and spirit. Lord! – they'd give me Jacks hell and they'd take a lot of killing. Tremendous battlers and very keen to live.'

The Master nodded affably, thinking it unwise to voice his thoughts on conservation. To hunt the otter with the creature on the danger list would have been criminal. No, mink didn't offer the same sport but they gave the dogs a chance to perform, season after season.

'Mink! Pah!' Courtenay snorted as though he'd glimpsed a Judas beneath Fisk's demeanor. 'Damned river rats! One of me Jacks could do the hounds' job, Master.'

But times certainly had changed for the worse, Fisk thought, glancing at Charlie Gutteridge. He recalled the Gutteridges' behaviour at the hunt dinner. They had revealed a whole new dimension of vulgarity. Yet the flashy spiv was worth a couple of hundred guineas a year, and the pack was an expensive luxury. In a smiling voice he said, 'Morning, Mr Gutteridge. Will the weather be kind to us?'

'I was hoping you'd kick-off up Woodburn,' Gutteridge said, hooding his eyes. 'The bloody mink grow on trees on my water.'

'Next time round, Mr Gutteridge. It think we've the power to make the mink jump.'

Gutteridge lit a cigar but made no reply. The mitigating euphemy of the middle classes got under his skin. Bloody ponces, he thought. Not a penny to scratch their arses with but enough bullshit for three guards' regiments. He looked sideways through his lashes at his girlfriend. She yawned and pulled the collar of her coney bomber jacket round her face. I should have stayed in bed with that, Gutteridge conceded. Guaranteed sport. He crumpled a fiver and dropped it in the cap held by a good-looking, upper-class youngster.

The meet had not been advertised in the press and there were no anti-hunt protestors. Many of the older members of the field wore the South Hams prussian blue jacket and matching stockings, and carried otter-poles of ash with metal tips. The notches on these staffs signified individual kills made by the hunt over the seasons. Fisk ignored the three motorbike louts lounging over their Yamahas at the roadside. He was hardened to abuse and at least they weren't a real nuisance like the anti-blood sport mob.

'Look at the wally with his walkin' stick,' one of them hooted and Fisk set his mouth. The ubiquitous council estate yob, he grimly reflected. The new world was anything but brave!

Leaning on his pole he regarded the patient progress of his animals. The pack was small – ten couples of elderly fox hounds and three couples of pure-bred otter hounds. He stepped briskly out, leaving the followers some way behind in a quiet, respectful group. Mink hunting, like otter hunting before it, was a leisurely business. It went so well, Fisk thought, with the rural scene: the little trout stream, the fields,

the leafing trees and the animals splashing through the
shallows. He loved to see his pure-breds work. They were tall,
muscular dogs, carrying narrow-domed heads. Five of the
dense, wiry coats were brown, the other almost black. The
foxhounds, who were no longer swift enough to run down their
natural quarry, lacked the otter hound's skill and deep voice.
Fisk would have liked an unadulterated pack but money was
scarce and everyone he knew had a cash flow problem.

'Why don't you hunt all year round, mate?' Gutteridge asked
Courtenay. 'I can't see the point of giving the mink a breather.'

'From November to March the water's too damned cold,'
Courtenay replied, looking askance at the Brummie and slowly
turning his back on him.

'Ponce,' Gutteridge murmured and he hooded his gaze. The
remark lacked malice. Charlie prided himself on calling a
spade a spade.

The medieval and the modern overlapped beside the river.
Big clouds sailed in from the Atlantic bringing dramatic
changes of tone to the farmland. The pack surged downstream.
Every once in a while the followers had to scramble over single
strands of barbed wire which had been strung across the water
to prevent cattle straying. Gutteridge's lady friend was
squeezed into tight jeans and yellow lace-up wellingtons, and
was getting her first taste of purgatory. But Charlie was enjoying himself. He was kicking up hell on someone else's
property and rubbing shoulders with a class whose token
acceptance he had courted for years. He had bought his way
into a select coterie and from there on he could only go up.

The sun twinkled on his gold rings and his smile which also
had plenty of gold in it. Gold watch, gold bondage chain round
his throat, sovereigns and gold fillings – and, it was claimed, a
twenty-four carat cigarette lighter and ballpoint pen! Captain
Courtenay grimaced. The fellow ought to go round in a
damned bullion van!

On the edge of Aishford the killing began. The pure-breds
started to speak and soon the pack was in full cry. The mink jill
had five kits hidden behind some ash roots up the bank away
from the river. Two couple of otter hounds found her ream –
which was hunt jargon for scent on water – and leapt ashore to
besiege her den. The animals were the pride of the pack and
many otters and mink had fallen to them. Their names were

Raleigh, Frobisher, Admiral and Amazon. Frobisher was the very dark dog that had lost half an ear to an otter in his younger days, and the sight of his left eye when a protester had jabbed at him with a stick.

Jack Russells were introduced to the den and the she mink wriggled under them and fled down to the river. Frobisher saw her and gave tongue. The mink was scrambling up the bank into the rushes and kingcups when the pack hit her and engulfed her. Above the baying of the hounds the rattle of the horn drifted through the mink's anguish. Great jaws were snapping and rending her body but before everything went numb and darkness closed in, she bit one of the lolling tongues and bore the hound's scream into eternity. Then the pack was worrying her carcass and the killing was over.

During the bloody finale the Jacks chopped the mink kits while red streamers flowed in the Aishbourne, clouded and were gone.

'Is that what it's all about?' Gutteridge's girlfriend enquired, 'Big dogs ripping a little animal to pieces?'

'It usually takes longer to find the sods,' said the thin, nasal voice which only a few hours earlier had been breathing endearments in her ear.

The hunt ran on. The hounds and hardiest members of the field waded under Aishford Bridge and came down Mill Leat. Bronze tufts were uncurling from the oak buds above them, and a coal tit fell from twig to twig uttering 'teachyou-teachyou-teachyou'. A solid mass of brown and black-and-tan hounds crashed along the leat scattering the calves in the adjoining meadows. And the first shower of the day whispered through the blackthorn and elderberry leaves, but only for a little while. Afterwards the sun shone with surprising intensity, lifting the fallen rain in steam off the lanes and roofs of the farm buildings. Stones and shillets were glinting underwater and the rocks glistened. Then, in the flags below Ramsdonsloe Farm, whose cob walls had seen nine centuries turn, Amazon marked the scent of otter and belled.

The 'drag', or scent-trail, climbed the side of the bullock field and the pack ran up it as they would run up a hill stream. The deep belling cries of his pure-bred hounds was fiercer and more passionate than Fisk had heard for many seasons.

'That's the ticket,' Courtenay muttered to himself. He was past running but the sight of hounds working still lifted him close to exultation.

*   *   *

Meeting the poacher at Chittlesford Bridge had thoroughly shaken Skerry. The bang and the flash in the dark had bewildered him because together they produced pain. He galloped over the fields beyond the Wash to cross the Aishbourne at Ramdonsloe. The old thatched farmhouse was dark and silent, and no dogs prowled around the outbuildings. Skerry nervously trod the cobbles of what was once the rickyard and came to the disused outside lavatory. The door hung on one hinge and the otter pushed past it into the deep, dry blackness. It was some time before he had ripped out the shotgun pellet and laid his chin on his tail.

The terrible voice of Amazon called him back to wakefulness. Uncoiling in one swift, sinuous movement he rose and stood facing the door. Amazon skidded to a halt and drove her muzzle into the gap. Her great snuffling gasps annoyed and alarmed the otter but the hound was also cautious. Skerry's crescendoing catterwaul raised her hackles and had her growling at her kennel companions. She thrust her muzzle again into the lavatory and shouldered the door as she advanced on her stomach. Skerry's yikker lofted once more to a screech. He darted forward and hissed at Amazon, then backed off and let out a deep, whining growl. Frobisher scrabbled at the door but one of the foxhounds blundered against him and the rest of the pack rioted.

A scrum of pure-breds collected in the doorway and began a prolonged chorus that brought the farmer out of his kitchen and Fisk into the yard. The whippers-in were close behind him. Now the hounds were trying to goad the otter out into the open.

'It's an otter,' the Master said. 'Whip off the hounds – quickly, gentlemen. And keep the field back, please.'

Obediently but without enthusiasm the hounds came to heel. Fisk pushed open the lavatory door and Skerry shot out and vanished between two sheds. Frobisher stood whining and quivering against the Master's legs. Rain fell and raising his eyes Fisk could not separate the clouds. The morning had turned grey and the cuckoo calling through the downpour sounded lost and uncertain. Courtenay was the last to arrive.

'Which way did the otter go, Captain?' asked Fisk.

'Upstream.'

The hounds milled around the Master, their cavernous music carrying many miles.

'They had him,' Gutteridge said acidly to a lady standing close by.

'But otters are protected by law,' came the patient reply.

Gutteridge shook his head in contemptuous disbelief and chose to look at the sky. He had never played anything by the rules and this always gave him the advantage over decent law-abiding people.

Clouds

The rain paused, the sky opened and closed again and pressed down on the hilltop. After his brush with the hunt Skerry was content to lie in the hedge bottom under the alexanders and blackthorn listening to the raindrops pattering from the trees onto the dock leaves near his nose. His breathing slowed, his eyelids descended and he slept. All day he remained unconscious to the world of wind, rain, flashes of sun and birdsong, and the crying of farm animals. Then after sunset he returned to Foxcroft and killed a trout by Bowcombe Pool. The fish was nosing up a feeding ground taking shrimps and pea mussels. Skerry also ate frogs which had come to the water over the fields to spawn, and he visited his sprainting posts to check for bitches. He had claimed the Aishbourne as his territory and was no longer a wanderer.

For a while he used two kennels upstream of the house; one in thick reeds on Orchard Island, the other in a hollow oak stump below Brent Copse. Revilious was heartened to find spraints and seals at the water's edge, but he no longer heard the whistling that had been a feature of Foxcroft dusks. News of the incident at Ramdonsloe Farm added to his anxiety and he wondered how long Skerry could tolerate such disturbances if indeed it was Skerry.

April closed coolly and little was seen of Gutteridge around Aishwell. Healey hinted at business problems in Birmingham and the vision of all those heavyweight urban sharks cutting into each other made Revilious's flesh crawl. But the brothers' absence meant quiet evenings in The Plough listening to Yelland's tall stories and watching the two old boys play crib. The journey home was heightened by the prospect of finding Skerry at the pond, and motoring down the final section on a frosty night he felt the rapture which appeared to rise from the moonlit countryside and take possession of him. Even the untenanted pool failed to dampen his spirits. Spring was undeniably in the air and on still evenings he heard hedgehogs snuffling around the flowerbeds. Then the perfume of the gardens lifted fine and strong and the blackbird sang to the edge of darkness.

Before bed one night he stood at the door, sober but pleasantly drowsy. Alcohol drummed up encounters with the unexpected and the good music and the firelight would not have been the same without it. Too many beautiful things were censored by logic. The dog otter whistled from some invisible trout-lie below Home Weir as if he approved of Revilious's philosophy.

There were sad little signs of Skerry's quest for a mate. Revilious found spraints deposited on twists of grass and prominently displayed in the hope some kindred spirit would find them and respond. The otter's rolling places were evident and Revilious discovered the remains of an eel chewed down to a stump the size of an expensive cigar. At the back of his mind was the fear of Gutteridge's shotgun, and one Sunday close to dawn he searched the Aishbourne from Woodburn Bridge to the Horridge Inn, dreading the discovery of a dead otter.

Nailed to a tree opposite Healey's chicken houses were the carcasses of three mink. Revilious came angrily down the fish swims and found some box traps and another mink strung up on barbed wire at a bend where a little marsh of Lady's Smocks grew. Cattle rose awkwardly from their knees when he approached and they ambled through the reeds blowing gently and stretching out their necks to sniff his jacket. The first black caps piped amid the bird cherry blossom and the chorus of native songbirds pealed down the coombe.

Revilious sat by the river. It was no use getting sentimental about the mink. They were pests and the shotgun and box traps would have been humane compared to gins. But Gutteridge's naked hostility riled him. The man was forever dipping into other people's reality with the sort of heartlessness that springs from self-dislike.

Light rippled all around him. A fish broke the surface and left a widening circle. He was nodding off and made no attempt to fight it. When he woke the shadows on the side of the coombe were announcing sunrise. Revilious came home through the wonderful melancholy of sabbath bells which reminded him of his childhood and walks beside the River Wye. House martins were hawking Old Bethlehem and a cuckoo called across the fields and copses. Maybe I'm dead, Revilious thought. Small white clouds sailed by. He opened the downstairs windows and the front door, and the distant church bells were like echoes from the England of Rupert Brooke.

Then Skerry was back at the pond giving the pike a hard time between building up his couch of reeds and twigs on the island and sleeping there in the sun. The dance of ephemerals over the glassy calm and the ploop! of rising trout created an idyllic atmosphere. But the rain returned, bringing with it a letter from the solicitors. Gutteridge had put in an offer for Foxcroft and Revilious instructed Bertish to convince the man he was wasting everyone's time.

'Cheeky clown,' Reg Yelland breathed into his tea. 'But he won't give up easy, maister. I saw un down Woodburn with his dogs yesterday. Those animals are wild buggers. Some of Charlie's meaness has rubbed off on 'em.'

We are born into a booby-trapped world, thought Revilious – me and Reg and the Afghan and the otter. And the magpie, mummified now in the hedge. Silent, heavy rain dribbled down the window, and the wet spring night seemed for a moment to hold all human grief.

'An otter, hey,' said Yelland as though he were addressing himself. 'Beautiful creatures. I didn't know they were still around Aishwell. Still, it could have come from the Wildlife Park at Cuckoo Cross over Sarson way.'

'No, Reg. This one's as wild as the wind.'

'Then I hope for his sake he keeps off Gutteridge's bit of water.'

'What makes Gutteridge so unpleasant?' Revilious asked Bob Maunder when the three met in The Plough after dinner.

'Christ knows,' Maunder growled. 'And I don't really care. Havin' all the details about Hitler's psychological problems don't help the Auchwitz victims. Charlie probably had a nasty dad or an uncaring mum or a sadistic granny. So what? As far as I'm concerned he's a pain in the arse.'

Some students were distributing Green Peace literature to a scattering of drinkers. Their passion and sincerity saddened Revilious for he recalled his own youth and the subsequent disappointments. Another booby trap, he mused – the adult world of jobs, apathy, conformity and resignation.

He took the leaflet and said thank you but Reg Yelland wouldn't give the time of day to 'hippies'. He had endured a war to secure his liberty and their's too as he was quick to inform them in blunt terms.

'Do you know what a five megaton bomb would do to Totnes?' a girl enquired pityingly.

'Improve it,' Yelland grunted. But the old man's humour made him hard to dislike, and he could be witty enough when it suited him.

A couple of teachers from a public school not far away occasionally used The Plough with their wives. Before long Revilious was wondering if Cadogan had been reincarnated. The academics were always so keen to advertise their superior intellects. Reg Yelland was courted with pints because he was 'the salt of the earth', the kind of bona fide yokel the trendies claimed to admire.

'If I were not Hawthorn,' one of them declared jokingly in a parody of Alexander the Great's words, 'I would be Yelland.'

The patronizing tone and daftness of the remark infuriated Revilious but he bit his tongue.

'Tom has written the definitive work on Hardy,' one of the women drawled. 'It's received some super reviews.'

'Think I'll wait for the one on Stan Laurel,' Yelland said.

The laughter was as hollow as the pub's mock oak beams.

*   *   *

The warmer weather flushed more crayfish out of the silt in pursuit of dragonfly larvae and Skerry often visited Lord's Pool to catch this delicacy. When colour sank in the sky he would patrol the trout-lies for whatever the river had to offer. Resting his elbows on the garden wall Revilious trained his field glasses on the otter and watched him go about his business.

Skerry loved the white water of Home Weir. He wriggled through it and gave himself to the current and let it play with him. But at night his whistling across the pond through the rain made Revilious's heart ache. Then everything whispered of the transient and the void after the creature had fallen silent seemed the fate of all happiness.

Walking the fields to Drang Cottages Revilious's eye was caught by something small and pinkish in the grass. It was a flower similar to the common orchid but much paler and with broader, plain green leaves. He regretted leaving his wildflower handbook at home but determined to consult it at the earliest opportunity.

The river was running brimful, clear and brown. Revilious swung his stick idly at the reeds and tried to recall the haunting refrain from Ravel's Introduction and Allegro. He climbed the hedge in the corner of Westerland and dropped into the lane humming to himself. The blue Cortina Estate stood in the gateway facing Healey's cottage. The young man was perched on the bonnet, arms folded, listening to Gutteridge. God, thought Revilious, hasn't the chap got a home to go to? Once more the life was leaving his knees. He wanted to turn purposefully and march off over the bridge but his feet had taken root. He had come to see Healey but the business could wait so why, he groaned inwardly, am I kicking around here like an idiot. On impulse he knelt and pretended to tie a bootlace. A furtive glance confirmed what he dreaded most. Gutteridge was bearing down on him with the alsations. Base macho, Revilious decided, employing the scale he had drawn up at Cavendish Towers.

'Wasn't my price high enough?' Gutteridge began. Revilious straightened and held himself erect in a moving ring of dogs. They were striding around him, placing their wet noses on his fingers, sniffing at his boots and regarding him from dark, inquisitive eyes.

'Foxcroft isn't for sale, Mr Gutteridge,' he managed. His hands had started to shake and Gutteridge also noted a swift greying of the face.

'But if you was to sell,' he continued softly, 'you could retire to some nice little Cotswold cottage far away from nasty bastards like me.'

Suddenly his eyelids slid upwards and the eyes of malachite green were wide and innocent. The man's self-confidence was irresistible and devoid of emotion, hawklike, Revilious observed from misery that welled and whirlpooled.

'Foxcroft is just a lot of aggravation,' the voice chimed. 'You'd be better off out of it!'

Revilious shook his head, and the malachite eyes slowly hooded and became knife-slits. A dog crinkled its lips and snarled. The long muscular bodies of the alsations passed back and forth across his thighs in deliberate provocation. He was terrified and was showing it. Gutteridge smiled.

'All this bother, Mr Revilious,' he whispered. 'And for what? It's so unnecessary.'

Drifting away from himself Revilious saw the magpie's ghost convulsing on the wet road.

'Revilious?'

Revilious lowered his head and shook it again. Some sort of signal must have passed between man and animal for one of the alsations planted itself in front of him and stared up into his face. A wave of dizziness was followed swiftly by nausea.

'You'll come round,' Gutteridge continued in a brotherly tone.

Then the Brummie was sauntering back to his car, whistling the dogs and hooking his sunglasses out of a breast pocket.

Before finally departing Gutteridge drew up alongside Revilious and said: 'A little bird told me you've been nosing about on my bit of river. Now that is definitely out of order, old boy, and if it happens again I may regard it as a declaration of war.'

The smell of the Ford's exhaust only lingered for a while, and Revilious sighed. Nothing had changed. Small green leaves shivered and settled once more into tree shapes. The river poured under the bridge and the pigs grunted and squealed. He wiped his fingers on his trousers and asked himself why he opted out of confrontations.

But Healey's wife agreed to come over once a week and do his cleaning. Her fresh round face had the flush of outdoor living. Revilious welcomed the small talk. His hands had stopped shaking and he spoke easily of Foxcroft.

'By the way,' he concluded. 'There's a pretty little pink flower growing in Old Bethlehem by Huish Brook. I'd say it was some sort of wild orchid.'

Mrs Healey confessed she had never walked on Foxcroft. It was private property. Her integrity touched Revilious. Old values endured, after all, and in a social class Major Shackle would have dismissed with boredom and contempt.

At The Plough

Revilious consulted as many books as he could lay his hands on and concluded the Old Bethlehem flower was the rare Military orchid. Further fieldwork uncovered another three and a telephone call to the local branch of the West Country Trust for Nature Conservation conjured up a botanist who made a positive identification. It was decided to keep the site a secret.

'You live alone, Mr Revilious?' the young woman said over a drink at the Horridge Inn. 'I only ask,' she hastily explained learning he had neither relatives nor commitments, 'because I wondered if you'd considered bequeathing Foxcroft to the nation. Our society would jump at the offer. These old properties are gold dust. Once they come on the market the developers move in and today's paradise becomes tomorrow's housing estate.'

Revilious argued his case for non-interference and the botanist conceded he had a point although it was evident she remained unconverted. She thinks in terms of wildlife trails, study-centres and parks, Revilious glumly decided – signposts, educational notices and human gregariousness in the search for knowledge and amusement. The botanist hinted politely at elitism and Revilious smiled. He was not prepared to elaborate on his idea of the Foxcroft stewardship or to go too deeply into the morality of creating a zone where plants and animals could exist with the minimum of human disturbance.

Bob Maunder resented Gutteridge's smear campaign as it slowly developed in The Plough. He had seen too many victims of pub talk. A special sort of malice crept out of the boredom and false bonhomie of bar society, and Charlie Gutteridge loved it. But he did not deceive the old ex-policeman.

For weeks tension had ticked away in Maunder's forehead. The scurrilous gossip reminded him of the police club after his divorce. 'Maunder losing out to a randy mick!' He closed his fist on the sleeve. Charlie Gutteridge surveyed his audience and muzak oozed from the speakers close to the ceiling, inanely, like the stuff they used to play between films in the cinemas of Maunder's younger days.

'What does Revilious do for a bit of skirt?' Gutteridge said. 'I mean, what's he up to at Foxcroft? Where's Mrs Revilious? Or is he –'

Leaving the sentence unfinished he placed a hand on his hip and pursed his lips. Someone giggled. Gutteridge frowned and minced out to the lavatory amid guffaws and hoots of glee. Bob Maunder collared him behind the door marked 'Gents'.

'You grubby bastard,' the old man snarled. 'Always chucking muck at people. What have you got against Revilious? Can't you get your own way for once?'

Gutteridge grinned and hooded his eyes.

'I've got friends in the force and if you keep harassing him I'll see you're put away.'

'You're still Old Bill then, Maunder.'

'Yes – and don't you ever forget it, Gutteridge.'

The Brummie opened his mouth, thought better of it and turned to the wash basin.

Bloody fascist, Maunder fumed, but he kept the encounter to himself and put on a cheerful face for the next time he met Revilious.

A light breeze from the east held the fair weather over the South Hams. Swallows swooped to drink on the wing from Foxcroft's pond. Then one day the swifts crowded the sky and their shrilling through the evening sunshine brought episodes of Revilious's childhood sharply into focus. Aishwell itself was one of those accidental monuments to nostalgia which big business exploits on television to advertise something bogus, mass-produced and unpalatable.

Revilious enjoyed walking up the hill to the square dominated by the church, and Bob Maunder supplied the best sort of company – silent, unobtrusive.

A couple of old border collies sprawled asleep in the road outside the post office and cabbage whites danced around the valerian sprouting from walls which had been built during the Civil War. Some of the day's heat was sandwiched between the buildings. Up ahead a farm worker drove three cows followed by a collie and a lame mongrel. The swifts screamed high against wisps of cirrus, so tiny and far off they might have strayed in from childhood summers. The absence of double yellow lines on the road helped create the illusion of timelessness.

Three farms spilled onto the village's one real street. The other thoroughfares were lanes and alleys and hidden cul-de-sacs whose names betrayed their origins – Leat Lane, Pump Lane, Church Close, Pill Drang. The church and the pub were historic but not glamorous enough to lure the tourist or day-tripper. No concessions had been made to tourism except the handful of holiday homes, for Aishwell was a working village aware of its own dignity. The architecture was South Hams utility – limewashed stone, some cob, paint in primary colours, a few bedroom verandahs, small terrace houses and cottages, and all thrown together in the sort of unruly cluster which modern planners loathe.

'It's a Godless age, Paul,' Bob Maunder grunted, hauling himself out of his thoughts and pausing to get his breath back. 'When a country turns its back on religion and morality it's doomed.'

Revilious glanced curiously at his companion but Maunder did not pursue the comment.

'Do you go to church, Bob?'

'Sometimes. Do you?'

'Sometimes.'

Maunder's advanced years and frailty were apparent now for all his bulk. He looked a worn-out, defeated old man living on the edge of an alien world. In his eyes anxiety was condensing, and Revilious knew then that his glimpses of the new, impending Dark Ages were not unique. They drank cider and took their bar snacks to Revilious's favourite corner.

'The beefburgers are the safest bet,' Maunder grinned. 'I tried one of their chicken curries once. Needed a magnifying glass to find the meat and the whole mess tasted like a disposable paper nappy – after use!'

'Egon Ronay would not enthuse over these baked beans,' Revilious said. Mercifully the music was not too loud and the bar was practically empty. They continued to make small talk until around six thirty when Maunder departed in time to catch a gardening programme on Reg Yelland's television. Revilious lit a cigar and blew smoke at a fly that was manoeuvring to land on the remains of his dinner. Almost telepathically the barman appeared and whisked away the dishes. Revilious tried to read but was too restless to concentrate for long. The swifts were screaming around the tower of Aishwell Church and whenever the music ended the blackbird's melody poured out of a nearby garden. And he felt an overwhelming desire to be home looking down on the pond.

He came out of The Plough and stood under the stippled sky. Little separate cirrus clouds were picking up the last of the sun.

Lord, it's a glorious evening, he mused. On and on the blackbird sang, and behind it a cuckoo, muffled by distance.

Cuckoo Cross Park

Revilious took his coffee to the verandah. The morning was fine and the rooks were swirling silently around the rooftop. Under the trees of Big Wood the ground was covered in bluebells. Revilious sipped the hot, sweet Nescafe while the Emperor dragonflies tacked and clicked across the pond. The birdsong was deafening.

Now the beeches were shaking out their almost transparent leaves and the trees, filling with the first breeze of the day, dappled the lane with shadows. Bob Maunder came groggily downstairs and unlatched the back door of his cottage. The right side of his head had gone dead and he had difficulty pinning down a thought. Unbelievably it grew worse and became a cold numbness that sucked each attempt at reasoning into a blank.

'Ruby,' he groaned. 'Ruby.'

The name screwed into his mind, distorted like something on tape played at the slowest possible speed. Then consciousness receded and long before the ambulance deposited him at the hospital in Plymouth the stroke had him in its sights.

By noon of that sunny spring day it had destroyed him.

'Dudn seem possible,' Reg Yelland whispered. 'Bob was such a big, healthy bloke.'

Jars of daffodils stood on the nearby mounds and a black cat rolled and purred against the wall of a tomb. The sun flushing the sandstone tower burnt Revilious's back despite the layer of dark worsted. Standing among the group of mourners he watched the first few shovelfuls of earth rattle onto the coffin before striding off, his turn-ups swishing in the grass.

* * *

The bell was tolling as it had in the time of John Donne, Shakespeare and Chaucer. Lifting his head from sleep Skerry sniffed the air and listened to the strange sound. He was curled up on the old straw of Hazard Linhay. Idly he snapped his jaws at a fly that drifted close to his muzzle. Then he placed his chin on his hindlegs and sank his nose in his tail and slept again. But with twilight hazing the watermeadows the ache returned and he pushed grumpily through the nettles and Fool's parsley into the orchard. The buzzards of Churchland's Wood circled Foxcroft, mewling to each other. And the emptiness around the otter's heart became a pain.

He ran up Horse Wrangler Hill trying to shake off the misery but it still pulsed in his chest as he came down one of the feeders off Beenleigh Brook to the hamlet of Sarsons. The circle of standing stones on a knoll nearby had given the tiny community its name. The megaliths looked like hooded saracens of which Sarsons was a corruption.

A short distance downstream was Cuckoo Cross Wildlife Park and its ponds and assortment of wildfowl and rare breeds. From mounting excitement Skerry smelled the musk of a bitch otter on heat and sent his call through the dusk. She left her sleeping box and ran down the ramp outside the shed that was her home and dived into the pool. Surfacing quickly she answered him, fluting small urgent cries. Skerry galloped across the paddock and stood upright against the fence of heavy wire mesh. The little bitch otter scrambled out of the pool and shook herself before coming to him and standing up to place her nose against his own. They exchanged the joyful yikkering of their kind but the fence was high and soon the touching of muzzles was not enough.

Her name was Cariad and she had come to Cuckoo Cross from mid-West Wales eighteen months ago. She had been badly wounded in the hind legs as a cub by a teenager trying out his new shotgun. The schoolteacher who found her had patiently nursed her back to health but she was ungainly on land and ran with a lopsided arching of the body. Attempts were made to return her to the wilds but she had cried after the man and would not be parted.

Cariad might have remained in Dyfed if her destructiveness around the house had not driven the teacher's wife to despair. The otter had broken crockery and china ornaments, chewed books and got stuck in the livingroom chimney. She had to go and Cuckoo Cross seemed like a good idea. It was owned by Tom Morgan, an exiled Welshman from the teacher's valley.

So the Welsh otter was brought to the Devon Wildlife Park and kept hidden from the public but despite Morgan's efforts no mate was found for her. Cariad remained a playful animal in an enclosure full of things which kept her amused. The place had been built to house a pair of Asian short claw otters but the deal had fallen through at the last moment. The stream running into the pool tumbled over a series of man-made falls, and she had a squeaky doll, numerous other toys and a slide. There were times, though, when she fell silent and stood up and looked towards an horizon only she could see. Then her soft whimpering cries sounded like the sobbing of a child and Morgan's heart bled for her.

Now she almost sang her joy and Skerry fell back on all fours and ran from side to side. But there was no way through or under the wire. He explored every foot of the fence with Cariad pursuing him on the other side. And their chittering brought Morgan to the diningroom window of his bungalow.

'Come here, Nell,' he said. 'We've got a new guest.'

His wife set the salad bowl down on the table and joined him.

'A dog otter at last,' Morgan breathed. 'Have a look at him through these.' He handed over the binoculars and smiled when she gasped.

'Oh, he's lovely, Tom! What are you going to do?'

'Open the enclosure gate and leave it open.'

'But she'll go.'

'Or he'll stay. I'd like to see them mate and move on. The rivers round here are crying out for otters.'

'Is it likely?'

'No. The visitors would put paid to all that. All the noise the trippers kick up would make Cari and her new boyfriend run miles'.

'Don't you mind losing her?'

'Yes – but she's a wild creature not a pet. I love her too much to want to hold her here on my terms. If she goes with him she has a real chance of surviving and breeding.'

The magpie geese were clamouring as he walked down the path to the otter pen. Skerry retreated to the trees and let loose his crescendoing screech of protest but Morgan ignored him and undid the gate.

'Live long and happily,' he whispered, and returned to the bungalow.

The spring night was drawing in and the scent of mown grass and wallflowers wafted off the garden. But before the light failed he saw the dark lithe shape of Cariad run with heart-wrenching awkwardness across the paddock to meet another dark shape. The cries rang loud and clear through the stillness, and the otters rolled together, paws round each other's necks until Morgan's labrador started barking. Then the paddock was empty.

'Well, that's that,' Morgan said, and his voice shook.

'Was it the right thing to do, Tom?'

He lifted his shoulders and let them fall again. 'My head and conscience say yes but my heart doesn't go a lot on it.'

'She was like a child, Tom. And the outside world's a pretty unkind place.'

Morgan placed a hand to his lips and blew gently through his fingers.

'Something will turn up, love,' he sighed. 'God, Nell – I couldn't keep her penned up, not after that little scene.'

'No, of course you couldn't,' she smiled, kissing him.

Salt water

Steeped in starlight the fields curved down into the shadowy coombe. The stink of garlic lay over the ramsons at the meeting of hazel scrub and water. Together the otters followed Beenleigh Brook to Whidden Bridge and caught eels. Dog and bitch played after eating, chivvying each other and rolling in the shallows. Then they left their spraints on a boulder which Skerry regularly used as a scenting post and pretended to hunt the little pools. But the commotion of the ducks in the nearby farmyard sent them galloping up the meadow to run their noses along the wire netting. Now the Khaki Campbells were really protesting and flapping their wings, and the otters darted about trying to find a gap in the fence. But the shot instantly put Skerry to flight with Cariad on his heels.

'Bloody foxes,' the farmer grated.

Skerry had intended going upstream to Foxcroft but the scare drove him and Cariad down beyond Aishford. The Aishbourne poured out of the coombe overhung with trees into the creek. Presently they were part of the broad, lazy Dart, drifting against the push of the flood-tide. They swam side by side, soundlessly, and often dived and rolled underwater. Her scent lay strong on the surface and he luxuriated in it, attentive and full of love for her.

They swam down the navigation channel of Long Stream, between tidal mudflats and sandbanks, past Middle Back cocklebeds opposite Stoke Mouth. Against the sky stood the tower of Stoke Gabriel Church and lights shone across Mill Pool. The waterway carried them into the many little bays and inlets beneath the outstretched oak boughs to surprise and kill mullet. And all the time between the hunting and eating they sparred, falling through the bubbles which broke from their coats to flicker in a sensuous ballet. Then they would rise and tread water and call to each other.

At Sandridge there were lights on the river and the low unpleasant noise of men's voices. The salmon fishermen were busy and the tide was helping to ease the one hundred and fifty foot long seine nets shorewards. Unseen the otters dived and swam for the opposite bank. They came across the silt beyond Lower Gurrow Point and glided among the yachts and motor craft anchored off Dittisham. Dog-paddling close to the Greenaway Quay their ears pricked to the cloop and slap of wavelets on gleaming white hulls.

Here the river coursed dark under wooded hills that curved steeply on each side. Skerry led Cariad in a game of chase around Anchor Stone but the little bitch was tiring and where Lord's Wood trailed down to the shallows of Parson's Mud he coaxed her ashore and waited for her to dry off in the ferns. Close by was a couch of dead bracken beneath a crab apple tree and they curled up on it, back to back, breathing gently.

When they woke a wren was trilling from the bramble thicket and the dawn chorus lofted from every corner of rural England. The glow of bluebells swept up into the trees and down on the river the waterfowl splashed and fluted.

Skerry and Cariad lolloped up the slope under the fall of crab apple blossom and stalked leverets in the meadows of Bosomzeal and Fire Beacon Hill. Mist was rising off the Dart and the cormorants that roosted in the riverside oaks beat swiftly downstream.

Cariad shook the dew off her coat and ran to him and held up her muzzle, delivering the broken, mewing cry. Then they slithered through the bluebells and splashed across mud softer than ground coffee into the river. A cock pheasant crowed and the first pale sunlight crept up the Dart to meet them at Higher Noss Point.

Motionless sailing craft were ranged along the deeps beyond Noss. Keeping under the shore the otters caught swimming crabs and more eels and ate them on a rock close to Britannia

Halt. The summit over the way was dominated by the Royal Naval College and the houses of Dartmouth clung to the hillside. Roofs and windows were gleaming against the sun.

Now the water was crowded with all sorts of craft and the otters swam beneath the surface rising at short intervals to vent. They met the surge of the floodtide at Waterhead Viaduct and frightened a mute swan into a flapping, noisy take-off. Beside the wharves and quays of Kingswear the flow was clotted with boxes and plastic garbage.

Pushed across the river by the tide they chased pollock amongst the seaweed of Halftide Rock and One Gun Point. For Cariad the journey was unbelievably exciting and having so much water around her played like a drug on her senses. An angler casting for bass off Deadman's Cove saw the otters surface, and the sight was ample compensation for a blank night.

Dog-paddling with the Channel swell Skerry and Cariad swam across the Dart estuary towards the wooded cliffs of Inner Froward Point. The light easterly was lifting the sea in long hogbacks that held bottle-glass twinkles. Waves enveloped rocks and slid green and transparent over ribs of mica-slate to explode silently below the surface. A small colony of kittiwakes sent a chorus of Punch and Judy cries down from the slabs of Old Mill Bay and fulmars skimmed by on rigid wings.

The otters hauled out onto a reef and groomed each other while the huge spring sun hung between the Mew Stone and Eastern Black Rock. The Mew Stone was a high pyramid of shattered slate about a quarter of a mile offshore. Its spine and spires and mallow-choked gulleys were white with gulls. On stormy, winter days it could look as grim as any Gothic castle.

A crabber chugging past Inner Froward to his pots off the Stone scared the otters and they dived. The drone of the propellers thrummed through their skulls. Skerry kicked and broke out of a swell, his valvular nostrils opening for air. 'Hah' he grunted. 'Hah'. Two glossy heads bobbed about like crab pot marker buoys before submerging once more. A jolt of love leapt between dog and bitch and they shot out of the water in twin porpoise leaps and dived deep to join the slow motion dance of the kelp.

The games and light-hearted attempts to catch pollock made their progress up a coastline of tall, gorse-clad cliffs and inlets sheer pleasure but the diving, often to depths of five or six fathoms, tired Cariad and left her cold and shivering. Swimming hard round a headland they entered Pudcombe Cove and came ashore onto a beach of pebbles and gritty shale. Fashionable swimming parties had once been held there by the residents of Coleton Fishacre and the little open-air pool up under the cliff had rung with laughter. Now it was choked with pebbles.

Skerry examined the cove and searched the grassy niches at the bottom of the cliff for a suitable kennel. The mallard duck whose nest was eight feet above the water watched him anxiously but did not budge. Twelve ducklings pressed against her. They were the colour of dead bracken and the soil, like their mother, and the entire family escaped detection.

The otters climbed the stone steps and paused uncertainly on the path. To the right lay the stream and landscaped gardens of Coleton Fishacre; to the left was a thick fir wood showing all the signs of neglect. Under the brush and fallen branches he made a couch big enough for them both. Then he returned to the cove and caught flukes and a ballan wrasse which he brought to her. The sun climbed higher and insects sawed and zithered around their hiding place. Glancing up from a cat-nap Skerry idly regarded the gull's white breast feather as it drifted down. Cariad ran her teeth through the hairs of his tail and his eyelids slowly sealed the moment.

*   *   *

They spent three days at Coleton Fishacre snatching fish from the cove and crabs and mussels off the tideline. The miniature heatwave continued but the nights were as cool as the sea. Sometimes they hunted by day but Skerry had to restrain the less cautious Cariad and emphasize many of the survival skills captivity had dulled.

Dusk was magical. They would lie awake waiting for the sky to darken, listening to the soft speech of the firs and the crisper sound of the sea crumbling on the beach below. On the final evening the house martins that nested in a cave roof along the coast were swooping across the cliffs and picking-off the mating hoverflies. The dense musk of gorse veiled the coast. A cuckoo hiccuped its D and D sharp over and over from the flowering almond in the lap of the estate as the otters cantered down the beach to the sea.

Before long they were diving and catching pout whiting off a sunken reef. Her tail brushed his face and he squirmed and turned back on her to nip one of her toes. Bubbles traced their twists and turns and sudden somersaults and undulations. Then he sank and pursued her underwater, letting her fool him with her dodging and corkscrewing.

Towards midnight instinct resurrected an image in his blood and he felt a compelling urge to return to Foxcroft. So he led Cariad out of Coleton Fishacre onto the open fields. Running at her pace they came over Kingston and Boohay to Hoodown, and were the safe side of Bridge Road with several hours of darkness to spare.

A little night music

The pain wasn't imaginary and Revilious resented being told otherwise. It did not come often but when it did it left him close to suffocation in a lather of fear. Once, moving a basket of logs, the sharp chest spasm sent him rocking back against the shed wall while his heart raced like the jammed throttle of a car. This time the doctor took him more seriously and a consultation with a heart specialist was arranged.

Before the actual examination got under way Revilious had
gone through the whole lexicon of fear but after the diagnosis
he was soon in a better frame of mind. Returning from London
on the train he had time to consider life from a new angle. One
day the angina would drop him like a poleaxed horse. It might
take a year or two, or a couple of months, and it could be next
week. Instead of panicking and collapsing in self-pity he
remained calm and detached, possibly because he could not
believe it was happening to him.

Poor old Bob Maunder had gone quickly but Bob had a few
years under his belt and had loved another human being.
Revilious sighed. And yet, one glorious spring day lived
through with joy and reverence was perhaps enough, or he
half-convinced himself this was the case. But the beauty of
dawn and dusk had a new, surreal quality and the nightingale
singing from the edge of the wood seemed to belong to the
After Life. How ironic, he thought, lying in bed enjoying a
last cigar before switching off the light. He had tried to see the
world so often through the eyes of pre-literate man and now
that vision was growing. He was living greedily through each
moment as it came, like a gunslinger waiting for the last
showdown. The romantic notion amused him and it was
comforting to know he would avoid the terminal ward.

*   *   *

Moving at fifty miles an hour the dragonfly tore into the
cabbage white and carried it into the virginia creeper to devour.
A solitary white wing fluttered onto the terrace and Revilious
shuddered.

'They girt old boys,' Yelland chuckled. 'They don't miss ort.'

The evening was warm enough to sit outside but the clarity
of distance suggested a change in the weather. And the wind,
Revilious noted, had veered north westerly again.

He refilled Yelland's glass. The cider had a strange yet most
appealing flavour, and for some unfathomable reason it
reminded him of an abortive walking holiday in Herefordshire.
Jane Wensley – God, yes! he thought. It was her, buried under
nearly thirty years of separation. Sweet, serious Jane. But the
holiday dynamited their relationship. Her enthusiasm for
sharing the same bed had shocked him. From pedestal to

mattress in a few moments! And I botched it, he lamented. Botched it because I'd never had a willing woman before. They'd drunk cider in a lovely out-of-the-way little pub and laughed a lot. Then the bedroom farce and her departure alone the following day after a breakfast eaten in silence. Lifting the glass to his lips he wondered what had become of her.

'You heard about the otter at Cuckoo Cross, Mr Revilious?' said Yelland. 'Her went off with a wild one. Morgan told me himself the other day when us met at the Seven Stars in Totnes. A dog otter got into his park and he let the little bitch Cariad run off with un. He reckons they'll breed. It could be the one on your pond.'

'That's more than likely, Reg. Skerry gets about. I hope they manage something. There's no pollution to speak of in the South Ham's rivers and a good few, like the Aishbourne, offer the perfect habitat.'

'If Gutteridge gets his hooks into 'em they won't last five minutes. Healey says he've got a bit of trout hatchery or something down Horridge way and you know what that means.'

'He'll be able to kill otters without fear of prosecution. Farmers and fish hatchery people are exempted from the Wildlife and Countryside Act.'

'Tez only a poky bit of water full of fry – tidn a real hatchery. Charlie's a cunning sod.'

'Yes,' Revilious swallowed, 'he never fails to amaze me.'

'Charlie don't write the poems for Mothers' Day cards and that's for certain,' said Yelland. 'Old Bob hated un.' He folded his hands clumsily on the table and added: 'Buggered if I don't miss Bob. He was a good old boy. But nothing can bring un back. When you'm my age you have to get used to death sticking his head in the door and messin' things up. Twadn like it when I was young but seems tez with you all the time as you get older. I s'pose age is all about losing things – hair, teeth, taste . . . friends, loved ones.'

It would be convenient to pretend the world is a construction of my own mind, Revilious thought. But there was an awful vanity in the assertion that nothing existed outside individual consciousness. Self as the centre of the universe!

'You know what I think, Mr Revilious,' Yelland went on. 'Bob wanted to die. He loved that maid – the one who ran off with the navvy. His heart broke long before his brain packed up.'

Revilious was out in the garden soon after sunrise. Along the borders the scarlet pimpernel were closing their petals against approaching rain. He squinted up at the sky and ran a fingertip through his moustache. The greyness was more menacing than sullen. Yet he felt almost foolishly cheerful. The wind was rising, blanching the willow leaves and raking the pond. It was as if the air had come alive. The entire coombe quaked and rippled, and birds on the wing were no longer images in a sickbed dream. The surface of the pond blurred. Ophelia would not have chosen the place for her drowning, he thought. Sluggish streams, weed, hot noons – those were the stage props of suicide. Suicide was the ultimate breaking of faith with the living world.

*   *   *

Healey paused in the porch of The Plough and took off his cycle clips. Rain dropped from the peak of his cap and a trickle ran down his neck.

'Back to normal,' Yelland grinned, pushing his empty sleever across the counter.

'I'll see to that,' Healey said.

While the beer frothed and clouded in the glasses he let his gaze wander round the public. At the far end a group of leather jackets were playing darts and a fat girl of sixteen or seventeen was pumping her pocket money into a one-armed bandit. A scattering of old and middleaged regulars occupied familiar niches and bar stools. The low hum of conversation would climb to a bellow around closing time.

'How's things at Foxcroft?' Healey said as they ferried their pints to the table under the mullioned window. 'I heard about they otters. I thought old Charlie would have a fit when I told un. But he didn bat an eye. Him and his bloody trout farm! Half a dozen minnows under a bit of wire netting that wouldn't cover a bog seat! Christ – he haven't half got it in for the bloke.'

'Only cos Revilious is Foxcroft. Charlie would go for anything belonging to the poor devil – house, car, wife, budgie. He's like one of they Great War generals. There's his objective and he's goin' to take it at all costs.'

'Idn he carrying it a bit far?'

'Charlie don't care about anyone or anything. He's got a deaf soul. I wouldn work for the bugger.'

Healey smiled and coloured.

'Some of us with families haven't got much choice, Reg. But I only look after his reach part-time.'

Yelland patted the young man's hand and winked and poured several inches of best bitter into his sly old face.

Healey knew most of the motorbike clique congregating round the fruit machine. They were OK, he decided, providing you didn't let them intimidate you with that leather jacket uniform and the hire purchase Yamahas standing outside the pub. He fancied a 500cc machine but not at the expense of everything else. All but one of the youths came from Totnes – a town that was not universally recognized as the mecca of Hell's Angels.

Returning to the bar he fished out enough coins for a packet of crisps. A couple of lads broke away from the dartboard scrum and swaggered up calling for double Southern Comforts and pints of Heineken.

'You takin' your bike, Dave?' drawled the tall, lean one with an untidy line of X's and the words 'CUT HERE' tattooed on his forehead.

'No machines. We do it quiet – Charlie's way.'

'What's in the bag?'

The stout teenager grinned through his acne and said 'Whatever it is matey won't like it.'

'Are we all goin'?'

'No, just you, me and Nos. When I leave you follow.'

They moved off and Healey heard no more, but he put two and two together and got Foxcroft.

'Something's on, Reg,' he confided. 'Those young sods are planning a surprise for Revilious. Has Charlie been in Aishwell today?'

'Can't say but Dan drove Charlie's Jag into the square earlier on, round tea time.'

'Delivering a bag for Dave Widger,' Healey murmured. 'A bag of what, though.'

And he related the leather jackets' conversation.

'A bag of bloody trouble,' said Yelland yawning like a pony.

'Think I'll cycle down to Foxcroft and wait for the boys,' Healey said. 'You phone Revilious and explain what's happening. Then soon as Widger and his mates leave phone again and warn us. I'll put the fear of Christ up they loobies.'

'By yourself, Ted?'

'In the dark I'd take on six of those scruffy berks. And Widger is a proper bloody Mary Ann.'

Yelland's George Formby grin lit up the bar.

Arriving wet and dishevelled at Foxcroft Healey was unprepared for Revilious's nonchalance. The tall, stooping figure merely nodded and smiled throughout Healey's account of the happenings and his suspicions. The sad face had lost its pallor and was quite ruddy, but it could have been the whisky or the heat from the fire. Whatever it was Revilious had a jaunty, defiant air and was keen to do battle.

He stood with his back to the blaze. A heavy-knit cardigan hung off his frame, exaggerating his boniness and angularity. His bagged-at-the-knees corduroys, cravat and Hush Puppies were up-market War on Want.

'Well, Ted,' he said briskly. 'Is there a plan of campaign?'

'It isn elaborate, sir – but when Reg phones I'll go up the drive and lay into the buggers before they can make their special delivery.'

'Fighting violence with violence,' Revilious sighed.

'I don't think it'll come to blows.'

'And what can we expect to find in the bag, Ted?'

'I don't know, but it won't be a birthday present and that's for sure.'

'I'll get my raincoat,' Revilious said.

'Better you stayed put, sir. No offence, but you'd only get in the way. They'm just boys and if I show 'em the big stick they'll back off.'

'Very well, Ted, but if you get in a jam – holler.'

Healey pondered on this. If it came to violence what could the gentleman do? He drank Revilious's fine smooth scotch and went out again into the night.

Among the hemlock and meadow sweet under the hawthorn hedge that was overhung with apple boughs he waited. The barn owls were screaming like they did in the autumn and the rain had at last stopped. The wind brought the drops pattering down off twigs and leaves onto broader leaves and grass blades. Up the drive he caught the babble of voices and clenched his fists. They didn't care about anything – people, property, animals, the law; everything got the boot if they gave it the thumbs down. But Revilious was old enough to look after himself. Even locked within his mind the platitude sounded bogus. You adopt orphan lambs, he thought, stray cats, sick calves, so why not human beings?

His eyes had grown accustomed to the darkness. Three figures came splashing through the puddles and one of them staggered and his companions giggled.

'Wayne's legless,' said Widger's voice.

'Wayne's always legless.'

'Lucky Wayne,' Wayne slurred.

The trio collapsed in helpless laughter, lurching about and grabbing each other in their efforts to remain upright. Healey shone his bicycle lamp on them and stormed out of the hedge.

'It's bloody Dracula,' Widger chuckled.

'Drop the sack,' Healey grated, feeling slightly foolish but holding his ground. 'Drop it now and clear off and no one'll get hurt.'

'But if we don't drop it and don't bugger off you'll get hurt,' said Widger without humour.

Healey strode up to him and put a knee in his genitals. Then Wayne closed swiftly but unsteadily, swinging windmill rights and lefts. The blow that stopped him loosened most of his front teeth and his wits. He sat down heavily beside Widger trying to work out what sort of creature was uttering the high-pitched mewing cries of distress.

'Now – drop the sack and get to hell out of here.'

'Twas only a joke, boy,' Nos complained. 'We were goin' to have a bit of fun with the old fella – post a few things through his letterbox, nothing else.'

The beam of Healey's lamp lit the retreat until a bend swept them out of sight. Before long they were yodelling obscenities and threats back through the darkness.

'Someone's going to be upset when he hears about this, Healey,' Widger bawled. 'And I won't forget what you did to me, you bastard. Can you hear me Healey? Healey?'

The young man started to untie the baler cord knotted round the neck of the bag. The contents fought the sacking like hungry ferrets. Tiny red eyes reflected the lamplight. With a grunt of disgust Healey swung the bag into the hedge and the rats rustled off, dragging themselves across the dock leaves.

They were disorientated and miserable and some had been injured during their captivity. But the night received them as it received all its suffering children.

'Rats?' Revilious grimaced. 'And they intended pushing them through my letterbox!'

'Charlie has some charming mates.'

'And I'm in your debt, Mr Healey. Won't this go bad for you? – after all, Gutteridge employs you doesn't he?'

'Only part-time. I don't suppose he'll be too happy but he won't let on or he'll have to admit he set it up. I'm good at my job and he's a businessman. He never does anything bent himself but sort of pulls strings and makes other folk dance to his tune.'

Like Iachimo, Revilious thought from cold recollection of Shakespeare's *Cymbeline*. Every age and society has its Iachimo.

'What makes a grown man hate so intensely?' he said.

'Charlie don't hate, Mr Revilious. Charlie don't feel anything. He does things coldly – like an insect. Everything's calculated.'

'And that makes it even more horrible. Look,' Revilious added. 'If it does turn sour – the river job and your dealings with Gutteridge – I can find you plenty of work in the gardens here.'

'Thank you, sir. I'll keep that in mind.'

Sunshine

Bluebells, red campion and comfrey bunched in a vase; rain drifting across the churchyard and swifts flickering among the gravestones.

'Bob was a rose grower,' Yelland said. He wiped his hands and stuffed them into the pockets of his gaberdine. 'But the wild flowers are a nice gesture, Mr Revilious. Tez easy to forget old friends after they'm planted. There's nort worse than a neglected grave.'

Long spells of rain helped the afternoon remain cool. Revilious drank a cup of tea at Yelland's and bought some odds and ends at the post office stores before walking home up the coombe from Woodburn Bridge. Keeping an eye open he was delighted to discover freshly minted spraints on two of the ten rocks above Lord's Pool. And the double line of seals in the mud and sand close by were also fresh.

Eagerly he glassed the pond but the only signs of life were the rings on the surface and the occasional flash of silver scales as something leapt and fell back. He sat for the remainder of the afternoon against the garden wall and watched the water gliding over Home Weir. But the otters failed to show and at darkfall the pond possessed little save shadows and reflections.

The stars provided the palest of light when the clouds scattered. Then the language of the great English poets took on

a curious relevance that couldn't be divorced from the beauty
of the sky. The deathless beauty. Lord, yes! They knew. They
knew. He wiped away the tears and buttoned his Solway.

The going was the easiest on the east side of the coombe
where ancient cattle creeps followed the contours. He trod
carefully and paused every dozen or so steps to listen. Finally at
Brockhill Field he was rewarded. From somewhere close to
Bowden's Pool an otter whistled and was answered by another
upstream.

'Dear God,' Revilious whispered. 'Let them mate and make
Foxcroft their home. Give all the clean Devon rivers back to
otters again. And let me live long enough to see the cubs.'

Later he dreamed of otters.

The universe was a vast pond and the constellations were
clusters and streamers of weir moss and water crow's foot.
Skerry melted into the Milky Way wearing his coat of many
bubbles, undulating through those raging fathoms of light like
the biggest and longest nebulae in the cosmos. Skerry and
Cariad swirling and twisting down the deeps of creation.

Revilious woke up choking and staggered to the windows
and flung them open to gulp the scent of leaves and water. The
pond was deserted and he crept back to bed and tried unsuc-
cessfully to recreate his dream out of a few vague recollections.
When Bertish phoned next day to tell him Gutteridge had
upped his bid for Foxcroft, Revilious was sufficiently irritable
to make suggestions that surprised the solicitor.

The otters were out there but refused to show themselves,
and if he trampled all over the place looking for them they
would go away. It was a frustrating business and Mrs Healey's
good nature only served to make matters worse. He did not
want to be cheered-up; but watching her go quietly and com-
petently round the house he racked his brains for a way of
helping her and her family without appearing to be patronizing. Then, after she had gone home, it was heaven to slip into
the silence of a poem.

The windscreen wipers stroked away the rain. Yelland sat like
a cigar store Indian and grinned vacantly at the countryside
that rushed at them and upon them and vanished in green
waves. They left a hamlet and motored slowly into Totnes.

The shower stuttered and faded into sunshine and a rainbow arched across the Dart. Eastward the clouds were steely-grey but blue sky was spreading from the west.

Strolling down a narrow street that steamed he hardly heard a word Yelland was saying. The people hurrying by visibly responded to the sunshine. Everything about him glowed. There was some great bonding force at work maintaining and generating its own power. Life flickered from being to being and the chain reaction reached back to the first dawn. Stopping for a moment to look in the window of a junk shop Revilious felt the wonderful solace of sharing such power and contributing to it. Death could only blow the dust away for the human spirit prevailed and was the true force, as indestructible as the sunlight. In the fog of horror and the renunciation of goodness on a global scale little acts of humanity shone through illuminating dark wastes of bestiality. There is always a human voice triumphing over the darkness. Ypres, Verdun, Guernica, Auchwitz, Belsen, Hiroshima, the Gulag Archipelago, Vietnam, Northern Ireland, Palestine, Lebanon, El Salvador. The candles flickered while the monsters came and went and were entombed in folklore. Hitler, Mussolini, Stalin and all the other minor satans who had dispensed misery on a scale too enormous to contemplate were gone but the light burned strong, inextinguishable. It was fed by music and literature and painting, by purity of thought, and compassion and love.

A butterfly brushed against his face. He stepped back and looked up at the sky, and the van driver leaned on his horn. Revilious lifted a hand in acknowledgement and rejoined Yelland on the pavement.

'Market day's murder,' the old man sighed.

But the noise and colour pleased Revilious, and the Elizabethan costumes worn by some of the townsfolk added a touch of carnival to the occasion. Then, browsing through the stalls, he came upon an otter's head mounted on a wooden plaque. 'River Exe, Summer 1929' – the gold lettering was still distinguishable. Jaws parted in a silent snarl of defiance the hunt trophy lay amongst discarded odds and ends of human homes: books, vases, cutlery, cups and saucers. A little girl rose on tiptoe to stroke the muzzle and touch the canine teeth.

'Poor doggy,' she said.

The moon in the weir

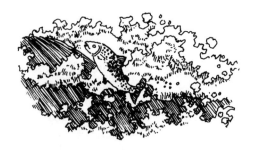

The flail mower rattled along the hedgeside chewing into the greenery and flinging pieces of twigs, stones, leaves, fledglings, pupating butterflies and the mangled remains of small animals onto the road. The shattered stumps of saplings and branches poked from the dirty yellow ruin left behind the machine. Torbay Borough Council was tidying-up the approaches to the Three Towns.

A red admiral butterfly, resting among the nettles, escaped with the loss of a wingtip and flew down a valley, crossed the Dart and came up the Aishbourne. Skerry saw the injured creature alight on a leaf above the water. He stared at it in the hot brightness between clouds until he forgot what he was looking at and returned his attention to his fur. Cariad still slept. Her eyes twitched beneath brown lids and every so often her toes stiffened and she yikkered softly.

They visited the pool while Revilious was sound asleep and made a determined but unsuccessful attempt to catch the pike. Life then was full and rich, and the water echoed their joy. It ran with them and swallowed them and held them within the rhythms of its own living. They journeyed through the scented night from the wellhead of the Aishbourne to the source of the Avon. The tang of granite and peat threaded amongst tussocks of deer grass and ling. But Dartmoor could offer only space and silence old with the shadows of man's coming and going. Sensing something violent around them the otters lolloped down the banks of the Avon below the reservoir and the dam. Here the river was narrow and exciting in its careless descent from the moors, and they spent hours searching out shoots.

The sun-flickery shallows were enticing and wherever the water deepened they could play chase.

Long Flow swept them under the Rings and Woolholes through a cleave to the in-country around Didworthy. A farm dog turned them west along Badworthy Brook to the coombe below Glaze Meet. They kennelled in a deserted sett and journeyed over the fields after dark, passing many farms and hamlets until Skerry led Cariad into the Avon at Bickham Bridge. The otters killed eels in the slack reach by the mill and surprised a doe rabbit and her young near the river. The sheep-grazing was pitted with rabbit burrows and the otters found other victims before first light.

After a luxurious roll in the grass he eased his body under an alder root and rubbed his back against it, repeatedly, eyes closed and lips parted in a little snarl of pleasure. A mink splashed ashore, took one look at the otters and returned hastily to the water.

Cariad lay on her side, ears pricking to the sound of the river and the surrounding countryside. A fly tried to settle among her whiskers but was instantly flicked off with a shake of the otter's head. Time washed over the farmland and the South Hams slept in its greenness. At Dimpsey a single star kept watch on the blurring meadows. Horses swished their tails and called to each other through their noses. Scents climbed and drifted. Dew and starlight lay on leaves, grass blades and flower petals.

They travelled the lanes between banks of foxgloves and hogweed into coombes and spinneys. Gates opened onto hilltop and sky. Passing the vegetable gardens of Tennaton soon after sunrise they stopped in the field corner to watch the starlings bouncing across a goose pen to stab the wet turf with their beaks. The smell of toast crisping under the grill wafted from a kitchen window. Then a disembodied human voice incanted a list of evocative names . . . 'Plymouth, Biscay, Fastnet', and a man in shirtsleeves sauntered down the garden path, whistling.

The otters moved on in a loop that ended at the Avon where it curved between woods of oak and ash.

Skerry snorted his grunt of delight. Six feet of limpid water lay between himself and the bed of the river. Dipping his head he followed it down into the clarity and weightlessness of dream. They found a torrent and shot out of it to wallow in the effervescence. Time and time again they rode the current until tiredness forced them ashore to roll and wrestle in the beginning of serious courtship.

Yet the wanderlust drove them back to the fields while the sun stood overhead and showers fell, but always far off. From the ancient tumuli on the 650 ft summit of Bickleigh Brake the hills of the South Hams rippled away to the bottom of the sky. Farmwork was caught in the glacial silence: a tractor creeping up a hillside; the tiny figures of men; unmoving herds of cattle and flocks of sheep dotting the distance. And Skerry drifted into sleep with the scent of her fur in his nostrils and the slow rise and fall of her body close to his own.

Dusk awoke in him a desire to see the Foxcroft pond again, and when the dog star gleamed in the puddles down the lane to Newhouse the otters departed more purposefully than usual. Cariad was still very playful and ran beside him, tugging at his shoulder and nipping the side of his muzzle. Briefly they tangled and rolled together and the car was upon them with a roar and flash of lights. Skerry flung himself sideways and squirmed unscathed into the hedge; but Cariad's instincts and actions were not so sharp. Something hard struck her haunches and smashed her against the bank and into the ditch. Her head cracked down on a rock and the pain in her body instantly vanished with everything else.

Skidding on the muddy surface the Hillman Imp came to a halt and the driver's door was flung open. The woman ran to the roadside and crouched over the still form of Cariad.

'Why?' she breathed, shaking her head in disbelief.

Tears sprang to her eyes and dribbled into the corners of her mouth. Christ! – to kill an otter and for what reason? Hurrying home to catch some bloody stupid soap opera on the box! Christ! Absently she stretched out a hand and stroked the twisted body and detected a flutter of life. The creature was breathing in faint gasps. Lifting it tenderly the woman carried it to the car and laid it on a blanket on the back seat.

'Don't die on me, you little beauty,' she whispered.

All the way to her house at Goutsfordleigh she prayed through clenched teeth. But Alice Larkin did not know how to beg for anything. She instructed the Almighty, using the tungsten-edged language she often employed putting down aggressive males. Alice was a big brunette, built to last. She had been a heavy, unattractive child, a handsome young woman and now fleshiness was cancelling out the good looks which had turned men's heads in the sixties. Her fine, large mouth was set in an expression of cynical yet amiable stubbornness, and the brown eyes held the perpetually surprised look of an adolescent. She had spent most of her forty years in and around the South Hams as typist or shop assistant. Yet her self assurance was an illusion. An unmarried mother bringing up a daughter in a tiny community like Goutsfordleigh could expect problems.

'How d'you know he's an otter, mum?' the child said, kneeling beside the settee.

'I seen some when I was a kid, and I saw a film about a Scottish otter.'

'Idn he lovely, mum,' from a whisper.

'He's a girl otter,' smiled Alice. 'And she's a sick little animal.'

'Have you sent for the doctor?'

'The vet, Jane. He'll be here as soon as he can, lovly.'

'Her idn going to die is her mum?'

Alice could only shake her head.

Cariad stirred and struggled to stretch out her hind legs but the pain brought her up sharp and she gave a cry, the sort of sound a cat makes when it sees a bird.

'Oh mum,' Jane said. 'Her really idn well.'

'We'll make her well, lovly.'

Alice trailed her fingers over the otter's muzzle and let them rest in the soft chest fur. Cariad opened her eyes, sighed and closed them again. Yes, the woman thought, stroking a small neat ear – like a cat, a beautifully ugly little cat.

It was some time before Skerry uncoiled from his fear. The grass whispered around him and the wind washed a terrible loneliness into his being. He stood erect and called to her, and cocked his head waiting for the reply. But there was only the whisper of the grass and quick beat of his heart and the wink of the stars. Again he cried out and dropped on all fours ready to run to her. The sharp double notes were insistent and close to grief.

Pushing through the hedge he landed clumsily in the lane and galloped to the shallow ditch where her musk was still sufficiently strong to swell his heartache and cause him to dart about whimpering. Every now and then he paused and listened. His eyes were round with desperation. Again the staccato wail broke from his throat and he cantered down the lane, stopped suddenly and returned to the spot where she had been hit by the car. Now the misery overwhelmed him and he crouched and buried his face in his forepaws.

It is one of the peculiarities of life that night can turn to nightmare between heartbeats. For hours Skerry ran up and down the lane his yikkering broken by sobs and the tears sliding from his face to bead on the tips of his whiskers. Then he needed the one place that had brought him peace since he had come to the South Hams.

But the roaming dragged at his nerve ends and sent the pain quaking through his body. Eventually he scrabbled up Home Weir, flopped into the pool and swam to the island. There his crying was piteous and full of loss. Time after time he lowered his head and let the misery burst free. Soon the wind took up his whimpering and rain breathed across it. And tears and raindrops dripped from his whiskers.

Revilious opened his eyes. Moonlight lay on the ceiling and the wind was bellying the curtains. From behind the wind came the whimpering cry. Revilious flung on his dressing gown and padded to the window. Shining across the trees the half-moon lit the pond and the island. Skerry's small upright figure was visible on his couch of reeds and the bleakness of his sorrow cut into Revilious's heart. On and on the otter fretted, stopping every once in a while to listen for the answer the wind could not bring.

Revilious was deeply moved. He stood at the window knowing something awful had happened to the otter bitch. His mind strayed from one possibility to another and always returned to Gutteridge. He had heard that inconsolable sobbing before. Often at Cavendish Towers he had listened to some unhappy boy crying himself to sleep in the corner of a dormitory. And history was full of similar cries. On the edge of everything man touched was a chorus of anguish and despair.

He went downstairs and poured a drink but the sobbing was in his head now, accompanied by a slow starburst of images.

Once, he recalled, he had forced himself to sit through a television documentary about seals and the fur trade. What brutalizing process enabled men to slither over ice fields clubbing the pups to death? What sort of man could ignore the pitiful cries? And for what? – more beer, a bigger house, a better car? He threw back the scotch but it did not swill away the horror. He was out on the ice where the wind failed to mask the sound of the seal pups calling to their mothers. Then the crunch of boots and the shadows falling across the helpless creatures.

Despite his pain Revilious returned to the bedroom trying to come to terms with the intensity of the otter's grief. But only the wind murmured in the trees and the couch under the scrub willows was deserted. The moon in the weir was broken into small pieces and when Revilious came to stand above the water he felt he was staring across yet another shattered dream.

Goutsfordleigh

'Have you seen the young vet from Aishford?' said Alice, resting an elbow on the table to pour the tea.

Her friend dropped lump sugar into her cup and sat shaking her head in anticipation of something worth listening to.

'He looks like Prince Andrew – only his teeth are smaller. Mr Copeland – young Mr Copeland.'

Dreamily her fingertips teased the sagging stem of her throat.

'And the otter?' asked the friend.

'Dislocated hip, concussion, badly bruised ribs,' replied Alice. Dipping into her handbag she produced a sheet of notepaper. 'I wrote down what he told me. Otters can slow their pulse rate. It's called bradycardia.'

'What does it do?'

'Helps them stay underwater and go deep if they want to. I didn't really understand all Mr Copeland was saying but because of the bradycardia he had a hard job putting her out with the injections so he could examine her. The anaesthetic didn't work straight off.'

'But she'll be alright?'

'In a day or so. She's all aches and pains, and she was lucky. There was a dead badger on the road by Hernaford Cross this morning when I took Jane to school.'

'I saw it,' the friend said.

After sunset a light wind sprang up. Cariad's ears twitched to the sounds drifting out of the evening. She lay curled in a dog basket on the settee and occasionally lifted her head when a new image flashed onto the television screen.

'Don't go too close, Jane love,' Alice murmured. 'Mr Copeland said they can give you a nasty bite.'

'But her's all sleepy,' said Jane, gazing into the otter's face. 'Can't we keep her, mum?'

'She's not a pet. Otters need their freedom — like children, like you.'

'But I live here and I don't mind it.'

'And you go to school and out to play. You wouldn't like to stay in this poky room all day, every day.'

'So where will her go?'

'In the river. The vet's getting someone to collect her when she's well.'

'No one else in Goutsfordleigh's got one.'

'That's because wild animals idn proper pets, lovy.'

'Darren Loveridge up Home Farm've got a fox.'

'That don't make it right.'

The child thrust her fingers into her brown curls and sighed and nodded.

By noon the following day the news had reached Aishwell and Yelland got on the phone to Foxcroft from the pub. Ten minutes later Revilious's silver Fiat was seen cruising past Murtwell en route to Goutsfordleigh. He drove slowly for fear of a blackout at the wheel.

Before answering the door of her semi-detached Alice parted the sittingroom curtains and scrutinized her visitor. Then he was shown into a room no bigger than Foxcroft's kitchen. It was furnished with typical, working class artlessness — a massive TV on castors in the alcove; a fireplace stacked with ornaments; wall-to-wall carpeting and a black vinyl three-piece suite.

Alice had a barmaid's gift for putting men at ease and by the time the second cup of tea was administered Revilious had spoken of the Foxcroft otters.

'I hope you won't mind,' she said, smiling over the rim of her cup, 'but after you phoned I got in touch with Mr Morgan of Cuckoo Cross. The vet thinks our lodger could be the little bitch otter that run off from the wildlife park.'

'And Morgan wants her back,' said Revilious unable to hide his disappointment.

'Idn it best for the creature? No cars are going to knock her down at Cuckoo Cross.'

'But she's got a mate now,' he said abruptly.

'You speak to Mr Morgan, love. If it's his otter she's bucking up no end. I've had to put her in the spare room. And don't her eat! The vet gave me her diet sheet but if she stays here much longer I'll have to claim extra off the social security. Where am I going to get eels to chop up? And raw minced beef idn exactly the sort of grub you'd give the cat. As soon as he mentioned the dead chicks I told him to forget it. The vet won't be cheap either – they never are.'

'Look, Mrs Larkin –'

'Alice,' she said softly.

'Alice. I feel responsible for Cariad. So – so I insist on paying the vet's bill and providing for her keep.'

'I won't argue,' Alice laughed. 'Bringing up a nine-year-old kid on the dole idn easy and I never reckoned on having a penniless lodger in the house.'

He borrowed a biro and scribbled out a cheque.

'A hundred quid!' said Alice. 'That'll buy a hell of a lot of minced beef, Mr Revilious. Do you want to see Cariad?'

'I'd rather wait till Morgan gets here. If people keep popping in and out of her room she'll get upset.'

Alice grinned and folded the cheque.

'Did I say something funny?' Revilious asked.

'Her room. An otter with a room of her own!'

'Animals tend to take over once you let them in the house.'

Morgan agreed. Revilious instantly took to the lean, balding Welshman with his nervous energy and passion for wildlife. A moment in the spare room was enough to convince Morgan it was Cariad that had come a cropper and he wanted immediately to take her back to Cuckoo Cross. But Revilious could be persuasive and Morgan did not need a lot of convincing. He followed the Fiat to Foxcroft wondering why the strange, well-spoken recluse drove so cautiously.

The estate proved unbelievably beautiful and the walk up
the Aishbourne ending with a scotch beside the pond finally
put his mind at rest. The otters stood a genuine chance of
survival in such surroundings. He could offer a sanctuary and
nothing more, but Foxcroft had the feel of the past about it –
like a piece of Edwardian England that had miraculously
survived the changes wrought by modern farming.

The Welshman listened attentively to his host's philosophy
and some of it struck a chord despite his conservation stance
and the realities of Cuckoo Cross.

'Good luck to him,' he grunted, watching his wife ladle
casseroled lamb onto the plate. 'It's a pity more landowners
don't think like that.'

'He can afford to be original.'

'Come on, Nell. He could be gallivanting round like the rest
of the bloody jet set, with nothing to show for it except bags
under the eyes and a passing mention in the gossip columns.'

'They say he can put away the booze.'

'So what? Where I come from everyone likes the booze. But
this bloke is doing something I admire.'

'There's no need to get on your high horse with me,' she said
cheerfully. 'Some people think it's a shame, that good farmland
going to waste.'

'You're not shedding tears for the farming community! OK
there are conservationist farmers like Mrs Marshall over
Lincombe way but the majority, the ones I know, put profit-
making before everything.'

'Like lots of other people.'

'Sure – only farmers are supposed to be holding the land in
trust for future generations. Do you want a countryside with
all the hedges grubbed-out? I love those little hilltop woods
like the one we go to on Stert Beacon. Agricultural vandalism
makes a hell of a mess, a permanent mess, and you'll never
convince me one man's livelihood is more important than the
land and the wildlife it supports. I don't want to live in a green,
chemically cocked-up desert.'

'Your soapbox is wobbling.'

'It needs to be said.'

'Not to me, Tom. I'm on your side.'

He gave a nervous laugh. 'Sorry, Nell – but there's a relentless greying-out of truth by politicians and bureaucrats. You only have to look at the behaviour of the Argentine government during the Falklands campaign to see how a nation can be deceived.'

'But only for so long.'

'Hedges have been vanishing for bloody decades.'

'Because so few people care enough to do anything about it and those like you, Tom, rant around feeling helpless and frustrated.'

He glared down at his plate and said, 'Farmers and farming communities are votes so the government can't afford to step on important toes. But if some farmers had their way we'd live to see a treeless countryside devoid of foxes, badgers and everything else that can't be milked, sheared or eaten. England would become an easily manageable, trouble-free prairie geared entirely to profit-making.'

'Farmers like old Whiddon of Beech Shilston, for instance?'

'Yes – the money-grabbing old devil. Remember when television interviewed him about the badger gassing? There he was, leaning on his gate, smoking his pipe and talking down at all us poor mortals. Lord! – I can see the bugger now and hear his drivel. "Badgers may look lovable to townspeople but –", then the prejudices trotted out like facts. The general public has been led to believe naturalists and conservationists and anyone else who protests about lousy farming, pollution, vivisection and what have you, are cranks, and farmers – being realists – have a direct line to God.'

'OK,' said Nell. 'We've been all round the houses. So,' and she sighed and puffed out her cheeks – 'Cari is going to Foxcroft under the wing of your new found St Francis.'

'That's it in a nutshell,' he said, smiling sheepishly. 'We'll give her a couple of days at Goutsfordleigh then bung her in Revilious's pond. Meanwhile I hope the dog stays put.'

Revilious drove down the straight lane with the most stunning display of wild flowers swaying on either side. Normally he would have stopped and cut the engine to stand for a while close to the dense cow parsley and grasses but his mind was on Cariad. Alice Larkin's friend Doreen had made the visit to

Goutsfordleigh uncomfortable. She had a way of giggling for no apparent reason whenever he had strayed onto some topic which did not touch her life. In a coarse, fat, middleaged woman the habit bordered on the grotesque, and he wondered why Alice bothered with the imbecile. But Yelland had spoken about Alice's affairs and how she had brought more than one local marriage to the divorce courts. Now she was ageing and losing her attraction, so perhaps it was natural that disillusioned with romantic love she turned to members of her own sex. He recalled the handful of women who used to visit his mother and whisper scandal behind drawn curtains.

Breakfast with Nos

The froghoppers had left their cuckoo spit all over the dogroses at the bottom of the garden. Little white gobbets nestled in the angle of stem and sucker. The scent of honeysuckle gusted across the morning and bees were beginning to hum around the apple blossom below the pond.

Revilious yawned. Ravel's Introduction and Allegro spilled from the drawingroom and the music captured the mood of the occasion. Blossom fell, treetops stirred in the first breath of wind and the songbirds sang with the sort of passion he felt for the new day. Then the urgent whistling carried from the pond reminding him again of a child that could not be comforted. He parted the curtains and looked down. Skerry's upright figure, frozen by misery into stillness, stood on the island. His head was raised and the trembling cries poured from him.

'She'll be back soon,' Revilious whispered. 'Hang on, boy. We'll have her in the pond in a day or so.'

Loving animals makes you vulnerable, he thought. Breakfast was finished and Skerry had fallen silent. He turned off the record player and went out onto the terrace. The birdsong had lost its intensity but a blackbird was throwing its familiar aria from the top of an apple tree. Revilious shuddered to think of all the grumbling and groaning which would be rising from the dormitories of Cavendish Towers as the prefects went round waking the boys. He smiled into his coffee. If he'd had an ounce of guts he would have turned his back on that petty confinement and walked into the future with nothing but a rucksack and his integrity. Life was ready to give to those who went out and searched.

He drew a deep breath and struggled to exhale. For an awful moment he stood at the table willing his lungs to function properly and the panic to subside. Afterwards he sat on the terrace steps. The morning had begun to lose its brightness and the wind had freshened to chop and slash at the trees. It really was futile, he reflected, to waste the end of your life dwelling on what had been and what might have been. But how do you learn to become a man of action after thirty years of spiritual impotence? Loving animals did make you vulnerable but it also kept you aware of creation's all-embracing brotherhood. Yet it saddened him to think that the destiny of every wild creature sharing the world was in human hands.

*   *   *

Nos and Wayne walked home for once after the landlord of The Plough had insisted they were too drunk to ride. Concern for their machines had eventually won and they had set off roaring and singing to ricochet off the hedges all the way down to Woodburn Bridge. Wayne possessed the homing instinct of a regular drunk but Nos was fighting nausea, weariness and rising self-contempt.

The teenagers lived with their parents in a small community a few miles the Plymouth side of Aishwell. They had got into the habit of saluting the arrival of their social security giro at The Plough. Wayne had been unemployed since he left school but Nos had only recently returned without a diploma from art college in the Midlands.

At the bridge the boys parted company. Nos lurched down to the river and urinated noisily all over his boots, and Wayne continued up the lane, burbling to a companion that wasn't there. Nos had a fleeting recollection of starlit water and the moon flashing through leaves as the alcohol-induced coma claimed him. He had overbalanced into the ramsons and grass of the hedge. And suddenly he was warm and comfortable. His eyes closed, his mouth gaped and he began to snore louder than the pigs he had disturbed in their houses on the opposite bank of the Aishbourne.

A sharp dawn brought him to his senses. He was shivering and his clothes clung to stiff limbs. From his hangover the world gyrated and spun like a video film of the nausea churning away in his bowels. He raised himself on his elbows and tried to shake off the searing headache. Sleep had gummed together the lashes of his left eye and he worked at the crusted mucus with fingers that trembled. There was a splash close by. Nos stared blearily through the grass stems and saw Skerry haul himself onto a rock in mid-stream where the river curved to enter the deeps under the bridge. The otter had caught a trout and Nos watched him eating the little fish. Then Skerry sprainted and sniffed at his scats. Struggling for a better view Nos brought on a fierce attack of nausea and he groaned and released a belch to rival any of the sounds coming from Healey's porkers.

Skerry vanished beneath a swirl and surfaced again and galloped up the shallows without a backward glance. The teenager had never seen an otter before. The sight of one in close-up left him feeling good even though he crouched on hands and knees and vomited. The otter was a mysterious, celtic creature, very much the spirit of the coombe. He got shakily to his feet and wiped his mouth. The headache made him squint. But he was beginning to feel something else turning in his guts, something he had not felt for a long time. The need to draw the otter and the river swelled to a kind of excitement. He walked into the water and doused his head. All about him the birds sang and the river ran through its own clatter and shine.

For Nos it was almost a religious experience – like waking and finding himself at the centre of a pre-Raphaelite dream. He did not have to go home. He could do anything he chose. So he waded up the river and slithered and stumbled over its rocky bed all the way to Lord's Pool. His legs were numb with cold and he came ashore to empty his boots and take off his socks. But the river would not let him go and he walked on up the bank until he reached Home Weir and sat amongst the bluebells letting the sound of the water sluice his mind.

Conflicting emotions were at work in Revilious. He was glad the otter's sobbing had ceased but he was worried in case the creature had abandoned Foxcroft. Pulling a cane chair to the edge of the terrace he drank some more coffee and flicked through an anthology of religious prose. A passage by Carlyle caught his eye.

> '. . . this earthly life and its riches and possessions and good and evil hap, are not intrinsically a reality at all, but are a shadow of realities eternal, infinite; that this Time-world, as an air image, fearfully emblematic, plays and flickers in the grand still mirror of Eternity; and man's little Life has Duties that are great, that are alone great and go up to Heaven and down to Hell . . .'

The wonderful, simplistic belief of the Gothic Age, Revilious smiled. He closed the book and left it beside his coffee cup and strolled down to the weir. Swinging open the iron gate and stepping into the orchard he was startled to see a stranger staring over the water at him. It was difficult to tell if the expressionless face belonged to a man or woman or indeed if it were human. The creature was bald and its face was all bone, bulging eyes and teeth. But it was also young and observing Revilious's alarm gave him a slow smile.

'I was down by the bridge,' it said. 'And I saw this otter and just sort of followed it up here. You're Mr Revilious aren't you? I idn looking for trouble.'

'Could you use a cup of coffee?'

'I'd strangle our mum for something strong, sweet and wet.'

'That probably won't be necessary. Come up to the house.'

He served a fried breakfast on the patio and the hairless youth ate with the exaggerated table manners of a curate trying to impress his bishop. It seemed so out of character Revilious could hardly restrain his laughter.

'You've got a name I suppose?' he enquired. A few months ago, he thought, such a conversation would have been un-imaginable – prep school master chatting to a skinhead who would probably turn round and mug him after polishing off the toast.

'Nos,' the youth said, lifting his death's head mask and pushing a forkful of bacon and tomato into it.

'Nos?'

'Short for Nosferatu – the vampire.'

'Ah yes! – how stupid of me. But what's your real name?'

'Eric Prowse. Eric don't go too well with the face and the head. I shaved it for fun and when they called me Nos I was sort of stuck with it. At least people notice me.'

'And that's important?'

The youth shrugged and reached for the toast. 'You've got to have a gimmick these days or you're nobody. I'm only a skinhead in the physical sense that I've got nothing but skin on my head.'

His off-the-cuff story interested Revilious who said: 'Being out of work must be pretty soul-destroying.'

'Not really. I don't want to be tied to a boring manual job five days a week for life. There idn anything smart about drudgery. Half your upper class sit on their asses all day livin' off shares and rents and things. And they're the ones who are always on about the workshy plebs.'

'D'you think I'm one of those people?' Revilious enquired cheerfully.

'No. You're doing something for animals. You're different. That's why Charlie Gutteridge wants to put the boot in. I was one of those blokes who came here back along to drop rats in your letterbox.'

'Why?'

'A bit of fun and a few bob. You get in the pub with the mob and things happen. I got this reputation for being a crazy bugger so –'

He shrugged and grinned. Like a Belsen survivor thought Revilious.

'What do you really want to do, Eric?'

'Draw and paint animals and birds and the countryside. I'm heavily into Samuel Palmer and Tunnicliffe's etchings – the ones he did on the farm.'

'Can you work quietly?'

'What d'you mean – quietly? And, look Mr Revilious, I'd prefer you to call me Nos.'

'OK, Nos. Could you creep round a place like Foxcroft and come and go unheard and unseen?'

'Is this some sort of game?'

'No. I'm going to commission some water colour drawings of the estate and its animals. I want you to do the river, the pools, the weir and the pond – the pond from one of the upstairs windows; the orchards, fields, the linhay and the house. Work as you choose, when you choose. Is it a deal?'

'Are you bloody serious? You've never seen my stuff.'

'As long as you don't disturb the otters you'll have my backing and my trust.'

'When do I begin, sir?'

'Sign off the dole today. Have you got the necessary materials?'

Nos nodded.

'If I like the first finished drawing I'll buy it – cash. You needn't spout it all over Aishwell. Then when you've done the lot we'll put them on show somewhere and where you go from there is up to you.'

That, Revilious decided, watching the thin figure lope off across Old Bethlehem, is better than cheque book generosity. The boy would retrieve his self-respect, providing of course he had some real talent. It was the first gamble he had taken and he felt six inches taller. Knowing Skerry was still active on the river was also a wonderful boost and he considered motoring over to Goutsfordleigh and asking Alice out to lunch. But by the time he had wandered up and down the coombe the notion seemed absurd.

Celebration party

'And she really is ready to be let loose?'

'You've seen her,' Copeland smiled.

'Oh she's frisky enough,' Revilious admitted ungraciously. The way Jane kept clambering onto his knees despite his obvious displeasure was most irritating. But the child's mother had eyes only for the young vet.

Good Lord! Revilious thought. I can't be jealous. He firmly rejected the idea and let the little girl jump about on him until Morgan arrived with the dog-grasper and travelling container.

'She's going berserk up there,' said Alice Larkin. 'The mattress in the spare room looks as if it's been hit by a bomb. I open the door and bang her food down in one second flat. Talk about edgy! That little lady can't wait to get out.'

But the Welshman was up and down the stairs before Alice's tea had brewed. Cariad could be heard yikkering angrily inside the metal box.

'Is her alright Mr Morgan?' Jane asked anxiously.

'She'll settle down – and it's only a short drive to Foxcroft.'

'Can we come and see her put in the pond, Mr Rev'lous?' the child said.

'Of course. We'll throw a celebration party. I'll get Reg Yelland and the Healeys to come over. What about you, Morgan?'

'Fraid not. I've too much on. You pop her in the water and let me have the box back as soon as you can. If I hang around it'll only make things worse. As it is Cuckoo Cross seems a hell of an empty place without her.'

'Cariad is a Welsh name, isn't it?'

'It means darling,' Morgan said.

Sunlight flooded the evening and it was warm enough to drink sherry on the lawn. The drone of bees muzzed the borage beneath the loganberry bushes and there was an occasional slow, downward flutter of blossom. With the dimming of light the bluebells on the far side of the coombe took on their familiar rich hue. Revilious was conscious of the growth of things all around him – crops, grass, leaves, creatures. And at dusk the fume of honeysuckle lapped the hush left by roosting birds.

'You have a very lovely home, Mr Revilious,' Alice sighed. She was fascinated by all the polished wood – the long tables, the floorboards, but mostly by the staircase. While the others took their places at the bedroom window she lingered on the landing. Like a Victorian courtesan, thought Revilious coming in search of her. One of Edward VII's trollops living out a brief fantasy before the bed claimed her and she ceased to be a person. But it was not possible to pity such a vital woman.

Ted Healey opened the container and placed it on the edge of the pond and beat a hasty retreat.

'Now watch,' Revilious whispered.

The otter bitch took three swift steps and sank through her own ripples. She remained submerged for a long time and the watchers marvelled at her gymnastics. Bubbles broke along the surface and soon the trout were leaping and plopping back to be chased again. Around the pond she went, leaving a broad wake to mark her passing. Now and then her head emerged and she gave a chirping cry that faded into a chitter.

'Like an old girl sighing in her sleep,' said Alice.

After a quarter of an hour of fun swimming Cariad clambered onto the island.

'Her's all spiky,' Jane giggled.

The otter shook herself and rolled and suddenly froze to press her muzzle to the willow stump Skerry used as a scenting post. Then she voided her own droppings and carefully inspected the couch among the reeds. What she discovered with her nose excited her greatly and she scampered around uttering her high-pitched cry and tripoding on tail and hindfeet to whistle into the darkfall.

'Where's her boyfriend?' asked Jane.

'He'll be along,' Revilious smiled. 'Let's go downstairs and have some supper.'

'But I want to see the boy otter.'

'He may not come for ages,' said Revilious. 'She may even have to go and find him.'

'Doannee want one of they prawn vollyvons and a glass of cider?' Yelland said, sweeping Jane up into his arms.

'What's a vollyvon, mum?' Jane laughed.

'Vol-au-vent,' Alice said from a broad smile. 'Little tubs of pastry full of creamed prawn.'

'Same thing,' said Yelland. 'I can never get on with bliddy French even when I hear it on the telly. Inky pinky parlee voo.'

'And jig-a-jig,' Alice said drily. 'That would be an essential part of a bloke's lingo.'

'Of course. I always get that right.'

'What it mean, mum?' said Jane.

'It's a funny sort of dance,' Yelland chuckled.

They're like members of a huge close family, thought Revilious. The working class family that can embrace everything and everyone in its warmth and yet remain as exclusive and ritual-ridden as any gentleman's club.

'Can I go outside and have a look at the otters,' Jane asked.

'No,' Revilious said. 'You'd frighten them off. They like peace and quiet.'

'I wouldn hurt 'em, Mr Rev'lous.'

'I know, Jane, but if I'm to share Foxcroft with them I'll have to do it on their terms. I'll have to keep out of the way and pretend they own the pond and the river.'

Cockchafers were on the wing. They clacked gently against the windows and whirred off into the night. The moon rose and the party assembled on the terrace breathing the scent of the honeysuckle.

'I didn know animals were like that,' Alice sighed. Behind her the wind climbed the creeper and the leaves whispered.

'Like what?' said Revilious.

'Devoted to each other. Full of love.'

'It's not exactly like human love.'

'I should hope not,' she snorted. 'Human love has a way of turning sour. But a couple of otters frettin' about each other – that's really touching. I never imagined they were capable of heartbreak or tenderness and – well, you know.'

Mrs Healey gazed at her from blank, unsympathetic eyes.

'Champagne!' Revilious cried, and he clapped his hands. 'This calls for Taittinger.'

'Champagne?' Jane frowned.

'Fizzy white wine – like lemonade. The bubbles go up your nose and make you sneeze.'

All the guests save Reg Yelland had departed before ten o'clock and the two friends settled at the fireside with a glass of brandy.

'You idn a TV fan, Mr Revilious?' Yelland observed.

'Fraid not. If you live alone television can become about as intolerable as the lodger who takes over the place.'

'Maybe, maybe.' Yelland smiled and added in a low, conspiratorial tone. 'I didn want to mention it in front of the others but I saw one of they motorbike yobs down by Lord's Pool. Dang me! if he weren't a proper ornament – bald as a coot and a face like a sick sheep. I think it was that Eric Prowse, the one they call Nos. I yelled at un to move on but he gave me the V sign and said he had your permission to do some drawings.'

'He dropped in on me yesterday,' Revilious said. 'He won't be any trouble.'

'He looks like something out of a horror film.'

'He's meant to look like something out of a horror film, Reg – a famous vampire.'

They laughed and the old man slapped his thigh.

'But do 'ee know young Prowse was one of the gang who tried to dump they rats on you?'

'Gutteridge used him.'

'Eric idn no saint, boy. He's been in court more'n once.'

'What for?'

'All sorts of mazed capers – like writing obscene poems to the parson and climbing the church tower to plant a po on the weather cock.'

'Pranks which suggest a mischievous rather than a malicious nature.'

'Posting rats is just a bit of fun, then?'

Revilious raised his palms, brought his hands together as if in prayer and let them rest on his knees again.

'Is Nos a nasty piece of work, Reg?' he sighed.

'No,' the old man chuckled. 'He may be mazed but he idn really crooked or unfeelin'. He's like his dad. There's too much imagination in the Prowse family.'

Something went bang and he woke with a jolt. A log had rolled into the grate and exploded like a fire cracker. It was nearly two-thirty and he was flopped in his armchair trying to salivate and clear the crust of alcohol from his mouth. Then he tottered to the kitchen and drank a pint of cold milk. The barn owls were calling across the coombe and standing at the bedroom window Revilious waited for the silence and stillness of the pond to reach up to him. Something large and white landed in the crack willow on the island. He put on the light and got into bed and tried to read. Then, for the first time since coming to Foxcroft he felt alone rather than lonely. The small print swam and blurred, and he reached for the switch.

Opening her eyes Cariad saw the soft golden rectangle of light in the blackness above her suddenly vanish. Nervous exhaustion brought on by all the shocks and trials of recent events had forced her onto Skerry's couch where she had sobbed herself to sleep until the owl dropped into the top of the willow and loosed its screech. Cariad chittered at the bird but it ignored her and flapped noiselessly over the river to quarter the meadows.

The otter bitch rose and stretched and caught the oily tang of his spraints. She hurried to the alder roots and fluted a chain of birdlike chirps. Sliding over the sluice Skerry pricked up his ears and hung, scarcely breathing, in the water. Again the cries cut across the sound of the weir and his own answering call burst from his throat. He dog-paddled towards the island and she swam to meet him. Then they trod water and their muzzles met and her front paws curled round his neck. In this embrace of joy they sank through the bubbles and began their courtship.

Charlie Gutteridge

He closed the wrought iron gates, got back in the Cortina Estate and drove fast up the drive to his brother Colin's house on the outskirts of Aishwell. The ceaseless barking of the alsations behind the wire mesh in the back of the car did not disturb him. Pop music blared from the radio. Charlie disliked silence. His parties were always the biggest and loudest, and his voice was heard above the din at strip clubs mouthing the sort of amusing filth his cronies admired. As he often boasted, Charlie had a nose for human weakness and Gutteridge Business Enterprises hinged on this intuitive grasp.

'Where d'you get them gates, Col?' he sniffed.

'From a public park in Spark Brook.'

'A touch of class, my son.'

They carried deckchairs onto a lawn that was exhaling the smell of freshly mown grass.

'How's Karen?' Charlie said, smoothing back a wing of bleached fair hair.

'Visitin' Sandra.'

Charlie's eyelids fluttered and descended.

'Perhaps you should be asking after Sandra,' Colin pushed on. 'When was the last time you saw her?'

'When was the last time I saw the kitchen sink?'

'It's that bad?'

'Good, bad – how should I know? It's just plain boring – her, the marriage, the house, every bloody thing.'

'So who is it now?'

'A bit here, a bit there.'

'And she knows you're playing away from home?'

'Colin,' Charlie said firmly, 'For Christ's sake knock it on the head.'

'I get on with Sandra. Me and Karen hoped you'd make a go of it this time – you know, have kids, stop buggerin' around.'

'Marriage is OK so long as you don't take it seriously.'

'Then why get married?'

'For a giggle. Sandra's Catholic and she really believes in all that Hail Mary crap. I had to marry her to give her one. She was a very tasty lady.'

'Jesus Christ!'

The subject was shelved. Charlie had more important things on his mind.

'Punters like the Spelling brothers and Archie Dalgleish have been askin' about the holiday village project,' he said. 'There's a lot of important bread waiting to be shipped our way.'

'But Revilious is some sort of nature freak. He won't part with Foxcroft.'

'You want me to tell that to Leo Spelling? "Sorry Leo – we can't get our hands on the place because this old queen is havin' it off with the birds and bees". Leo is not a sensitive man.'

'Do we really need holiday chalets and bloody health farms and wholefood restaurants?'

'There's a few bob in it if you box clever. But for once you're right, my son. It's not worth the hassle. The Spellings and Dalgleish want in alright – into our other interests. Dan should've kept his mouth shut.'

'So why give Revilious bother?'

'When the old girl died I went and had a poke round Foxcroft. It's me, Col. I've set my mind on havin' it.'

'The poor sod.'

'I guarantee the poor sod will be out on his ass by Christmas.'

'The otter's not important, then?'

'What otter? Geeing up Revilious is a bit of a giggle – but if you get what you want in the process, you're doing alright. Life's that simple, my son. Everything's a giggle.'

The rain they could see falling over Kingsbridge was heading their way. They sauntered into the house and sat in the spotless but rather cluttered lounge waiting for coffee to be served.

'You always pull it off, don't you Charlie,' Colin said. 'Even when we was nippers you got the bit of Christmas pudding with the tanner in it.'

'Winning,' Charlie confided. 'That's the name of the game.'

Colin grinned and went over and tapped the barometer with a knuckle.

'By the way,' Charlie continued in a colder voice. 'You heard about Healey?'

Colin assured him he hadn't and was given the details of the leather jackets' abortive raid on Foxcroft.

'Healey knew he was crossing you?' frowned Colin.

'Do me a favour! If I'd been there he wouldn't have had the bottle to step out of line but Widger and the other clowns would get up the pope's nose. I'm givin' Healey the benefit of the doubt. He's a good bloke to have round the river. But if he cocks things up next time –'. He broke off and twisted the rings on his fingers, one at a time, like a mechanic tightening screws with a spanner.

'What I don't understand,' Colin said, 'is why you keep rabbiting on about the holiday village if you've no intention of building it.'

'Local support – or rather, Yokel support. With Aishwell behind me bawlin' for jobs and trade the pressure will really be on maty. But once I take over I won't get planning permission, will I. Meanwhile some of the lads will pay him surprise visits to ginger him up. I'll be movin' my furniture down the road in the New Year.'

Colin cleared his throat and said: 'Karen likes otters.'

His brother's lids inched up to reveal the pale, expressionless eyes.

'Healey says the one on the Aishbourne ain't takin' your trout, Charlie.'

'So?'

'So why not leave it alone?'

'Because,' Charlie said slowly, like a teacher talking down at a stupid child – 'Revilious cares about it. If I get at it I get at him and he's well on the way to packin' his bags. Understand, Brains? I got nothing personal against otters. This is business and animals are just animals. I eat bits of animals every day and so do you and Karen and everyone else we know. Why don't that upset you?'

The rattle of rain on glass drew him to the french windows. Behind the rain was a broad expanse of blue sky. The shower moved slowly across the farmland like a colossal car-wash, slicking down leaves and grasses, and giving everything a shine. Then a black and white bird fluttered onto the back of one of the deckchairs and began to chatter.

'Magpie,' Colin said. 'They nest in the big fir round the back, Karen feeds them.'

Charlie sipped his coffee and said: 'You ought to paint them gates silver.'

*   *   *

It was the bedroom light going on and off that eventually caused Cariad to inspect holt sites further upstream. At first the pond satisfied all her needs but the mysterious golden shape suddenly materializing from the night began to disturb her. She was conscious of new sensations in the blood and was instinctively aware of the consequences of Skerry's attentions.

The cool, wet days were full of violent movement uncharacteristic of an English June. Flags and rushes, trees, fields and water showed dark and glaringly bright with a savagery the otters loved. The flags curled and quivered and the wind racing across the pond shattered images it could only borrow. Noise, light and shade fading and growing, and the constant movement of things sharpened the otter's responses.

Yelland forecast another flop of a summer but after a week or so of rain the sun shone and the swifts were screaming in a blue sky. The rutting dog otter took his bitch to Hay Creek and caught flukes for her and killed the mullet whose flesh pleased him almost as much as the taste of eel. At dawn with the air still holding some of the previous day's warmth they raked crayfish out of the cress beds under Ramsdonsloe Farm. The reeds fringing the water were covered in the cast skins of mayflies. Born without mouths the doomed insects flew over the reach laying their eggs. And the brown trout leapt and snatched them.

Skerry narrowed his eyes and pricked his ears at every splash of rising and falling fish. A dense sea mist rolled in to hide the

South Hams but the otters could feel the sun waiting to break through. The silent countryside made them edgy and they lay-up in a bramble clump on the hillside overlooking the mill leat not far from Aishford.

Soon after Dimpsey the fog thinned and Sirius appeared in the blue haze. Skerry and Cariad crunched through the grit and pebbles and entered the river. By dawn they were back in the coombe scattering the trout all the way up to Brent Copse. On either bank the undergrowth was thick with nettles, loosestrife, campion and comfrey, and the sunrise brought out the insects. Cariad snapped her jaws at the dragonflies tacking over the pool. Her flat pug face broke out of a raft of crow's-foot so that leaves and flowers trailed from her ears and the water boatmen danced away on the skin of the surface. The great hawker dragonflies, sporting their double sets of transparent wings, fascinated the otter bitch and she tried to catch them until she was too cold to swim. Then Skerry was waiting nearby at the drying-off place to groom her; but whenever his tenderness turned to lust she drove him off and left him swishing his tail in frustration.

The hunting which never failed to excite him took on a new significance. Together they killed more efficiently and had begun to take a serious interest in the Foxcroft pike. But the raids became courtship play and the underwater sparring reprieved the giant fish. For Skerry the whole universe centred on the little Welsh bitch. He was her slave, bringing her eels and the occasional mink; and after a brief separation she would run to meet him, allowing his amorous advances to go no further than the grooming or the rolling together. If he attempted to abuse the ritual she chivvied him and chased him off. Although fully recovered from the accident she was not ready to receive him and her play was an elaborate contrivance to keep him obsessed until her body chemicals urged her to surrender.

*　　*　　*

'This is good, Nos,' Revilious said shrewdly eyeing the watercolour. 'A lot of wildlife art is dead – photographic, insipid. But this is bathed in light. And that colour! It's luminous, shimmering.'

'Are you looking at the right picture?' Nos grinned. 'I idn
exactly Turner or John Sell Cotman.'

'Seriously. It is good.'

'I'm into exploring higher keys of colour,' Nos admitted.
'Colour and design. The otter is part of the pattern. Do you
paint, Mr Revilious?'

'No, no,' laughed Revilious. 'I'm not a creative person but I
can recognize genuine talent in others. There were boys at
Cavendish Towers where I used to teach who were very gifted.'

'They said I had talent at college.'

'But you didn't get your diploma?'

'Unwillingness to work, Mr Revilious – not inability to do it.
I was just a lazy, know-all bastard.'

Revilious held the picture at arm's length and said: 'How
much are you asking?'

'I haven't given it a lot of thought.'

'Then you must. Putting a price on your work is part of the
business.'

'OK – fifty quid.'

'I'll give you seventy-five, and if the others are all this size
and quality we'll make it a standing order. Don't look so
surprised. I'm the lucky one. Now leave it with me and I'll get
it framed. Oh yes, and while I think of it,' he added counting
the notes into Nos's palm, 'I'd be grateful if you'd stay well
away from the river now. The otters have settled and I don't
want them frightened off. Did you draw the one in the picture
from life?'

'I used the stuffed model you can borrow from Paignton
Zoo,' Nos grinned.

'But you've brought it to life.'

'The tricks of the trade, Mr Revilious. The kiss of the
vampire.'

The youth ran his fingertips gingerly across the brown fuzz
that was sprouting on his head.

'It must be a bit cool without hair,' Revilious chanced.

'I'm growin' it again,' Nos said. 'My old man reckons I ought
to cover my dome in horse manure.'

'Think of the mess it would make of the pillows,' laughed
Revilious and he began to cough as the pain tightened round
his heart.

'Damned bronchitis,' he wheezed apologetically.

'Mr Revilious,' Nos said in a sudden loud voice. 'You idn doing me a favour or feeling sorry for me or – or –'

'Don't be daft,' Revilious said kindly. 'You've done a job and you've been paid for it. Keep up the good work.'

Alone again he sunbathed on the terrace while the heat swelled. He was dozing off when a commotion close at hand jerked him up in the deckchair. A sparrow fledgling was on the wall being goaded by its parents into flight. After much hesitation it fluttered over the flowerbeds and managed a groggy return to the virginia creeper.

Revilious came back to the drawing room and opened Nos's folder. Then he stood the watercolour against the back of an armchair and called Mrs Healey down from her bathroom chores.

'What do you think of it?' he asked.

'Beautiful, and that water's real. The otter looks like he's floating in it.'

'Nos has got a very clever eye.'

'Nos did it! Eric Prowse?'

'Eric Nosferatu Prowse.'

'Get home do, Mr Revilious! – you'm pulling my leg.'

'I bought it off him this morning.'

The woman's upper lip curled. 'Pity he can't get a proper job,' she said dismissively. 'He's always on the scrounge.'

No use arguing, Revilious thought. No use asking her to define 'proper'. A 'real' man, a 'proper' job, a 'bad' boy, a 'loose' woman. He pressed the panama gently down on his head, straightened the brim and went for a walk. Poor Nos! – born into the booby-trapped world of village life with all its restrictions and prejudices. He wasn't his own man. He was a consequence of his environment and moment in time. A cuckoo started to call from Churchland Wood and Revilious smiled at the creature's timing.

The lane of tall, white hawthorn hedges was hung here and there with dogroses. If he climbed the bank and pressed his face to the small pink flowers he could breathe their scent which was never very strong. Dogroses, hayfields, the distant cuckoo and a blue sky! God, he sighed to himself, is there a lovelier place or a lovelier season? Devon, the South Hams and the coombe.

A slow drizzle of chestnut blossom fell on the lych gate of Aishwell Church. The breeze lifted it again like confetti and broadcast it across the square and all over the blue Cortina Estate where it stood in front of the pub, its expanding metal work creaking under the afternoon sun. Colin Gutteridge emerged from The Plough and drove off. The chestnut blossom continued to fall and drift.

'There's more than one way to skin a frog,' the salmon fisherman grinned. He rested on the oars and the flood tide held the skiff in the neck of the creek. Charlie Gutteridge unscrewed the top of the whisky bottle, half-filled the plastic cup and passed it to the old man. The wind sweeping off the river lifted his wispy hair like a pale golden crest.

'A good malt, Warren,' he said.

"'Ansome, boy.'

'You were skinning a frog,' Charlie coaxed.

'Well, us would baish they otters on the haid with our oars if they got in the net. And old Wilf Endicott back along always had a two-two on board. He used to pot seals as well as the odd otter. Course you didn't see an awful lot even in those days, but they was buggers for the salmon. Have you tried gins, Mr Gutteridge.'

'I've got dogs, Warren.'

'Then your best bet's a small mesh net. I got some back in the shed. String it cross the stream like a curtain and let it hang loose in a girt tangled mess and a cow won't get free. The bugger'll get all snarled up and drown. Sometimes it happened when us hauled the seine. Put un at the neck of a pool where the water comes in fastish.'

'This is our little secret, Warren,' Charlie smiled. 'Buy yourself a pasty to go with the scotch.'

He leaned forward and stuck a fiver in the chest pocket of the old man's overalls.

'You idn fussed about a trip down to Sandridge then, Mr Gutteridge.'

'Not today. Show me this net.'

Taking sides

Skerry led. Beyond Woodburn Bridge the heavy odour of cattle masked the shallows where the animals had gathered to cool off. Cariad nosed about under the arches, examining the mink scats on the sills and sinking every so often to flush trout from the weir moss. Flexing his rump and rudder Skerry dashed through a pool overhung with alder and hazel. Then he lay on the surface watching the leaves quivering above him.

Cariad called and he answered. The leaves were motionless now in a sky that was picking up the pale glow of dawn. The chomp of feeding cows floated across the hush. Skerry dived and the gush of white water shot him out of the pool into the folds and loops of the net.

It was suspended between two alders, a few inches below the surface. Curving his spine Skerry passed under one skirt of nylon mesh and found himself wrapped in great billows that embraced him and held him. He writhed and kicked. A hind foot was instantly entangled and a front paw became trapped but he managed to work it loose. Fear jolted to his nerve ends. He uncoiled and kicked with his free back foot and broke surface. Loose net covered his head and body. He gulped air and yikkered and tore at the orange nylon with his teeth. Then the other forepaw was caught fast. After a moment of blind panic he lay still and rested his chin on the taut cord supporting the net and whimpered.

Cariad galloped along the bank and plunged into the deeper water the other side of the net. He was leaking fear but she came as close as she dared and cried at him to join her. But

Skerry was aware only of the thin nylon chewing into his flesh and the weight of the net seeking to drag him down. He gazed at her from his misery while she swam to and fro, begging him to follow her.

The sun came up and the shadow of Churchland Wood reached down the coombeside. Gutteridge opened the gate above Woodburn Bridge and whistled his dogs. They danced around him and then dashed off to sniff the rabbit runs and cock their legs. Charlie smiled and called them by name: 'Laddie, Buck, Shane – come here, settle down now.' And they obeyed without hesitation.

Cariad sank and drifted away on the current. About fifty yards downstream she wriggled under some alder roots and waited for Skerry. The idea of him failing to appear did not cross her mind. He was half her life now and a world without him was inconceivable. Something large and heavy forded the stream close by and she pricked her ears until the noise subsided. But the alsations suddenly gave tongue and Cariad's hackles rose and she hissed. Her breath sent a chain of bubbles along the surface to meet the flow and sail off.

Ted Healey pushed through the flags and shaded his eyes against the sun. The twelve-bore lay across the crook of his arm and a brace of woodpigeons dangled from the baler cord knotted round his waist.

'Bugger,' he said softly as the dogs started to bark. The last person he wanted to meet on a beautiful June morning was Charlie Gutteridge. But the big Brummie was leaning against the fallen willow waving at him.

'We've got an otter, Ted.' Slowly the lids fell, adding a stony aspect to the hard, blank face.

'An otter, Mr Gutteridge?'

'Behind you.'

Skerry had sunk but his nostrils and the top of his head were visible under the orange netting.

'How long's that been there?' Healey said.

'The net? – me and Dan set it up last night.'

'And the otter? Are you going to kill it, Mr Gutteridge?'

'Not yet. I'm goin' to stick it on a lead and walk it down to old Revilious. He won't like that, Ted.'

'Nor will the otter.'

'Sod the otter!'

He produced a collar and leash from his fishing bag and stepped into the water.

'What you're doin' idn only wrong,' Healey said, 'it's dangerous. The animal won't let you handle un, Mr Gutteridge.'

Charlie waded out into the trout swim. The water was waist deep when he reached the net and the trapped animal. Skerry's mouth gaped and he flung himself from side to side and his tail lifted the net and smacked down on the surface.

'Don't stand there like a spare dick at a wedding, Healey,' Gutteridge said. 'Tap the sod on the head with your gun.'

'No. I don't want nothing to do with this.'

Charlie smiled and half turned to peer under his lashes at the young man. Skerry hissed and let out a terrible catterwaul and spat at him – like a drowning tom, Charlie thought. Once he'd got the collar over its head he'd have the bugger. The otter floated and regarded him steadily. Charlie felt in his pocket for the clasp knife.

'Mr Gutteridge –' Healey began.

'Shut your mouth and keep it shut.'

Charlie stuffed the collar and lead down the front of his denim jacket and transferred the knife to his right hand. If he held the cord and hacked a hole two or three feet wide in the mesh he could grip the otter behind the ears and slip on the collar. As the blade flashed Skerry tried to dive but was held by his snared front paw. The man was ready now and thrust his hand into the gap he had cut and attempted to clamp his fingers round the otter's neck. Effortlessly Skerry twisted and drove his canine teeth through flesh and bone until they met. There was a dull, crunching crack followed by Gutteridge's shriek of agony. The knife slipped from his grasp and sank.

'Shoot the bastard,' he sobbed. 'Kill him – kill him.'

'No,' Healey said.

'You're sacked, finished. Christ – I'm goin' to make life difficult for you, my son.'

'I'd get that hand seen to before it turns septic,' said Healey, but Gutteridge was staring wildly at the alsations and what he had in mind was transparently obvious.

'If you set the dogs on the animal I'll shoot them,' Healey added calmly, releasing the safety catch.

Gutteridge's face had gone taut and white and blood was dripping from his wound into the river.

'I could set them on you,' he grated through clenched teeth.

'Try it.'

But Gutteridge clambered slowly out of the water and said nothing. He was squeezing the injured hand in an effort to check the blood. Dragging air through his teeth he stood crookedly and lifted his face to the sky. Healey thought he was going to howl like a sick dog but there was just the sound of his breathing harsh with the effort to master pain. Then the blue-veined eyelids quivered and Healey's skin prickled. Gutteridge was watching him from the secrecy of his lashes, and the malevolence lodged within the knife slits of those eyes was as intimidating as a burst appendix. But he departed quickly and silently.

'How on earth did you free Skerry?' Revilious asked.

Healey raised the mug of tea to his lips.

'I cut the supporting cord at each end and hauled the net ashore – otter and all. Then I chucked my coat over the poor thing and caught hold of un real tight and chopped away with the knife. Christ! – didn he shift once I got the thread off his back leg. He hit the water like a tank and I heard un going full blast downstream.'

'I hope Gutteridge hasn't scared him off for good. Did you see Cariad?'

'No – but they'm together again. After breakfast I walked down the river as far as Horridge. There were two sets of otter tracks in the mud by the copse. If this had happened on your place, Mr Revilious, you'd have cause to worry. But the Aishbourne the other side of Drang is far enough away from the holt site. In fact, I'd bet money on 'em running back here. Nothing bad happens at Foxcroft. It's the outside world that keeps messin' them about. The coombe is their place.'

'You aren't just saying that?'

'If they'm mated the bitch will be making a home for the cubs. Her knows the river at Foxcroft. There idn no Gutteridges or what-have-yous here. And animals idn daft.'

A post of honour

His solicitor was not happy arranging a loan on terms which seemed generous to the point of lunacy. But Revilious was adamant. Healey needed independence and heavy interest rates would drag him down quicker than anything. And arguably he was a good risk. The acquisition of the two fields next to Drang would enable him to expand his market garden and make it pay. More land meant more pigs and profitable garden crops as well as room for bigger hot-houses. Healey wanted to be his own man and taking wages was for him the worst kind of bondage.

'Buy No. 2 Drang Cottages,' he concluded. 'I want it let rent free to the Healeys.'

Bertish sighed and lifted the phone to set the appropriate machinery in motion. Then, staring from the office window at the pigeons on the roofs opposite, Revilious was aware for the first time of the terrible power of money. Even after his release from Cavendish Towers he hadn't appreciated what he had at his fingertips. Now he was in a position to do immense good, and he left Totnes feeling warm inside, recalling with a smile Scrooge's happiness on that Christmas morning Dickens had placed beyond the reach of time.

The Healeys were dumbfounded by their change of fortune. The two toddlers sat on the settee watching television while Revilious gave their father the details. Of course Joan Healey would not have the time to come to Foxcroft anymore. Already she was working out in her mind how many free-range fowls she could manage. But Ted's face dropped when he started costing the machinery and equipment he would require: a small tractor and plough, sprinklers, a van, cloches, the glasshouses and pighouses, fencing.

'All part of the arrangement,' Revilious said reassuringly. 'I lend you the money for investment in the smallholding and you spend it as you please. The monthly repayments remain the same. Who owns the cottage next door?'

'It's a holiday home,' said Joan Healey. 'Belongs to a gentleman up north – a nice man. Him and his missus come here round July and August and the odd Christmas.'

'They won't object to being surrounded by pigs and chickens?'

'Lord no,' she grinned. 'They idn dainty. They like the real country.'

The children wanted the television turned up and Mrs Healey glared at them. But Revilious found it perplexing trying to conduct a conversation against bursts of laughter and a comedian cracking unfunny jokes. Ted was a pleasant easygoing man but Revilious saw the makings of a shrew in his wife. Her tongue had a sharp edge and she was forever teetering on the brink of argument. Maybe, he thought, the market garden will mellow her.

Before leaving he reminded Healey of the work he needed doing at Foxcroft. He wanted new gates hung and the lawns and vegetable garden required attention. But the pond and its approaches were to remain 'no go' areas.

He climbed the hedge and dropped into Westerland. Under the hawthorn and hazel was a small private world of beauty. Garlic mustard grew against granite rocks which were covered in moss, hart's tongue ferns and pennywort. Dogroses, bramble and briar trailed over the blue germander speedwell and cuckoo pints. To this cameo a peacock butterfly added the splendour of its outstretched wings.

Revilious searched the meadow and found several fading orchids. The day was cloudless and the sun caught the distances in unsteady images. Hedgebrown butterflies and common blues were passing jerkily as though they had just learnt to fly. Revilious lay face downwards and rested his chin on his forearms. He was marvellously happy. Dylan Thomas was right, he thought, when he wrote 'Death shall have no Dominion'. Close to his nose were the flowers of bugle, clover, buttercup and sorrel. On a poignant gush of nostalgia he was hurried back to a summer afternoon in the 1940's. Lying in a meadow beside the Monmouthshire Wye under the scent of grass and the sound of churchbells and looking up into his mother's face. Her smile was gilded with buttercup gold and her arms reached out to him like – like – 'Angel's wings' he whispered. But the tears sprang from happiness, not regret or a sense of loss.

Rolling onto his back he watched the grassheads swaying on their stems across the sky. The silvery green seeds were flushed tawny. They rustled when he stirred. And his heart was suddenly big with the love of Foxcroft – the fabulous untouched meadows, the copses, orchards and the brown river gliding ceaselessly through the coombe like the source of all its life.

'They'm back,' Yelland smiled, opening the iron gate and stepping aside to let him into the garden. 'I saw 'em – dang me if I didn! I was leanin' on the wall down there and they come up the weir like a couple of porpoises, splash! splash! – gone. My God! Can't they move!'

Revilious patted the old man on the back and wrapped an arm round his shoulder.

'Fancy some cider, Reg?' he said.

'Seems like a good idea, Paul.'

'It's a beautiful bit of the world,' Revilious sighed. The cider oozed into the tumblers, clear and amber. They drank reverently and Yelland was given an account of Charlie Gutteridge's misfortune.

'Serves him right,' the old man said gleefully, and he smacked his lips. 'This stuff's fit for God's mother. Beautiful.'

'Have you any secret ambitions, Reg? Is there something you'd like to do or somewhere you want to go before you die?'

'I fancy a trip round the world callin' in at all them exotic places; Hong Kong, the Nile, Sri Lanka, the Great Barrier Reef, the Statue of Liberty and so on.'

'An Odyssey?'

'My own Ulysses adventure,' chuckled Yelland. 'Do'ee know I haven't been further than Exeter? Always been too busy workin'. Even in the war me mates were in North Africa fighting Rommel and I was down Blackawton plantin' bloody spuds. Your mate Charlie is forever flyin' off to Spain or Bermuda and places us only sees in films. They say there's no peace for the wicked but him and the Devil aren't doing so badly.'

'Yes, it does make you wonder,' Revilious said. But he thought he had detected a desperate self-doubting streak in Gutteridge's bravado. Was it possible for a man to live out his entire life unaware of his inner ugliness? Yet so many bullies managed to live without consideration for the dignity of their fellow human beings. Was it a genuine inability to perceive something divine watering the roots of our existence? What had Addison said? 'When vice prevails and impious men bear sway, the post of honour is a private station'. But why hadn't the death sentence cured his cowardice? He was still timid and he still retreated into corners when threatened. He never imagined a person with cancer could possibly care about toothache. In the end, though, Iachimo would have to be stopped.

He refilled the glasses. From mounting elation he knew his otters would survive. There was a peculiar, all-pervading optimism in the sunshine. Everything seemed possible. Then he remembered he was living out his last summer but his mood remained unchanged.

'Charlie won't chuck in the towel,' Yelland said. 'Why doan 'ee get blokes like Piper of Woodburn Barton Farm on your side? He's a shrewd old sod. Right, so he'd pick a tanner off a dog's turd with his teeth but he's straight, boy, and straight blokes is pretty thin on the ground.'

'Isn't he a hunting man?'

'He don't ride to hounds but he idn anti. He's mad about rough shootin' and up to a few years ago used to do a bit of fly fishin' on his own water. Gutteridge rents his stretch of river from un.'

'The coombe from Woodburn Bridge to Horridge belongs to Piper!'

'Didn 'ee know?'

'Do you suppose he'd part with it?'

'Never. He's as mazed about places as you are. But,' the old man continued with a sly lowering of the voice, 'he might rent it to you if you was to offer him more than Charlie.'

'Fight dirty, eh Reg?'

'You can't fight dirty against the Devil. Drop in on Piper. Rattle some loose change in his face.'

'I thought you said he was straight.'

'A straight businessman, Paul. If he gives you his hand you'm there.'

'I'll phone and arrange a meeting for tomorrow.'

'Do it now, boy. Walk up the river and just drop in on him. He don't get about much. Meantime I'll look after this drop of scrumpy.'

'I'm sure you will,' Revilious smiled.

He was sweating by the time he had pushed through the long grass of Bowden Field and taken the path above the river to Forders. The water looked delicious. He could not recall the last time he had gone for a swim yet it was one of those sweltering June afternoons of hush and insect chirr with cattle lying in the shade twitching their ears at the flies. Revilious lifted his panama and wiped the sweat off his brow. Monet would have celebrated the day in paint but marching along the track to Woodburn Barton Farm confidence joined the alcohol leaking from his body. Supposing Piper and Gutteridge were on good terms? Gutteridge would step up his campaign if he learnt resistance was hardening. Let him, he said defiantly to himself. He was playing Russian roulette with death and all he had to do was struggle through his cowardice and let Gutteridge get on with it. Yet there he was again close to panic, like a rabbit in a car's headlights.

The farmyard was deserted. On one side was an enormous block of hay bales half-covered by a sheet of black polythene, and some long, low outhouses with asbestos roofs. To his right were a couple of silos and a big square tank containing diesel fuel. The lifeless atmosphere of the place was not helpful. But the stackyard that had not seen a haystack for over fifteen years led him up to a traditional white-washed, half-slated farmhouse. He tapped on the open door and a sharp, female voice, coming he guessed from the kitchen, asked him what he wanted. Revilious explained and was told Piper was over Wadstray looking at the sheep. Wadstray was pastureland sloping under Dinnicombe Wood on the east side of the valley. Revilious smiled. It was a decidedly odd conversation but by no means unusual for the West Country.

Piper leaned impassively on his stick. The sheep trotted away from Revilious and gathered at a safe distance. The shearing had just finished and they were conspiciously white and thin. How curious, Revilious thought, they're wearing Piper's expression of disinterest.

'I was told I'd find you here.'

The farmer sucked his lower lip up under his top teeth and nodded. He had a boyish face, smooth and suntanned, which some men collect on the way to a handsome old age. The metal-framed glasses bestowed an air of scholastic calm that put Revilious in mind of the poet Philip Larkin.

'I'm from Foxcroft,' he continued.

'What do you want, Mr Revilious?'

'I want to rent your stretch of river from Woodburn Bridge to Horridge.'

'It's already let to Charlie Gutteridge.'

'Until when?'

'July 12th. The trout season begins in March but he came here one July and seemed keen enough to make me a good offer.'

'And he's settled up for another year?'

'That's between him and me,' Piper said.

He drew in his lower lip and waited for Revilious to go on.

'I'm prepared to pay you double not to re-let it to him.'

'Are you a fly fisherman, Mr Revilious?'

'No. I'm only interested in the otters.'

'You sound like my boy, Kevin. He's always on to me about keepin' bits and pieces of the farm for wild animals and birds.'

'Like the copse down by the river?'

'That's cover for the pheasants. Otters doan get preferential treatment here, but I wouldn harm 'em. I don't keep poultry and Kev would give me hell if I shot an otter or snared a fox.'

'Gutteridge netted an otter.'

'I idn goin' to let him have the Bridge water again and I don't want your money. Charlie Gutteridge has got too much lip but he won't rub me up the wrong way. I'm giving that bit of river to Kevin for his nature study. The mink hunt won't like it but that's Kev's business now he's home from college.'

'He sounds a remarkable young man.'

'There's more to him than meets the eye, Mr Revilious. He don't say a lot but he's deep. And he's taught me things about life. Anyway,' he sighed. 'It's done.'

'Old Piper idn a bad sort,' Yelland said. 'But he can be an awkward bugger when he likes. Charlie must have put his foot in it.'

After all the words have been spoken, Revilious thought, it comes back to the Bible. If only they hadn't been so keen to sacrifice animals at the drop of a hat. He could not reconcile it to Christ's love of every living thing.

'You're winning, Paul,' the old man laughed. 'Charlie's going to be greener than a cooking apple when he hears he's lost his trout water.'

'He'll get another bit, Reg. He'll probably buy Lake Windermere.'

'Or Loch Ness and catch a really big bugger – or get caught by a big bugger. Dang me! – I'd give a year's pension to see his face.'

'I'm not very good at resistance and heroism, Reg. There's bound to be trouble.'

'Still, I wouldn like to see 'ee back off now. I reckon you'm one of they quiet blokes who picks up the V.C.'

*   *   *

The green river flowed through a tunnel of green light and poured over the weir to swirl around Zion Pool. Revilious entered feet first, very slowly, gasping all the way. But when the water closed over him his body soaked up the lovely bubbling cool and he opened his eyes on the real world of the otter.

Alice

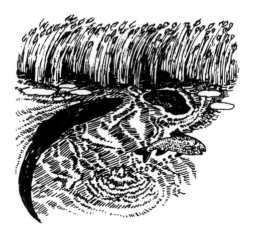

Rising under the slow, sensuous glide of the eel Skerry seized the creature in his jaws and bore it thrashing to the shallows where she was waiting. Her scent laced the water reaching in a loop of provocation from one bank to the other. They had mated for the first time among the shillets below Forders, then he had taken her whenever enjoyment of her company turned to lust. Now she ran at him and bit his muzzle and the eel was forgotten as he caught her and pinned her down.

Then the eel could be eaten in peace under the jerky, angular flight of dragonflies and the morning song of the wren. Another sunny day was breaking from the mist hazing the coombe. A mink plopped into the water nearby and floated down the runnel to hunt the scrub willow of Orchard Island for birds' nests. A little before dawn the badgers from Furze Copse had brought their cubs down to the Aishbourne to drink. Their paw marks were clearly printed in the mud. Woodpigeons crooned and a green woodpecker sent its yaffling cry across the treetops.

The mist lifted and vanished, and Cariad inspected every corner of the holt in the dead ash stump but did not lie-up there. Beneath the matted woodbine, goosegrass and brambles was a couch of dead bracken. Skerry joined her and she groomed the paw which the nylon net had cut, and removed the crumbs of grit from between his toes. A sparrow-hawk roosted in the crab apple tree on the far bank and it was preening itself, wearing a crazed, ruffled look. Every so often it shot its mutes onto the bramble leaves.

Skerry sniffed the air. It smelled of sunlight and dew-wet greenery. Mink slid in and out of the shadows, and between the leaves of his kennel Skerry would sometimes glimpse a sleek head or a back. Despite the sun the air under the trees had taken on some of the water's coolness. Skerry slept with his head on her haunches and the golden light of the west changed swiftly to silver and winged insects danced above the Aishbourne wherever water hung in slack reaches. Among the trout were bullheads and elvers. Some of these found their way into Foxcroft Pond and were eaten by the pike. Reg Yelland was itching to toss a hook at the giant fish but Revilious refused to abandon his principles. The old man stood at the garden wall in his shirtsleeves, braces and corduroys after a couple of hours weeding the vegetables. For him it had been a labour of love – thrusting his fingers into the soil, seeing the infant plants rising under his care. Wordsworth's priest, Revilious thought and that evening when Yelland was bent over the *Western Morning News* he re-read Clare's 'Remembrances', picking out lovely little pieces of the poem and savouring them.

'I was out watching the pike last night while you were in the bath,' Yelland said suddenly. 'And a bit later your bedroom light went on. It didn exactly startle me but it made me look up. If I was Cariad I wouldn go a lot on that light being switched on and off. The little bitch otter probably cleared off because of it. Now why don't you change rooms and keep the one above the pond for observation purposes – no lights, no noise?'

So it was done but the otters did not return to the island and Revilious regretted his blindness. He walked through the heat which the humidity had turned into a penance. The streets of Aishwell were generally deserted during the day with the men at work and the women sunbathing in their back gardens. Once in a while teenagers sauntered by in twos or threes chatting and laughing or listening to a transistor. Dogs came and went on private missions and if he glanced over his shoulder he would sometimes see an old lady withdraw into a doorway and feel her eyes following him as he strode on.

These elements helped accentuate the surrealism of the occasion and his awareness of time immobilized. The blue sky was neurotic with the noise and movement of swifts and martins. White buildings cast geometric shadows which shifted as the day progressed. And Revilious encountered a peculiar loneliness which he had hitherto only partly discovered in the paintings of Magritte and Dali. Sensations frozen solid within the aesthetic form, and a car parked half in shadow, half in sunlight became a piece of sculpture – aggressively modern yet standing at the frontier of the nineteenth and twentieth centuries.

Revilious ambled up Pump Lane and there ahead of him was a motionless, faceless figure in black with three equally still black dogs. But when he paused to flick the sweat off his eyebrows the figures disappeared and he arrived uncertain and insecure at the village square. On the limewashed walls clumps of pink and white valerian were snarling softly as bees arrived and departed. He turned the corner. Half a dozen motor bikes were facing him, head on. Their riders were clad in black leathers, crash helmets and visors. They sat astride the machines watching him with the awful clinical interest of predators. Somehow Revilious forced his legs to carry him through the lych gate into the churchyard. He sat on a bench and tried to keep the nausea under control. Then there was a roar of engines and the motorbikes were ridden off at speed into the countryside.

Nos was stripped to the waist sunbathing in the middle of Zion Field. Beside him lay a sketch book, a twenty pack of Rothmans and a box of matches.

'Getting it all down?' Revilious smiled.

The youth nodded but without enthusiasm. It's the heat, Revilious thought. Lord! – it was sticky. They were in for a thunderstorm and the swifts seemed to confirm this by flying low down the coombe.

'Have you done a lot of travelling, Mr Revilious?' Nos said.

'Not much. What I've done has mostly been in Britain. I'm not overkeen on foreign tours.'

'I'd like to get out of this poky hole.'

'If you've got talent it'll take you anywhere you want to go.'

'But if you're in a hurry that's no help. What's it like being really rich?'

'Awesome. Gutteridge is really rich.'

'Charlie's a pratt but you're different. It must be great to have enough cash to buy anything you want.'

'Earning what you want is more satisfying, Nos.'

'That sounds like a load of cobblers. I reckon the toffs have to put it about in case the peasants try to grab some of the high livin' for themselves.'

'You are probably right.'

'People like the royals and the oil sheiks have got it made.'

How, Revilious thought, will we bring about a universal change of values, offer moral compass bearings and become less acquisitive and more caring? A society that worships money will produce its crop of discontented, self-hating have-nots. He spoke sadly about the motorbike gang and Nos gazed at him unsympathetically.

'They idn necessarily out to gee you up,' he said. 'They've got nowhere to go. All they've got are their bikes and themselves.'

'Hanging round street corners menacing people won't win them many friends.'

'They don't need friends and I tell you what, Mr Revilious, most of what you believe is pure bloody fiction. Old Charlie's got you scared of your own shadow. If you want peace of mind stay away from The Plough and places like that. You don't see many rabbits kipping in the ferrets' hutch.'

Revilious stood up and sank his fists in his trouser pockets.

'Two world wars,' he murmured, 'to produce a society like this.'

'Well, you don't see a lot of it locked up in Happy Valley,' Nos said petulantly.

'You think I'm running away from life?'

The youth shrugged and lifted his ugliness to the sun.

'Someone else was on the estate about an hour ago,' he said. 'But you needn't worry, Mr Revilious. It was only the Spazzie from Woodburn Barton.'

'Spazzie?'

'Spastic. Old man Piper's boy Kevin. He speaks like one of them horror film hunchbacks who help mad scientists. They say he's harmless but I wouldn't like to meet the mazed bugger on a dark night.'

'Has Charlie met Kevin?' Revilious asked intuitively.

'You haven't heard about it then?'

'No. But I can guess. Charlie is a predictable gentleman.'

'Him and Dan was up The Plough and Kevin comes in for a bottle to take away. So Charlie starts pickin' on him, doin' his Quasimodo act. A lot of villagers were pissed off but the lads thought it was really funny. Charlie's a heartless bugger. If old man Piper had been there there would have been hell to pay.'

'But Mr Piper found out?'

'I suppose so. The bread roundsman told my mother and he delivers up Woodburn Barton.'

Revilious recalled Piper's defensive references to his son and sighed. And Gutteridge's nastiness had back-fired. It was curiously providential as if nature was fighting back and calling up the most unlikely forces.

'I wouldn let the spazzie come on Foxcroft, Mr Revilious. He'll only do something stupid like fall in the river or scare off your otters. He gives me the creeps.'

How is it possible, Revilious reflected, for a narrow mind to conjure up such lucid and magical visions of nature? All the windows were wide open and Beethoven's Ninth had reached the adagio molto e contabile. The music tugged hard at his emotions. He sat in the armchair with the plate on his knees forking up the chilli con carne. But a knock on the door brought him wearily and reluctantly out of his thoughts.

Alice Larkin rarely phoned to warn him of her impending visits and this was one occasion when he preferred to be alone. The child was lovable but inquisitive and noisy, and had to be watched or she was all over the house.

'Us saw a 'edgehog on your lawn, Mr Rev'lous,' she said breathlessly. 'Doan 'em make a racket!'

'So do you,' said her mother.

But the child's bubbling cheerfulness soon put Revilious in a good mood and he smiled and let her ramble on while he finished his meal. Over the lawn the ghost moths flickered and dusk softly gave way to night. But there were no stars and the first loud crack of thunder rattled across the South Hams.

'Us spent the day at Slapton,' Jane said. She had a lively mind and did not require massive doses of television to keep her amused.

'The only thin wrong with Slapton,' said Alice. 'Is it idn too safe for kiddies to swim. The beach shelves so steep and tis all pebbles.'

She was seated decoratively on the edge of the chair eating crisps. Revilious switched off the record player. Beethoven could not be expected to compete with all that munching, he thought, pouring her a large neat whisky. Her reading glasses were perched on top of her head and her eyes looked small without the customary mascara. She dipped her hand in the bag and transferred the crisps noisily to her mouth. Revilious had never heard anyone eat so unselfconsciously. But the bag did not last long and she was pouring the remains of the cheese-and-onion flavours into her palm before tipping them into her mouth. Then the bag was crumpled and placed on the coffee table, and a fingernail probed the gaps between her front teeth for any fragments which had escaped her molars. Meanwhile the child gossiped on.

Tolerating such a performance night after night was inconceivable but he could not permit his prejudices to spoil his plans. Now the night outside was disturbingly silent. If I invited her to become my housekeeper, he mused, would she respect my privacy? Would she stick to her rooms? The terms of employment would have to be made very clear. Without peace and quiet his life would be purgatory.

The thunder pealed again, distant and muffled, and he imagined the otters pricking their ears and curling deeper into their kennel. Another giant rumble burst from the south west and raindrops pattered against the window.

'We'd best shut those,' Alice said, dashing across the room. Jane was apparently unconcerned but her mother was far from happy.

'Bloody thunder,' she said. 'I hate it. Hate it.'

Rain hissed down now in thick, straight lines, making the metal table on the terrace sing and rattling on the leaves of the virginia creeper. Lightning played around Horse Wrangler Hill and the thunder was as loud as an exploding volcano. The flashes in the sky were followed by detonations which ended with grumbling roars. The rain hammered down, crushing flowers, flattening the grass and bouncing off the terrace in a fine spray.

'Bloody thunderstorms,' Alice said for the umpteenth time, and he took her hand.

The lightning continued to split the darkness pursued by the shuddering boom and crack of thunder which seemed to intensify the fury of the downpour.

'You can't drive home in this,' Revilious said. 'You and Jane are welcome to use one of the guest rooms.'

'What will the neighbours say?' Alice enquired with a coquetish smile and a toss of the head. She squeezed his hand and slipped from his grip. Revilious coloured and groped in vain for some sophisticated retort.

'Bugger the neighbours – that's what I always say,' she laughed. 'Show me where it is and I'll put Jane to bed. Can you spare another scotch?'

Half an hour later the sky was clear and the fallen rain was holding the moonlight. The river in spate roared over the weir.

'Seems funny to be in a room without a telly,' Alice said. She sat on the hearth rug and hugged her knees to her chin.

'Do you find silence intimidating?' he asked.

'It don't trouble me now but it would if I had to put up with it night after night. Don't you ever feel lonely, Paul?'

She had used his christian name for the first time and hearing it on her lips thrilled him.

'Yes – I get lonely,' he faltered.

'You haven't got a girlfriend?'

'Heavens no! Look at me. I'm a wreck.'

'But you're not. If you had your hair cut and up-dated your clothes you'd be an attractive man.'

'You're very kind, Alice.'

Again she laughed. 'I've been called many things but never that.'

'I don't suppose you'd consider coming to Foxcroft as my housekeeper?' he stumbled on. 'You could keep your place at Goutsfordleigh and have a couple of rooms here. You aren't working are you Alice?'

'No. Do you need an answer right away?'

'When you're ready.'

'I'll talk it over with Jane and let you know as soon as I've made up my mind. It would set a few tongues wagging – you being a well-off bachelor and me being . . . me.'

Again the colour rose in his cheeks.

'Alice,' he said in a comical croak.

'Do you want to go upstairs?' she murmured.

He nodded and watched her climb briskly to her feet.

'Here,' she giggled as he led her up the staircase, 'I thought you were going to say yes please you looked so bloody grateful.'

I nearly did, Revilious thought opening the bedroom door with a hand that would not stop shaking.

——— Darkness before night ———

She surprised him by making early morning tea and he sat up in bed in his pyjama trousers, marvelling at his audacity. Then she dressed lazily, easing into the clothes she had discarded without haste or embarrassment the night before. Brush and comb raked the thick brown tresses and sent them tumbling over her shoulders.

'You have beautiful hair,' he said woodenly.

'Out of the bottle,' Alice grinned. 'The roots are as grey as a badger.' He wondered how Byron would have handled the situation. Alice had a way of killing the poetry by simply being herself.

'Won't Jane ask questions?' he said.

'Why should she? She's asleep.'

'You're a good lady, Alice.'

'Kind, good – I'll be a bloody saint in a minute. I don't want to talk about last night. It was a bit of fun and life's too short to bother about hell-fire or raised eyebrows – although sometimes I have to admit neighbours make you bloody miserable. People are an unforgiving lot. More than a few women I know hate me because I do what they'd like to do if they had the guts.'

'It's all very Freudian,' he smiled.

Alice was a creature of impulse and needed no persuasion to join him on a trip to Dartmoor. He drove with all the windows down but the heat was still phenomenal. Cars swelling from distance had the wobbly wetness of mirage about them and the country, despite the storm, was dusty and tortured looking. Jane hung out of her back window catching the wind in a cupped hand.

'Have you met Kevin Piper?' Revilious asked. He swung the Fiat off the motorway at Buckfastleigh and rolled leisurely up the main street.

'I've never heard of him.'

'His people farm Woodburn Barton.'

'And Kevin?'

'He's handicapped – a spastic. Gutteridge made fun of him at The Plough recently, and Nos is scared of him. He called him a spazzie.'

'Bloody typical!' Alice fumed.

Then he told her about the magpie and the net and Gutteridge's loss of his fishing rights.

'Why don't you contact the water bailiff?' she asked.

'I never see him. The water authority has nothing to do with Aishbourne. It's small, unimportant and privately owned. And to be quite honest I don't want to involve the law if I can avoid it. Entering into a sort of Sicilian vendetta wouldn't trouble Charlie one bit. He's dying to have a real go at me.'

'Oh yes,' she agreed. 'He's a vicious yob. But you can't let him get away with it, Paul.'

'Perhaps if he discovers he's banging his head against a brick wall he may pack it in.'

'Nice things only happen in pantomimes, love. Charlie's a big rat. He'd roast his mother if he thought it'd bring him closer to what he wants. All he understands is this!' She held up a clenched fist. 'Soft pedal with him and he'll boot you where it really hurts.'

On the other side of the cattle grid past the village of Holne the in-country met the moor. Sheep were grazing amongst the bracken and gorse and Jane squealed when she saw the pony foals. The swelling landscape of prairie-like sweeps of grass, whortleberry and heather, and deep cleaves was crowned here and there by granite tors. Sharing it with another human being made the experience sweeter for Revilious. The draught from the window tugged at Alice's hair and she kept closing her eyes and laughing everytime he said something amusing. He had never played the clown before and was beginning to enjoy it. Glancing up into the driving mirror he saw a face that radiated cheerfulness. It was suntanned and animated, and it belonged to him.

After a pub lunch they lay on the riverbank at Two Bridges overlooking the West Dart. Larks were singing and a buzzard circled the far hill.

'Nice and peaceful,' Alice breathed. 'Like the epilogue on telly.'

Jane went in the water and half an hour later came shivering to her mother to be dried. Her thin little body aroused something protective and paternal in Revilious. He felt part of a family. Through the white trembling heat the larksong registered and once again he was conscious of the glory of life.

Alice's warmth enveloped the child and Revilious's throat was suddenly dry. He recalled how she had sucked him into her passion and he shut his eyes on the disagreeable replay of lust and abandonment as the images grew. Beyond her ample, crooning figure the river was picking up his thoughts and carrying him back to old loyalties. Skerry, Cariad; Adam and Eve, the children of chance pushed into a booby-trapped world.

They had a strawberry and cream tea in Moretonhampstead and cruised between hedges covered in bramble flowers to Bovey Tracey.

'I'd like to stand on Hay Tor,' Alice said. 'The view's lovely. You can see for miles. Miles,' she sighed dreamily. 'When I was a girl us used to get our blokes to bring us up here Sunday afternoons. When you'm young you don't realize how bloody lucky you are. Being young's marvellous.'

But Revilious had no special memory to quarry into. Novels and poems had been enough in the past. He had spent a lot of his mature life in other people's dreams. For no particular reason he thought of the poetry of Keats which reflected what seemed to him a bogus love of nature. And the irritating wet Philomel was forever creeping in and out of that sort of verse.

Gradually the tourists drifted home leaving the great pile of granite rocks to Revilious and his 'family'. Dusk glazed the lowlands blue and lights were coming on all over South Devon. A herd of the half-wild ponies and their foals crowded round them begging food. The mares advanced with bowed heads, snuffling gently and fixing them with heavily-lashed brown eyes.

'Kin I take one home, mum?' Jane whispered.

'And who'd clean up the mess in your bedroom?'

'A pony wouldn be no trouble, mum.'

'Have 'ee forgotten what the otter did?'

They dined at an inn which snob magazines recommended in their good food columns. Alice's pleasantly suntanned figure and Marks and Spencer's frock were decided embellishments of place and proceedings, Revilious thought, watching her gingerly probe the lamb and sip the Moselle.

'Like Christmas idn it, mum?' Jane said on the homeward journey.

The night sky was blue and hazy and sprinkled with big yellow stars. Whistler, Revilious thought – 'Battersea Bridge'. A world observed from other people's art, he smiled.

Jane was singing when he put on the handbrake and cut the engine. She climbed out of the car, pushed open the garden gate and ran along the terrace. Alice squawked and beat the air above her head.

'Bats,' Revilious laughed. 'Pipistrelles by the sound of it. They won't hurt you, Alice. All that rot about getting them in your hair is absolutely unfounded.'

Then Jane screamed – a long drawn-out rising cry of horror and fear. Alice was first to reach her. The child was sobbing through the fingers she had crushed to her face. Her whole body was convulsed.

'Jane. Janie baby,' Alice whispered. 'What is it love?'

'The door,' Jane cried. 'The door. On the door.'

To crucify the badger sow it had been necessary to break her forelegs. Six-inch copper nails had been driven through the pads into the oak panels. The animal's head was slumped on her chest. She was dead and the blood had stopped leaking from the wounds.

'Dear God,' Alice gasped, and she knelt and folded her arms round Jane.

Revilious wanted to speak but emotion got in the way of the words and all he could do was stand there swallowing like a sleepwalker emerging from nightmare.

'Come on, lovie,' Alice said, gathering up her daughter. 'Let's go home.'

Revilious turned the key and the door swung inwards. He snapped on the light and waited for the numbness to tingle out of his knees. The badger's lifeless eyes were fixed on him. Revilious sat at the telephone table and flicked through the pad. Then he dialled the number and spoke to the desk sergeant who calmly took down the details as though badgers were found crucified to people's front doors every day of the week.

The RSPCA Inspector did his best to reassure him. 'Look at the blood around the animal's muzzle,' he said. 'It was dead before they nailed it to your door, Mr Revilious. It was probably knocked down by a car – an all too frequent occurrence, I'm afraid. Otherwise we could do them under the Badger Act.'

'And the actual crucifixion?' said Revilious.

'A pretty unique business,' the policeman admitted. 'But if we catch the person or persons involved all we can charge them with is criminal damage to a door.'

'But I told you it's part of a wider campaign of intimidation.'

'I'm sure the CID will look into that, sir.'

'What about Gutteridge?'

'He's in Spain.'

'Hitler was in Berlin but the commandant of Belsen still got his orders.'

'Proving it in court won't be easy – assuming Mr Gutteridge has something to do with this.'

'Yes, I'm sorry.'

'Make out a statement, sir, and we'll take it from there. When Mr Gutteridge comes home we'll interview him.'

'One thing, officer. I don't want the press in on this. They'd come up with some lunatic black magic stuff and bang would go my otters' privacy.'

If he flicked the stamens of the weed named pellitory-on-the-wall they coughed little puffs of pollen.

'It had to come out in the open eventually,' Yelland said gruffly. '– Charlie's threats, the rats, the netting, this. But he's as slippery as an eel and he's worth a bob or two. Don't expect anything earth-shattering – like justice.'

'All I expect is trouble.'

'You'd have got that anyway – coppers or no coppers. Stirring it up for Charlie will make it easier for you in the long run. If Bob was alive he'd have gone to the police ages ago.'

'I can't forget the look on the little girl's face.'

'Don't fret, boy. Her won't dwell on it. She probably sees worse things on the video.'

'But it doesn't make it right,' Revilious grunted, flicking the pellitory again. 'Only a truly warped mind could have dreamed that up.'

'Old Charlie's twisted alright,' said Yelland. 'Dang me! but I wouldn piddle on him if he was on fire.'

'Of course we have Nos,' Revilious smiled. 'If he makes a clean breast of the part he played in the rat affair we're off the mark.'

'Don't count on un, Paul. Nos won't be keen to go to court and drop his mates in it. And Charlie wouldn exactly be over the moon either. Then you have to think of Ted Healey. He assaulted two of the boys and that would look bad – 'specially if Charlie gets one of they smart city lawyers.'

'Whoever hung that badger on your door idn goin' to own up. Widger and Wayne Steer are about as popular with the police as a couple of pork pies in a synagogue.'

'I'm having second thoughts about this, Reg. Maybe it was a mistake to call in the law.'

'The only mistake you made was leavin' it this late. If Bob was alive he'd give you a piece of his mind. You've let Charlie call the tune.'

The badger was buried in the orchard by the weir and Revilious came to the grave in the evening when the may-flies were passing over the pond and the rising fish were ruffling the hush. Tomorrow he promised himself he would go to church. He felt close to a darkness that had nothing to do with his impending death. Dying itself had brought him nearer to God and deepened his love of life and respect for living creatures. But in Gutteridge he was confronted by something terrifyingly negative.

'Dear God,' he prayed, sinking to his knees amongst the loose-strife. 'Watch over me and help me serve you. Protect and comfort all wild animals and let them find peace according to their needs beyond the reach of evil men.'

If I'm not careful, he thought sheepishly, I'll be going to bed wearing a necklace of garlic cloves.

The evening was very warm and still, and he waded through the undergrowth to the river's edge and gazed into the weir. Then a breeze sprang up and swept through the lap of the coombe and started the trees hissing and roaring. A grey squirrel sailed across the chasm between the riverside willows.

For a little while Revilious stood in a churning green and silver cauldron of noise and violent movement. Pain clamped his heart and he balled his fists and hammered them against his chest until he could breathe normally again. The breeze died and the stillness of twilight took him by surprise. Only the river gliding under its own music convinced him he was not imprisoned in some colossal painting being observed by eyes which were not human.

Shortly after midnight the otters were swimming in the pond and chirping their contact calls. Their joy was infectious and he remained at the window for nearly an hour while they played in the light of a moon no bigger than a toy sickle. His anxiety had faded to a queasiness which he took to bed. But he could not sleep. What he and Alice had done together filled him with revulsion now. He had never entered into a casual relationship with a woman before. 'Hypocrite', he whispered into the pillow. She was blameless. Then he laughed. Yesterday he had come close to asking her to be his wife. It was unreasonable to expect her to share his love of the coombe and the wildlife. But supposing he died intestate? What would become of Foxcroft? Who would fight Gutteridge? He couldn't leave everything to Alice. She meant well but was too irresponsible and would go off with the first good-looking waster that turned up. He wasn't certain of Nos, and Reg was too old – although at the last resort he was the best bet.

It was a pity about Alice but provisionally, at least, Yelland would have to be made his heir. He did not like the Healeys sufficiently to consider them despite Ted's stoicism. Beneath their apparent charity he thought he had located a certain grasping peasant meanness, which in the long term might be bad for the otters. Whatever happened he would make a will that would reinforce his wish to preserve Foxcroft's unique rural character. No tidying-up of riverbanks, no grubbing out of hedges or copses; no fishing, shooting or trapping. The birds and animals would always come first and whoever took over from him would run the estate on those terms. Anyway, he thought sadly, I probably won't see Alice and Jane again.

'Damn you, Gutteridge,' he groaned. 'Damn you to hell.'

Heatwave

'I can't do it,' Nos said, and he drew his fingernails savagely through the stubble on his head. 'Christ! – if I did grass on Wayne and Dave the gang would brand me as King Crap. Then Charlie would lean on me, heavily.'

'I'm sorry,' Revilious sighed.

'Tidn that I don't want to, Mr Revilious; only, I'm bloody scared as it is. I've been gettin' some aggro up The Plough and Dan Gutteridge nearly run me down the other night. I had to jump in the hedge to get out of his way.'

Revilious felt as helpless as a child in the undertow of heavy surf. The familiar pattern of failure was evolving.

On Sunday he went to church and was disappointed. The vicar was a doddering old man who mumbled his way through Mattins like a bored courier on one of those London sightseeing tours. But the nave was cool and the tiny congregation allowed plenty of time for private prayer and meditation.

Walking down Top Field through the heat of noon under the lisp of house martins and swallows he saw a young man laboriously ascending the far side of the coombe on walking sticks. Nos was sketching on the lawn, resembling a strawberry and vanilla ice-cream, Revilious thought, with his sunburned back and white front.

'Part of the wall and the iron gate,' Nos said, and he held aloft the drawing.

'Plenty of pre-Raphaelite detail,' murmured Revilious. 'But it's unlike you to be working on a Sunday.'

'I'm usually in bed sleeping it off,' the youth grinned. 'I had to come over Foxcroft, Mr Revilious. I got something important to ask you.'

Revilious removed his panama and used it as a fan. Then he took off his jacket and rolled up his shirt sleeves. The sparrows were chirping in the virginia creeper and rook fledglings clattered about in the oaks behind the pond cawing for food.

'There was a young man the other side of the coombe,' he said absently. 'I think I know who it was.'

'Kev,' Nos grinned. 'The original K.P. That's what the lads call him up The Plough. Kevin Piper, K.P. – get it?'

Revilious stared uncomprehendingly at him.

'K.P.s a brand of salted peanut. So, K.P. – nut.'

'You can't refute that sort of logic,' Revilious said gently. 'But isn't it cruel and mindless to keep baiting him?'

'It's a joke,' Nos said, closing his sketchbook. 'If you took life seriously all the time you'd go crazy. When I was a nipper I used to laugh at cripples. I felt sorry for them but couldn't stop laughing whenever I saw one. I'd curl up. Sometimes I wonder why God allows them into the world. Maybe he gets a laugh out of it as well.'

Revilious had to visit the lavatory and Nos followed him into the house and stood admiring the landscapes in the hall.

'That Brianski knew how to use oils,' he said when Revilious rejoined him. 'Bags of romantic atmosphere. I bet they're worth a few bob. And talking of money, sir, I was hoping you'd let me have a small loan.'

'How small, Nos?'

'Three hundred and seventy-five quid – as soon as possible.'

'Are you in trouble?'

'Not with the law or anything like that. I'm behind as hell with the payments on my bike and I want a new drawing board and easel, oils, good water colours, brushes, canvasses, paper. I'm piddlin' about at the moment and I can't do what I want to do.'

Revilious nodded.

'To pay you back I'd knock up the next half dozen pictures for nothing.'

'And how would you live?'

'I'd do other work. If I'm going to make it I've got to widen my field.'

'I see. But I think it would be more sensible if I paid you every other picture then you'd have a guaranteed income as well as the chance to work off the debt.'

'So you'll lend me the money?'

'Yes. Be here at noon tomorrow and I'll have it ready.'

'You won't regret it, Mr Revilious. I'm going to work my ass off.'

'I should sign your masterpieces Eric Prowse. Nos would look a bit trendy on the bottom of a painting. Posterity mightn't understand.'

*   *   *

Skerry dragged himself under the arching ash root and rubbed his back against the bark. The water level of the Aishbourne had dropped as the heatwave poured sunshine into the coombe. But the pools were still deep enough to interest the otters and the undergrowth each side of the river walled them off from prying eyes.

They hunted by day while the sound of tractors and the
tchak of daws floated from the distance. Then it was heaven to
wallow in the green reflections of the trees listening to the
collar doves and the song of the blackcap.

One evening Skerry was coming up the shallows between
the two upper pools of Foxcroft when he was met by the scent
of a dog otter. He had left Cariad lying up in the scrub under
Forders and he called to her now with a piercing whistle. She
poured out a rising chitter of alarm, and Skerry crashed
through Bowden's Pool and galloped along the badger path
beside the river, his spiky coat adding to his air of ferocity.

The rival dog, who was in his third year, stood ready and
began catterwauling. He had chosen a large, flat rock in
midstream and had sprainted defiantly through Cariad's musk.
For such a prize he was prepared to fight but the vision of
Skerry exploding from a cloud of spray suddenly wrecked his
resolve. The growling cry he dredged up was drowned beneath
Skerry's screech of rage. The otters met and tangled with the
concentrated fury of all mustelids. Rolling over Skerry held the
stranger down and bit his shoulder. Then he sprang back and
snarled while his swishing tail beat the rhythm of his anger.

Hissing and chattering all the time the intruder retreated
backwards until he had created enough distance to turn and
run. Skerry strutted after him but only in token pursuit and
contented himself with a final scream of triumph. But before
he joined Cariad he patrolled the northern boundaries of his
territory and sprainted and raked up earth and grass with his
claws.

At nightfall he led her downstream through the scent of the
sleeping countryside. Healey's pigs chugged softly from their
houses and the otters crossed the open meadows by starlight,
stopping and pricking their ears whenever an owl screeched or
a cow shifted in sleep. Cariad was eating less and playing more
and both animals lusted after really deep, muscular water.

In Hay Creek the tide was up, pushing the smell of the river
across the farmland. Skerry killed a mallard duck beside a
boat-house and ate only the breast. Sometimes the otters separated and pretended to lose each other in the black waters.
Then the reunion of entwined bodies and muzzle pressed to
muzzle was a small ecstasy.

Returning up the Aishbourne they caught eels in the bend of the river above Woodburn Bridge and came on through the dewy grass to wriggle under the gate into Old Bethlehem. But Revilious missed them. He crouched against the stone wall overlooking the weir whose voice had been reduced to a whisper by the heatwave. The solitude held the frail light of dawn. Once again he shook his head and smiled, recalling how he had considered sharing Foxcroft with Alice. In fact, he had spent too much precious time on people like her, the Healeys and Nos. Reg was different. He was a kindred spirit, but Alice! Revilious grinned. What were her problems? How to get the Hillman Imp started on a cold morning. What dress to wear. Whether or not to have her hair long. Her failure to take fidelity seriously amused him only because he would never suffer from it. Why, he smiled, straightening his stiff legs, can't I meet an attractive cultured lady who subscribes to *The Listener*?

But he had made his will and Bertish had told him there was enough in the kitty to meet the death duties without carving up the estate. Could Yelland cope? – and would he be prepared to after a lifetime of hard work? Certainly Gutteridge wouldn't relent. If that man got his hands on Foxcroft everything would vanish including the otters. Revilious closed his eyes and gripped the grass in his fists.

'Stop him,' he whispered. 'Stop him.'

He was reading *The Mabinogion* on the terrace when Kevin Piper pushed wide the iron gate and came across the lawn dragging his left foot and walking almost on tiptoe. Both legs were deformed and the young man banged down the metal walking sticks to take the weight of his body and maintain his balance. Moments later the introductions had been made, hands had been shaken and he was sipping tea at the garden table.

'I saw the otters,' he said with the curious flat diction and frayed consonants of the cleft palate. Like a deaf person using a language he can't hear, Revilious thought.

'They crossed the field and went in Brent Copse.'

Lolling back in the deckchair he gazed solemnly through his spectacles. Although not more than twenty his black curly hair was thinning at the temples and his jowls were darkened by a permanent five o'clock shadow.

'My father sent me over, Mr Revilious,' he added quietly. 'I should have asked permission before gallivanting around your property.'

'You have it – so long as you keep away from the river.'

'Is the otter bitch going to have cubs?'

'Hopefully. If she's left alone she will. The next couple of months are crucial.'

'No one's allowed to hunt them anymore,' Kevin said. 'When I was a boy I saw one killed. The hounds cornered it under Huxton Bridge. I remember the blood in the river. Now they go after the mink. Dad says you're against that, too – the mink hunting.'

'For all sorts of selfish reasons but mainly because of the racket they kick up. Otters hate din and if you have fifty dogs and the same number of people charging up and down a stretch of river the otters will go.'

'I'm trying to get dad to stop the foxhounds and the mink hounds coming on our land but he does a lot of business with hunt folk,' said Kevin. 'I did prevent him sluicing the silos into the river. Conservation is just about the most important thing, Mr Revilious.'

They discussed the problems of maintaining a traditional countryside and Kevin listened to Revilious proclaim his primitive Taoism.

'But the land needs looking after,' the young man said, propping his elbows on the table. 'Copses need managing if they're to stay healthy and I noticed a lot of good hay has gone over in your fields. I'm sure I can create a peaceful environment on my bit of land without forgetting it's part of a working farm. Good husbandry can provide a good environment for wildlife without going to extremes.'

'But Foxcroft isn't a farm. It's a piece of wilderness,' Revilious said patiently. 'Otter country.'

'As a farmer's son it's difficult for me to see it in that context,' Kevin smiled. 'I'll cut hay on my land and run a few cows but I'll let the hedges grow and get rid of the barbed wire. You won't catch me using chemical sprays and there will always be plenty of cover on my riverbanks. I've aired my views at Young Farmers' Club meetings but generally I don't pack much political muscle. They call me K.P. in some quarters – like The Plough for instance. You've probably heard of my run-in with friend Gutteridge.'

'You seem remarkably unperturbed.'

Kevin shrugged. A greenfly had settled on one of his lenses. He took off the spectacles and gently blew the insect away.

'But there's more to Gutteridge than meets the eye, isn't there, Kevin? – you sense it. I sense it.'

The young man drew down his eyebrows in a frown and waited for him to continue. Then he was told the entire story from the bag of rats to the badger's crucifixion.

'Wildlife as tools and victims,' Revilious whispered. 'Yes, Gutteridge is different.'

'Horribly different,' Kevin said.

'When I heard he was having a go at you I thought you might have seen it.'

'Seen what, Mr Revilious?'

'The dark side of the man – for want of a better phrase. Sometimes I feel he's not really interested in me or the otters. It goes deeper, and I can't put my finger on it.'

But Kevin Piper shook his head and Revilious was content to let the matter drop.

The bow bridge

Nos's absence from Foxcroft eventually prompted Revilious to enquire after him.

'You didn lend the bugger money!' Yelland said in slack-jawed disbelief. Then it came out. Nos had borrowed from the vicar, the landlord of The Plough, Healey and Charlie Gutteridge.

'And he stole off his own mother,' said Mr Prowse from his chair in the front room of the pebble-dashed council house at Uddern. 'Eric thinks the world owes him a living. Oh he got talent but he hates work.'

'The gentleman don't want to know them things, Russell,' said his wife shifting her gaze from Revilious to the mantelpiece and a photograph of the schoolboy which Eric had once been.

'Tis fatal to give un a penny before the job's complete,' Mr Prowse continued. 'Eric isn wicked – he's weak. The vicar paid him fifty quid back along. It was an advance on the mural he was supposed to be doing in the church hall. Eric took it and went off on a spree. The mural never got done.'

'How much exactly did he borrow off you, sir?' said Mrs Prowse. She was a squat, unsmiling woman with dark down on her upper lip that would coarsen into a moustache as she aged.

'Nearly four hundred pounds,' Revilious said.

'So him and Widger could take off on their bikes on a bloody joy ride,' Mr Prowse snorted. 'They've gone to Scotland – or so

he says. Going to pick fruit! But they'll be home when the cash
runs out. Then he'll have to pay you back – every bloody penny.
Us haven't got a cent, sir, or we'd settle up now. I suppose
you'll be goin' to the police.'

Revilious shook his head. 'No, I'll put this one down to
experience and try not to get caught again.'

'Lendin' large sums of money to boys idn on, Mr Revilious, if
you don't mind me sayin' so,' Mrs Prowse offered as a passing
shot.

Wading up Hay Creek at low tide Warren Palfrey began to
impale flukes on his three-pronged fork. It was something he
had done well since a twenties childhood. He found the little
flatfish with his toes and lifted them squirming from the sand
on the end of the fork. Each catch was popped in a sackcloth
bag slung from his shoulder.

Mist was creeping off the mud banks to meet the sunrise.
Stealthily the old man worked up the channel keeping a wary
eye on the tide and measuring the distance between himself
and the skiff anchored near the mouth of the creek. The otters
surfaced close to his bare knees, stared up at him for a second
or two then twisted away, turning and diving to vanish.

'Jesus Christ!' the old man gasped, and lost his balance and
sat back in the water.

'Bloody fitches!' he squawked, trying to retrieve the fish as
they spilt from the bag.

When Skerry surfaced again he heard the thrashing and curs-
ing behind him in the mist. He swam unhurriedly and joined
Cariad on the broad apron of shillets and stones.

The Aishbourne trickled through a runnel which a man
could have straddled comfortably, but a little further up the
fresh water was deep enough for them to bathe and shake off
the smell of the tidal river. They dog-paddled on to the brisk
flow under the bow bridge. Here the sills were littered with
evidence of mink activity and Skerry and Cariad made a
thorough examination of each scat.

Wharton laid the shotgun across the jacket he had folded on
the parapet and waited for the otters to appear. The poacher
had walked the river from Aishford to Hay and could have
killed pheasants, duck and hares but had resisted the temp-

tation. Beside the mill leat he had discovered the fresh seals of otters and Charlie Gutteridge was offering a hundred pounds for a carcass. Luck was a funny thing, he reflected. Not long ago he had stood miserable on the bridge dying to light a cigarette when suddenly a couple of otters had emerged from nowhere like the answer to a prayer. Now he was ready to turn them into hard cash.

His tongue slid across his lips and he thumbed back the hammers. A vehicle was coming down the lane from Totnes. 'Shit', Wharton hissed through teeth he had clenched on his tension. The otters splashed about under the arch immediately below him. Maybe the noise will flush them out, Wharton thought. Come on, you little sods, come on. The sound of the engine droning in third gear grew louder and a red mail van crept round the corner and drew slowly to a halt on the bridge. Wharton gestured wildly for the driver to remain still but the postman got out and slammed the door behind him. He was a big bear of a man with thin blond hair and a ginger-and-grey streaked beard.

'What are you bloody up to, Wharton?' he growled.

Despairingly Wharton placed a finger to his lips in a plea for silence.

'You're not shooting salmon,' came the gruff response.

'For Christ's sake be quiet,' Wharton whispered.

The postman joined him as Skerry and Cariad left the safety of the bridge and splashed noisily into the shallows offering the easiest of targets. But a hand like an irate giant spider pressed the gun barrels to the parapet and another unhooked Wharton's trigger finger.

'You mazed berk, Trevisick,' the poacher snarled.

'Another word from you Wharton, and I'm going to ram this right up your arse.'

A fierce swing was enought to shatter the stock on the stonework. Then the ruined twelve bore was dropped in the river.

'If you had shot those otters you'd be joining it,' the postman said, stabbing a forefinger repeatedly into Wharton's chest. 'And if I ever hear you've hurt an otter I'll come looking for you. Understand?'

The huge forefinger continued to peck at Wharton's rib cage.

'You bastard, Trevisick.'

'Yes – a mean bastard and don't you forget it. Don't give me
any lip. Just keep your mouth shut and go. Not . . . a . . . word.'

Wharton compressed his mouth into a thin white line and
spun on his heel. Trevisick watched him depart before turning
his attention to the river. As anger subsided satisfaction
swelled. He was a keen amateur naturalist and had not seen
wild otters since his Cornish youth. Now there were signs they
were secretly in possession of some South Hams rivers and
once in a while he had heard them whistling on the Avon. But
a sighting was a special bonus.

*   *   *

Charlie Gutteridge replaced the receiver and studied his reflection in the hall mirror. With the sun tan and ash blond hair
he could have passed for a twenty-five-year-old. Shaving off the
side pieces had certainly helped but the beergut filling the front
of the modern drainpipe jeans his girlfriend had persuaded him
to buy was definitely council estate darts team. Dan said he
looked like Tweedledum.

'Wharton nearly bagged a brace of otters this morning,' he
mumbled. 'But some wally of a postman stuck his oar in.'

'Do you ever get the feeling things are going wrong, Charlie?'
Colin said.

'Old Bill left Rattlecombe thinkin' the sun shone out my
ass,' his brother replied. 'Who gets copped for a tickle on the
vicar's lawn? You can bet money I won't end up without laces
because some old queen opened his mouth.'

'The badger was bad news.'

'Who for?'

'You, Charlie. Revilious wouldn't have called in Old Bill if
you hadn't got Widger and his mates to do that. And how come
you lost the fishing?'

'The spazzie must have put the boot in. Taking the piss out
of him was just bad timing.'

'But Revilious helped. He's not as thick as he looks.'

'But it's him not me who's goin' to end up in a paper hat.'

'And that's important?'

'No – it's a giggle. This is what it's all about, my son.'

Charlie slid a wad of tenners from his pocket and peeled one
off. 'This separates blokes like me from wallies like Widger,
Healey and Revilious.'

The lids descended and he gently rubbed the scar on the back of his left hand.

Alone on the motorway behind the wheel of his Rover Vanden Plas Colin recalled Charlie's words and let them resurrect an image his subconscious had guarded for twenty-five years. He was on the settee in the flat not far from Villa Park. The upholstery smelled of cat's urine. Dan was arranging the dinky cars on the carpet when Charlie came in. It was like an excerpt from a silent movie – lots of gesticulation but no noise, not in his daydream. Then Charlie picked up the cat and bent his head to kiss it. Lifting both front feet the animal raked his face, leaving horizontal claw marks. Charlie did not say a word. He put the cat down gently and stared at her while the blood flowed. The following day she vanished and was never seen again.

Colin also remembered how Dan had collared him in the bedroom before breakfast one morning to show him the swollen eye Charlie had given him.

'He ain't our real brother,' Dan said coldly. 'They adopted him because mum thought she couldn't have kids. Then I came along and they wished they hadn't taken the nasty little bugger.'

But Dan didn't mean it. He loved Charlie and would do anything for him. Charlie was a kind of cult figure. As a boy he had done things that had alarmed the police and the school authorities.

'The secret,' he confessed once to Colin, 'Is not caring about nothing. Nothing.'

Scents and sounds

From the edge of Venn Copse at the top of Brockhill Field Kevin Piper could glass the river from Bowden's Pool to Wotton's Pool. A magpie sent its rasping screech down the orchard more like a knife being sharpened on a grindstone than a bird. The light around him came from the coombe itself. But the otters demanded all his concentration. They were splashing about in Bowden's Pool and their cries were soft and confident. Eventually Skerry broke surface with a large eel and the bitch chivvied him, trying to tug the fish from his jaws. And he let her have the prize and followed her to the shallows.

The river was as low as it had been in the drought of 1976. Kevin turned his binoculars on the island at the Forders end of Brent Copse and saw the strand of orange nylon knotted to the blackthorn stump. It vanished ominously into the trout swim. If the water had been higher he might have missed it.

'So in that sense,' he said, 'the drought's a blessing.'

Revilious made him comfortable on the lawn and hurried upstream with Yelland. Beyond Brent Copse they uncovered three nets – one showing above the water where no allowance had been made for the dropping level, and two cunningly concealed below the surface at Forders. Barbed wire had been woven into the top net and Yelland spat out his disgust as he hacked it free.

'Whoever did this meant business, and that's a fact. The bloke hasn't heard of the Geneva convention.'

'It's obviously Chárlie's brainchild,' Revilious said. 'Have you any idea who could have set them, Reg?'

'Wayne Steer, the Langley brothers, Wharton. There's lots of local rubbish willing to do anything for an easy couple of bob. But we've got allies. A postman stopped Wharton from shooting a couple of otters down Hay the other morning. I know the boy. He delivers your letters sometimes.'

They searched the length of the river. There were no more nets but gin traps had been tilled in the shallows below Lord's Pool where the banks were heavily overgrown. Revilious yanked them out.

'We're dealin' with craftsmen, Paul,' said Yelland. 'You can't see this bit of water from the field. The iron was perfectly placed.'

Healey agreed to patrol the valley from Forders to the Horridge Inn but with the otters in residence his usefulness was limited. Most evenings and mornings Kevin and his binoculars were strategically placed high up the coombeside, and Yelland had taken it upon himself to stroll down to Drang occasionally and look over the southern end of Foxcroft.

At last Revilious felt he was making some headway. Yelland told him he had seen Charlie on the local evening news shaking hands with the show business celebrity who was opening his new betting shop west of Plymouth. Apparently Gutteridge was also extending his video empire across Wales.

'Now he can't bung his worm in the Aishbourne,' Yelland said wickedly, 'there's no reason for him to hang round the village. You'm winning on points, boy.'

The heat bounced off the garden. The grass was blond and parched, and the lawn hard underfoot.

'If it don't rain soon the river will be down to a trickle,' the old man sighed.

'Then the otters will move on,' Revilious said miserably.

'Don't fret,' said Yelland. 'I've never knowed the Aishbourne to run dry.'

'Everything's weighed against them,' Revilious said. 'Noise, people charging about, toxic chemicals in the rivers, nets, guns, cruelty, stupidity. The poor animals are running blind across a minefield.'

Placing their feet among the strands of pink convolvulus Skerry and Cariad emerged from the thistles and waddled across the cart track into a meadow full of poppies. The hedges were veiled in traveller's joy, honeysuckle and bramble blossom, and shadows were blueing a little with the advance of dusk. Sparrow flocks flighted noisily from one field of grain to the next, and swifts were chasing over the roofs of Huxton Manor.

The otters swam under Yetson Bridge and left the river to run along the bullock creep to Huish Bridge and were beyond High Aishbourne when darkness descended. Then they turned from the water and explored the fields and open moor between the Aishbourne and the River Erme.

Cariad's wanderlust was insatiable and she spent a lot of time nosing about in disused setts and rock clitters. Whenever Skerry showed his impatience she growled at him. But the Erme was a busy little river and once she was in it her mood changed.

Racing downstream they caught a salmon that had been injured by a poacher's harpoon gun, and later they killed a brace of goslings despite the old goose's clamour and the yelping of a chained collie. Although the hunting was good Cariad was uneasy quartering water which might prove hazardous to cubs. Her play was half-hearted for her thoughts were back at Foxcroft where no dogs barked and the nights were riddled with comforting sounds and scents.

*   *   *

'Honeysuckle,' Alice sighed, joining him at the door. 'The air's full of it.'

'I'm glad you called.' Revilious said.

'I like it here – and so does Jane.'

'Then you'll take the housekeeping job?' he faltered.

'No, Paul,' she said, catching his hand in her arm and dovetailing fingers. 'Goutsfordleigh is my home and I don't want to move in on you. I've burnt too many bridges. I'll pop over every Saturday if you like, but I'm not moving in.'

'I never imagined I had the pull of a pop star,' Revilious smiled. 'Saturdays will be fine, Alice.'

'Don't keep knockin' yourself,' she scolded him as he locked and bolted the door. 'You are a kind, loving man.'

'But I don't – as they say – turn you on.'

'Few men do, love. If it's any consolation I enjoyed sleeping with you. I really fancied that young vet David Copeland but Christ! – what a non-event he turned out to be. All that advertizing and nort to offer when the wrappings came off! Keep it casual, keep it friendly. I genuinely like you, Paul. Idn that enough?'

Later he returned to the terrace and sat listening to the darkness. Sparrows were chirping in the virginia creeper and the river rippled over the weir. It was nearly midnight, warm, star-hazed with the countryside holding its breath. Alice had gone home after a conversation which had lapsed into the sort of gossip he found irksome. In fact the entire evening had been arduous. Uneducated people were under constant bombardment from trivia and their talk ranged across the mundane. He sighed and made a brief return to the drawingroom. Then the record player clicked and Bach's St Matthew Passion lapped his thoughts and the light from the windows revealed little diamonds of moisture on the grass.

He had fallen asleep but something woke him with a jolt that cricked his neck. Something warm and moist was curling round his fingers. The alsation lay beside him slavering over the hand that had flopped down beside the deckchair. Horror flooded Revilious's nervous system. I'm still asleep, he thought, but the record player was on automatic and Bach was competing with the rush of the weir. Oh Jesus, Revilious cried from the darkness of his mind. The dog gazed up at him and stopped washing his fingers. Its eyes were full of curiosity.

Revilious's tongue darted across the roof of his mouth but could find no saliva. Slowly he began to raise his hand, curling the fingers protectively into a fist. The dog growled and showed canine teeth which were curved and sharply pointed. The hand was lowered but remained clenched and quivering on the tiles. The alsation laid his chin possessively on it and whimpered.

Sweat broke from Revilious's scalp and ran down his forehead to fall in drops from his nose and eyebrows. The pain pressed around his heart like broken glass and he was suddenly struggling to breathe. He could drag air in but could not exhale.

In his panic the dog was forgotten. He scrambled out of the chair and tottered down the steps onto the lawn. Now the night was swimming away with his senses and his knees had given out and he was flat on his back under a swirling sky. He closed his eyes. The dog's breath was unpleasant. Carnivore's stink, he thought, allowing the giddiness to have him. Briefly he looked up, hoping the universe had steadied. Sirius dilated and contracted and was eclipsed by a tall figure. Then everything vanished like it did when he turned off the bedroom light.

The dappled stream

The slender starlings crowded the margins of the lawn. Yelland glared at them and let the curtain fall back across the window. Starlings were not his favourite birds.

'There's no trace of any dogs,' he said, 'no tracks or muck, nort. And no human footprints. I gave the garden a thorough going-over.'

'But the alsation and the figure, Reg,' Revilious said.

'Funnier things have come out of a whisky bottle, boy,' Yelland grinned.

'I only had a night cap.'

'Listen,' the old man said soothingly. 'When I'm worried and nod off all sorts of queer things happen in my head. Trouble breeds trouble.'

As if to confirm this maxim Kevin phoned to say the mink hunt was meeting at Cockstone Bridge. It was the raw, desperate voice of someone imprisoned in his own body. But the morning was blue and sunny and the blackbird's melody seemed heartless against the background of unhappy human affairs. In the top branches of the pine overlooking Churchland's Wood the buzzards were feeding gobbets of freshly slaughtered rabbit to their young. And at Woodburn Barton Farm Mr Piper and his labourer were dipping the sheep which would soon be on their way to market and the butchers' slabs.

Revilious drove through the lanes to the Dartmoor in-country and reached the bridge as the hunt moved off. So many jolly sunburned faces and all the birds and animals, insects, leaves, grasses and flowers breathing life into the earth and sky! Never before had Revilious been so agonizingly aware of the living world and his ancestry.

The hunt itself possessed a pagan vitality. The dark blue uniforms moved down the stream, the horn yelped, people laughed, the whips brought the rioting pack under control. The hounds splashed on beneath the rowan trees, past a forestry commission plantation of larches into a valley with a long, narrow, oak wood on the righthand side.

Revilious and Yelland tramped behind the field.

'What do you intend doing, Paul?' the old man asked. 'There's a lot of rough boys here today and to be perfectly honest I haven't got much sympathy for the mink. The hounds chop 'em quickly and animal killin' animal strikes me as natural.'

'The whole business is contrived,' Revilious said in a tired, flat voice.

'So's everything else, boy – marriage, education, war, funerals. But I wouldn like to see this crowd of hypocrites chop one of our otters and that's why you'm here, idn it, Paul?'

'Yes, I'm afraid they'll find them on some exposed tributary and kill them on open ground before the people can interfere.'

'The master idn stupid.'

'And hunting isn't an exact science, Reg. In any case, if Cariad encountered a pack of dogs she'd run miles and probably abandon the Aishbourne altogether.'

They overtook half a dozen elderly followers absorbed in the sort of small talk Revilious loathed. Coffee morning chat glazed the venality of the occasion with a callousness reminiscent of the awful socializing that attended public hangings. Then the hounds spoke from the bottom of the sloping meadow. Revilious had a fine view of them. Most of the pack were in the river and the remainder ringed a young ash tree. Their clamour filled the valley, drowning the lark song and the bleating of sheep.

The mink clung to the thin top branches and its agitation made the leaves shiver and twinkle. Several hounds stood on their hind legs and clawed at the trunk. Their pink mouths gaped like the maws of giant fledglings pleading for titbits. A boy in breeches and blue woollen stockings darted forward and climbed halfway up the tree and began to shake it. The mink's hind feet lost their grip and the animal swung with twisting body until it anchored on four points again, spread between two boughs that bent like fishing rods under its weight.

Urged by the crowd the boy climbed higher and gripping the branches pushed them apart. Again the mink's back feet were jerked free but this time the force of its body whipping back sent the creature spinning helplessly down. It ricocheted off the boy's shoulder and crashed into the massed hounds.

'A quick death,' Yelland said gruffly.

'But hardly sporting,' Revilious remarked loud enough to turn a few heads.

'Disgraceful,' barked a lady in a headscarf and tweeds. 'Shameful conduct!'

'If you're determined to come home after a day in the country with the blood of an innocent creature on your hands,' Revilious said, 'does it matter how you go about it?'

The woman stared through him as the hunt surged off once more. Two or three young men dropped back to keep an eye on Revilious.

Wading thigh deep down a Devon river on such a day reminded him poignantly of boyhood adventures. He was hurrying now and steeling himself for the belling of the hounds and the sight of Skerry and Cariad vanishing under the pack.

'Ease up, boy,' Yelland gasped. The old man grimaced and rubbed his left knee. 'If they find an otter us won't be able to do much about it.'

'But I can make it difficult for them, Reg – bloody difficult.' Yelland looked at him. The tall, lean figure was quivering and the normally placid eyes blazed.

A row of dead elms guarded the approach to High Aishbourne. Swallows hawked the water meadows and fantailed doves clattered down amongst the roofs of the village. A crowd thronged Kittaford Bridge and the hounds and master were getting a noisy reception.

'They're not locals,' Yelland said.

'How can you tell?'

'Them on the bridge are all youngsters, students. High Aishbourne is full of wealthy, retired old fogies.'

The whips forced the pack under the bridge to shallows flanked by paddocks and cottage gardens. Closing in behind them the followers were pelted with abuse and a couple of eggs were thrown.

'Your hunt saboteurs mob,' Yelland grunted. 'Now we'll see some fireworks.'

It was not a peaceful demonstration. The protesters' strategy had been carefully planned. The coach had crept into High Aishbourne half an hour after the start of the hunt and no one had been posted at the village to warn the master.

Revilious and Yelland trotted round the houses to the public footpath that ran beside the river. A gang of teenagers barred the way.

'Please let us pass,' Revilious said.

'Want to be in at the kill?' someone sneered.

'You cheeky young bugger,' Yelland roared. 'Mr Revilious idn a hunt supporter.'

'Prove it,' came the cool response.

'I don't have to prove anything,' Revilious said. 'This isn't private property and unless I'm misinformed this is still a free country.'

'When we get a socialist government there'll be no private property and no hunting,' piped a girl wearing a CND badge on her sweater.

'Unless bloodthirsty morons like you want to hunt each other,' said a ginger youth.

Yelland struck a straight left in his face and put him on his knees nursing a bleeding nose.

'Now move,' the old man said, shaping to pick off another youngster.

'Fascists,' the girl cried but the jostling stopped and they were allowed to pass.

'I didn't know you were handy with your fists, Reg,' Revilious said, caught somewhere between admiration and dismay.

'Even in my fifties I was a rough handful,' Yelland winked.

Protesters had linked arms and were standing in a line across the river. Larger groups were assembling on the banks.

'Pro or anti?' The question was too blunt and aggressive for Revilious's stomach.

'Anti,' he said. 'Anti-bloodsports, anti-violence, anti-extremism. But I'm on the side of the animals.'

Yelland's jaw jutted dangerously.

'We won't interfere,' Revilious continued. 'When it comes to extremism we're non-aligned.

'Like the Swiss?'

'Isn't this getting a trifle melodramatic?' Revilious sighed. He gripped Yelland's arm.

Then the hounds were churning up the mud and advancing in a tight wedge until they met the human wall. There was a lot of tail-wagging and sniffing and prowling up and down.

The master tried to weigh the situation. Behind him was a growing anger and frustration. What a mess, Fisk thought, recalling happier days.

'Go right through the rabble,' Captain Courtenay thundered. 'Send the lot of 'em running back to Moscow.'

The captain invariably opted for simple solutions. Fisk cleared his throat and realized he had nothing to say. To make matters worse the protesters started chanting slogans and insults. The old hound Amazon stood upright and placed her paws on a student's chest. Despite the heat the boy was wearing a reefer jacket and Fisk soon discovered why. The student had a round, white face rendered sinister by a pair of narrow sunglasses. Dipping swiftly in his pocket he produced a plastic container of washing-up liquid and squirted it at the dog. Amazon tumbled back and her yelping cry of pain became a full-blooded howl. Along the line similar containers were produced and a dozen hounds thrashed about pawing at their eyes while the hunt supporters charged into battle.

'Get back,' Fisk shouted, and he turned to face the hotheads.

A girl with short, fair hair jumped in the river and demanded the containers. Her indignation reminded Revilious of the boy Julian Lomax who captained Cavendish Towers first fifteen. A lad with a surfeit of integrity and no guile.

'Leave them to it,' Yelland said.

Revilious shook his head and waded out to Amazon. The hound snapped at him but he stood astride her and held her firmly by the scruff of the neck. Green washing-up liquid ran bubbling down her muzzle and a paw kept jerking up in an attempt to brush away the terrible irritation that had closed both eyes.

'Help me, Reg.' But the old man was already alongside him, dipping his handkerchief in the water and applying it to the dog's eyes.

'I'm sorry this happened,' said the fair haired girl.

'Apologize to the poor bloody animal,' Yelland said.

The hound wrenched free and nipped his leg and stood plunging its head in and out of the water. Elsewhere blows were being exchanged as protesters and supporters skirmished. Revilious tripped over and landed on his hands and knees. Then he was kicked in the ribs and winded. Yelland and the girl dragged him to the bank.

'What a sad business,' he gasped.

'Brought about by people like yourself who think it amusing and exciting to kill wild animals,' said the girl.

'You're wrong,' Revilious said. 'Very wrong. But isn't a hound an animal? Doesn't it have rights? If you can harm dogs in this way you're no different than the hunt bigots.'

Before she could reply a brawling mob rolled over them and swept them into the mass of militant protesters.

'Let's get out of here,' said Yelland. 'Before the police come. Don't worry, Paul – the hunt idn goin' nowhere now.'

The heat thickened and lofted, pushing the swifts so high their screams were hardly audible. It was a long way back to Cockstone Bridge and the hard slog and excitement left an ache around Revilious's heart.

Horse Wrangler Hill

A day or so later he came back from a walk over the fields, ate a seafood salad and finding the insects troublesome in the garden brought book and cider to the drawingroom. The clock ticked across the silence and the faint cawing of rooks crept back whenever he emerged from the celtic mythology. It was also comforting to raise his eyes to the large Frith-like oil above the mantelpiece and let the mind wander through the clutter of the Victorian household. Attentive gentlemen and crinolined ladies were sipping port after a day's shooting. Woodcocks, hares and mallard were given pride of place beside the gun dogs on the carpet.

All the occupants of the room were dead and he was surprised to find the realization had the power to chill him. I suppose, he thought, you can only come to terms with dying on a purely day-to-day basis. What begins as a great adventure in the morning can deteriorate into hopelessness and despair at dusk.

Revilious lit a cigar and came onto the terrace. The ghost moths danced around his head and the lawn was collecting starshine. He stared into the universe from glistening eyes. He had visited the place before. It was the delta where sensation became consciousness and the stream flowed on into the divine. Standing there he experienced some of the rapture that blazes in and out of childhood. Then he recalled the terrifying episode with the black dog and returned to the drawingroom.

What sort of soul-life had the otters? He had forgotten the joy of looking down on the pond. And they were together, weaving their patterns in the water, whistling along the surface where stars shivered. They rose and leapt and raced around the island. Blearily behind his eyes Revilious saw the mink falling into the hounds' jaws and Amazon writhing in an attempt to wipe the washing-up liquid from her eyes. But on the pond the celebration of life continued and he went to bed with mixed feelings. Beneath all western thought since civilization had triumphed ran a deep seam of brutality and squalor. Slowly the mink fell from sunlight and running water, scents and sounds, and the shadows closed and the lark was rising unheard and unseen.

The thunderstorm did not materialize. Cloud piled up, threatened, sent down a few heavy drops, then rolled on with a boom and a crackle to leave the sky clear and the heat oppressive.

'We will get a storm,' Kevin said, discarding the walking sticks and lowering himself into the armchair. 'You were right, Paul,' he added. 'This place is a paradise for animals. It makes wildlife parks like Cuckoo Cross look shabby and contrived.'

He spoke of the vixen and her cubs, how she brought them the wild duck's wing as part of their hunting education.

'In a few weeks cubbing starts,' he said. 'And you won't be very popular with the hunt. A coombe full of young foxes! That should raise the eyebrows.'

'I have an amazing talent for raising people's eyebrows,' Revilious said.

'So have I,' chuckled Kevin.

Pushing up on his arms he rose from the chair and stood like an actor impersonating Richard III, the toe of his right foot pointing at the heel of the left one and the leg bent at a grotesque angle.

'Let me give you a lift back to the farm,' Revilious said.

'No, no, the walk up the coombe is a tonic,' Kevin assured him. 'I may look an absolute crock but there's nothing wrong with the inside. Rolls Royce engine. I'm not interfering with anything am I?'

'Lord no. If you didn't drop in on me I wouldn't know you were on the estate. You're part of Foxcroft.'

He traced the young man's departure through the binoculars. Kevin's movements were slow and he often paused and looked about him, and sometimes crouched awkwardly to peer into the grass at his feet. Revilious had seen cats crossing fields in a similar manner – reaching out with their instincts, touching everything.

It dawned on Revilious that Kevin was feeling his way through the coombe alive to whatever it had to offer. His twisted body was not suffering and could be forced on at a faster pace if he chose. He was living each moment as it came.

Revilious lowered the glasses and Kevin vanished behind some trees. Vision clouded by intellect. He sighed and raised the binoculars again and swung them slowly up the side of the coombe. Beyond the last hedge Horse Wrangler Hill was a sunburnished dome. Caught in the heat three hawthorn trees squirmed on the horizon. At their feet he was startled to discover the shape of some sort of ancient structure under the grass. It was marked FORT on the ordnance survey map.

Revilious collected his panama from the hall and strode purposefully up the coombeside. The humidity clung to him and his shirt was wet by the time he had left Foxcroft and was climbing the hill. He winced at the memory of tackling Tryfan unfit. God! – that harmless Welsh peak had put him on the rack. His thighs and groins were aching. The slope was longer and more severe than it had appeared through the glasses but that foreshortening was a typical hill country illusion he recalled.

Why am I hurrying? he thought, slowing and removing his hat. The heat struck him with such ferocity that he looked up. A huge cloud was filling the sky above the hill and angling the sunlight. Then the sun was gone and the cumulo nimbus swirled and billowed across the South Hams. Now the hilltop was dark, almost black. It was only a field away but seemed much further.

He pressed on expecting at any moment to be drenched by the downpour hovering over him. But the clouds were veined with silver and the thunder when it began was muted. Lightning played and brightness swelled inside the clouds. A scattering of raindrops burst on his face. The damp heat was debilitating and he was near collapse despite the rain that soon faded after a moment or two. A long, low peal of thunder stammered away and the light continued to go on and off in the clouds.

And Revilious was cold. A chill ran through him, goosepimpling his flesh. He plodded wearily up to the row of thorns. They were gaunt and leafless but alive in a wintery sort of way. The fort under the grass was forgotten and Revilious knelt before the trees while the wind freshened and darkness deepened. He had stopped shivering and the crack and thunder of the breaking storm did not alarm him. Down came the rain in a deluge and he felt it running off his body into the grass. Then he was shouting words without meaning and a force older than language was rising from the earth all around him.

Suddenly it was pitch black and the girl at the wheel of Charlie Gutteridge's new BMW craned forward for a better view of the lane. Rain burst on the windscreen and streamed away and the wipers could not cope with the volume.

'Soddin' weather,' Charlie said. He had been drinking all lunchtime and was the worse for it. Slack in the passenger seat he puffed out his cheeks and blew his frustration through capped front teeth. A flash illumined the muddy tarmac ahead of them, leaving white spots dancing before his eyes. But he saw the hare dart into the headlights, freeze and leap back into the hedge. The girl also saw the animal and responded automatically. The car skidded and slid on and hit the rocky bank.

'Jesus wept,' Charlie shouted. The engine coughed and died but Radio One continued to bellow pop music. Another burst of light fizzed and dissolved and the girl collapsed over the steering wheel.

'You stupid bitch,' Gutteridge snarled.

'There was a rabbit on the road, Charlie,' she sobbed.

'So bloody what? You've wrecked my new motor. Next time you see a rabbit you bloody flatten it.' He stared morosely at the rain hammering on the windscreen.

Visitors

The otters swam the spate to Home Weir after sunset while the sky cleared to grasp the last flush of day. The roar of water bucking and kicking into the race below Foxcroft House drove them crazy with excitement. They darted over each long arm, riding the muscles of the Aishbourne and tangling to be pushed by the flow into Zion Pool. But Cariad was not the all-giving, joyful playmate Skerry had grown accustomed to. When they crawled out of the river to dry off and rest she snarled at him and would not submit to his advances. So he crouched and swished his tail. The moon came up and the weir tossed it about like pieces of ice.

The rain which had fallen for most of the afternoon had scented the air and the drops pattering through the leaves of Charlie Gutteridge's shrubbery at Rattlecombe ticked as regularly as a dripping tap. Gutteridge stood in the pergola and whistled his dogs. They bounded past him onto a lawn the size of a football pitch.

'Fine animals, Mr Gutteridge,' said Charlie's companion.

The Brummie gave a nodded grunt of agreement and wrapped an arm around his guest's shoulders and led him back into the lounge. Stronger men than detective constable Nathan had been overwhelmed by Charlie's apparent warmth. The whisky in the policeman's glass was best highland malt, his cigar had a pedigree and the manilla envelope on the coffee table was bulky enough to set his adrenalin pumping.

Once they were settled in the room that looked unlived in – possibly due to the attemps of Mrs Gutteridge to cram it with onyx and brass – Charlie said, 'Revilious, Phil. Now there's a punter worthy of your professional interest.'

'Why? Is he bent?'

'Not in the criminal sense.'

'Queer?'

'That's for you to decide, my son. But you don't have to be a bloody genius to put two and two together. You know the set-up at Foxcroft – funny old bloke living alone, entertaining weirdos like the Piper kid and Nos Prowse. I'm sure a smart jack like you could dig something up.'

Nathan sipped his Glenfiddich and said nothing.

'You don't have to pull him. He needs leaning on. Let him know the aggravation is coming from all sides.'

'I take it he's bothering you, Mr Gutteridge.'

'Leave off, Phil!' Charlie grinned. 'This is a giggle. I'm chasin' a mouse round a pisspot with a mustard tipped knitting needle. That's all. A giggle.'

He pushed the envelope across the table and Nathan transferred it to his inside pocket. Charlie's smile broadened. He liked smooth business deals. That's how the world was run – backhanders, mergers, doublecross, the marketing of honour.

'Play it your way, my son,' he whispered. 'Only don't drop me in it. I got friends in the force up in Brum and they are very big fish. Lean on the old queen.'

'Just for a giggle, Mr Gutteridge.'

Charlie chuckled and reached for the whisky decanter.

Revilious left his solicitor's feeling he had made the most important decision of his life. The thunderstorm had done its best to freshen up the countryside but the fine weather had returned and the long-range forecast predicted drought. A slip of paper on the passenger seat caught his eye. It was a prescription for heart tablets. Revilious glanced at it and screwed it up and dropped it on the floor. Anyway, I got out of Cavendish Towers just in time, he thought. Although dropping dead in assembly might have caused Major Shackle some embarrassment. He smiled and drew the tip of his tongue along the bristles of his moustache. No one came to visit him. That was significant. All those years and not one real friend.

'Good folk are as scarce as hen's teeth,' Yelland said.

The old man had needed no encouragement to join Revilious on Horse Wrangler Hill. They sat with their backs against separate hawthorn trees looking down into Foxcroft. Unperturbed by their presence the hare continued grooming itself on the grassy ramparts of the fort.

'Kevin Piper is as close as you'll get to a good bloke, Paul. Maybe it's something to do with his disability.'

A crow flopped onto the long swell of grass where the outer wall of the fort had once stood. Revilious looked up at the sky through the thorn branches and felt the slow spin of the world. The day was calm, still and very hot, and the sky empty. The swifts were gone, en masse, abruptly as they departed every year, and he wondered if he would see them return.

Haze lent romance to the far-off hills of Dartmoor. Faintly from Aishwell way came that most summery of summer sounds – the snock of cricket ball meeting bat. And suddenly he was aware of the ephemeral: the six struck and lost forever, the blur of the sparrowhawk passing through the hedgerow leaves, sunlight catching the scales of the leaping fish, a child's smile veiled in the blue petrol fumes of a tractor. Memory could only fix part of the experience. The muted discords were heard as they faded.

Slowly he returned to the moment and the glaring landscape hurt his eyes. To be part of its stillness instead of an onlooker was attractive. To go beyond the appearance of things.

They strolled down to Drang and met the north country businessman ferrying suitcases and cardboard boxes from his car into the holiday cottage. He and his wife were charming and Revilious invited them to tea at Foxcroft.

'Mr Wilkinson is OK,' Yelland said.

Beside the river Healey's pigs were half-buried in the mud. The water level had dropped again but the Aishbourne still smelled clean and stony.

'A lot of folk from up north are loud, rude buggers,' Yelland continued. 'They call it being blunt. But Mr Wilkinson is a gennelman.'

'So are you, Reg,' Revilious said with a smile.

'Get home do! Sit me down to dinner with a lot of toffs and I'd soon show myself up.'

'And a lot of them would too – in different ways.'

Near the top of the lane, parked against the hedge was a Y registration Fiesta.

'Nathan's car,' Yelland said. 'I'm danged if that young copper don't raise my hackles. But I s'pose it's only because he hangs round the Gutteridges. Funny, but I've never seen un out this way before.'

They parted company at the junction and Revilious swung along the road humming the tune of Widecombe Fair. When he stopped to obey a call of nature standing against a field gate he checked both ways to make sure he would not be interrupted. But afterwards his shirt got caught in the zip and trying to free it he hopped back into the road.

'Are you touting for business?' said a voice with a lot of south east England firming the vowels.

Revilious lifted a red face and was confronted by a thin young man of medium height wearing an expression of disgust.

'Touting for what?' Revilious laughed.

'That's funny is it? Indecently exposing yourself to other men is funny. Do you do it often?'

'For God's sake!' Revilious cried. 'I stopped for a pee and my zip stuck.'

'You were exposing yourself,' the flat tone persisted. 'You saw me coming and stepped back with it in your hand – soliciting.'

'This is absurd,' Revilious said. A final tug released the shirt but also broke the zip and left it gaping.

'Is that what you do at Foxcroft when you get the boys in?'

'Who are you?' Revilious faltered as the life left his knees.

'Detective Constable Nathan.' The I.D. card was produced and slipped back into the officer's pocket. 'Sods like you make me ill, Reviliious,' he sneered.

Now the confrontation was assuming aspects of nightmare for Revilious. Heat curled off the road, warping the hedges. Printed on the gleaming tarmac was the Magritte figure with its jacket folded over an arm.

'Do you and the boys do it at Foxcroft?'

'Which boys?'

'Skinheads like Eric Prowse. Disabled kids like Kevin Piper. Do you and Reg Yelland hold hands and other things in the woods?'

Revilious shook his head slowly in disbelief and revulsion.

'I stopped to relieve myself. Nothing more. If you think I've tried to interfere with Nos and Kevin you'd better question them. All you'll get from Reg Yelland is a black eye.'

'Oh I'll be speaking to them,' Nathan said. 'But there's still this business, isn't there? You have indecently exposed yourself to a police officer.'

'And I say you imagined it. Or was it wishful thinking, officer? Maybe you're looking for –'

'Christ! – you bloody pervert. I've a good mind to knock the crap out of you.'

'It would cost you more than your job.' Anger was edging into Revilious's fear. 'I was watering the gate and this isn't exactly a very public place. If you take me to court I'll call you a liar and you'll find it difficult to blacken my character. I taught without a blemish for twenty-five years so if you've finished insulting me I'm going home. Any further abuse will be construed as harrassment.'

'We'll see what Prowse says,' Nathan retorted.

'He can say what he likes. I shall continue to invite my friends into my home whenever I choose. If you're so desperate to hook homosexuals may I suggest you put on a guard's uniform and parade around Kensington after dark. Now, get out of my way.'

'You'll slip up, Revilious,' was Nathan's parting remark. 'You perverts always do.'

He had put ten or eleven yards between him and the policeman when his courage failed and he stopped and stood droop-shouldered.

'Please,' he said without turning. 'This is just a misunder-tanding. I don't want any trouble.'

But Nathan's footsteps receded slowly into silence.

Revilious decided not to mention the encounter to Yelland for fear of jeopardising their friendship. He was worried, though, what Nos might say if Gutteridge bribed him and Nathan threatened him. Kevin would be left alone. The last thing

Nathan wanted was outspoken honesty. Then Alice dropped in
that evening and he opened his heart to her and she gave the
best sort of consolation.

'Tell everyone you're knocking me off,' she said. 'Don't look
so shocked, Paul,' she laughed pushing him back on the bed.
'They all do it – all the young rugby club rams. It inflates their
egos.'

'Basest of base macho,' he grinned.

'So what? It'll get Nathan off your back.'

'I couldn't Alice.'

'OK – take me to dinner at the Horridge Inn and we'll let the
gossip spread from there. I'll give you the lover boy treatment.
We'll set a few tongues wagging.'

'You'd really like that, Alice?'

'I'd really like dinner.'

Revilious did not see Yelland again until the weekend. Kevin
Piper also called then and suggested they pay a visit to Hazard
Linhay to see the young barn owls. He set the pace and con-
versation flowed.

'By the way, Paul,' he said when Yelland had finished ragging
Revilious about his affair with Alice. 'Have you called in the
police?'

'Why?'

'A detective dad knows was hanging round the top lane early
on. He gave me a really odd look as I left the farm.'

'Probably something to do with salmon poaching,' Revilious
said, colouring. 'Poachers dynamited stretches of the Avon last
night.'

The stab of anxiety faded and Revilious was surprised to
discover he was quite proud of his new sexual status. Yelland
called him a sly old stag. If only Cadogan had been around to
see Alice clinging to him in the bar after the meal. Good Lord!
he thought. I'm strutting like a farmyard cockerel. Well,
perhaps there's a little of Cadogan in us all.

They were approaching the Linhay and had paused to allow
Kevin to take the strain off his arms when Yelland pointed up
the coombe and said: 'Who the hell are they?'

Figures were hurrying down the hillside from Furze Copse.
Half-running and marching Revilious and Yelland cut them off

but they would have reached the Aishbourne if they had not blundered into the blackthorn scrub. It was a group of youngsters carrying wire-cutters, crowbars and spades.

'The bloody anti-hunt mob,' Yelland panted.

Revilious had also recognized the fair-haired girl he had clashed with at High Aishbourne. Honesty shone from her eyes but like her comrades she was at the mercy of her emotions.

'What are you doing on my land?' Revilious blazed. 'Come away from the river, please, now.'

'Or you'll do what?' she demanded.

'Call the police.'

'By the time you get to the phone we will have found the mink and released them,' said the girl.

'What mink?'

'The animals you've got penned up somewhere on your property.'

'This isn't a mink farm,' Revilious said, exasperated.

'No, it's worse than that,' the girl replied. 'It's a reservoir of living creatures for the hunt.'

'And I'm the pope's wife!' Yelland roared. 'You daft young buggers! Foxcroft is a wildlife sanctuary and if you storm around like elephants you'll mess up everything Mr Revilious has worked for.'

'We had a phone call saying you were keeping caged mink on the river ready to release if the hunt had a blank day,' said the ginger-haired youth Yelland had punched during the mêlée on the upper Aishbourne.

'Rubbish,' Revilious grated. 'Whoever told you that is a cold-blooded, mischievious liar. At the moment you are close to disturbing a pair of otters – closer than you think. But don't take me at my word. Come quietly down the water and see for yourself. No mink but bags of wildlife in genuinely natural habitat. Of course you could end it all by creating a song and dance.'

'Bullshit,' someone said. 'You want us near the house while you call the fuzz.'

'Go on alone if you like, but use the other bank and keep fairly high up the coombeside in case the otters are in the water. Then wait for me by Woodburn Bridge.'

The girl turned and spoke to her companions. There was a brief, sharp exchange before Revilious was asked to lead the way.

Yelland was to hear his friend speak passionately about Foxcroft and the otters. All round them the evidence of his sincerity was growing green and untamed in the hedges, fields and copses. By the time the house was reached and jugs of cider brought onto the lawn Revilious was entertaining converts. Kevin lumbered up on his sticks to dispel any doubts the more sceptical may have harboured.

The girl turned out to be Beth McCormick, the leader of an animal liberation group which drew its members from all over South Devon. She was one of those irritatingly cool young people who project maturity until a close inspection of the eyes reveals confusion. But her commitment to animals could not be faulted even though Revilious failed to disguise his dislike of extremism. The dialogue was crisp and unfruitful despite mutual respect. Revilious was anti-violence; Beth was a militant.

Their verbal sabre fighting amused Reg Yelland who had picked up most of his opinions second-hand in the tradition of his class. Yet he remembered pub disputes when truth was always trampled underfoot and egos clashed like prehistoric monsters. This row lapsed into small talk and Yelland was impressed. No punches were thrown, no voices raised.

The girl departed apologetically and Revilious went indoors for something finer than farmhouse rough.

Ghost moths

The kestrel perched on the telephone wire beside the main Totnes – Kingsbridge Road scrutinized the dance of white parachute seeds plucked by the draught of passing cars from the wayside flowers. Revilious kept the bird in his driving mirror for as long as possible then gave Mrs Healey a glance. Whenever he called at Drang she greeted him po-faced. Keep off, that look started. Leave us to live our own life. She probably hates being in my debt, he thought. And her husband was also reluctant to do his bit where the river was concerned.

Revilious had visited Woodburn Bridge three mornings in succession before the Healeys were awake; and by the time he had tramped to Horridge and back Ted was hoeing his vegetables or feeding the pigs. Self-absorbed, self-serving – but Revilious stifled the notion before it could grow into bitterness.

Mrs Healey mumbled a thank you and went into her home without a backward glance. Revilious blushed and turned the car around. A horn sounded and he braked. The white Fiesta crawled by and Nathan did not bother to take his eyes off the road.

I'm not really important to anyone, Revilious thought. He was acutely conscious now of the flesh on his face losing its firmness, hanging off the bone, surrendering. But do I want to slide into lonely old age, through the indignity of my own decay? He drove slowly and was prepared to meet Nathan at the Bullenford junction. An empty road lay in wait yet his unease persisted and he found Nos sitting astride a motorbike on the forecourt at Foxcroft. The youth's black leathers and helmet with its tinted visor were as menacing as any of Gutteridge's dogs. Revilious tried to control his nervousness. He got out of the car and slammed the door.

'You still upset about the money, Mr Revilious?' Nos said.

Mr Revilious. Revilious cynically considered the import of the words. If he were a hard-up schoolmaster no one would consider calling him Mister. The worship of money invoked all sorts of dishonesties. 'Bilious Revilious', Cadogan bawled from his corner of hell.

Nos was a robot soldier from a science-fiction film. Everything was correct: the honey-coloured house, rooks cawing, summer heat, and the alien creaking in its black carapace.

'Yes, I'm upset,' he managed, willing the pain to withdraw from his heart.

'Can't we go on as we used to, sir? I'll do the drawings and pay you back. I didn mean to let you down.'

'All I want from you is your immediate departure.'

Nos nodded. 'You know what they're saying.'

'They?'

'The lads, other folk down Aishwell.'

'I don't want to know what the lads are saying.'

'Dc Nathan had a word with me. He thinks –'

'He can go to hell and you can join him,' Revilious said.

'It's OK, Mr Revilious,' Nos said quietly. 'I may be a bad bugger but there are some things I wouldn do. In any case if I went along with Nathan I'd drop myself in it. Everyone round here would think I was bloody gay.'

'I'm not interested. Just – just go,' Revilious said, lowering his eyes and letting his shoulders sag.

'Charlie's behind this,' said Nos. 'Don't show your back to the bugger. And thanks for not going to the law about me.'

He was watering the alyssum along the rockery and the soft, shuffle of footsteps on the lawn took him by surprise. Nathan removed his sunglasses and stared at him. Then he lifted a finger, pointed it and said: 'Eric Prowse and me had a heart to heart about you. And I've come to the conclusion –'

Revilious ran up the steps into the house and grabbed the telephone. By the time Nathan arrived at the door the number had been dialled and Revilious was asking to speak to the senior officer. During the pause before he was put through he said: 'I'm calling your bluff, Nathan. Don't come through that door or you're in serious trouble. Now get off my place and don't come back unless you have a warrant. Tell Gutteridge he's failed again.'

Nathan opened his mouth and closed it. Then he replaced his sunglasses and departed.

About the middle of the day two other members of the CID visited Foxcroft. Both were dressed casually in sports jackets and ties and the senior officer wore the sort of spectacles elderly civil servants favour. The men put Revilious in mind of a couple of post office counter clerks on holiday. But they listened to his story.

'And you think Dc Nathan's alleged harassment is part of Gutteridge's attempt to hound you off Foxcroft, sir?'

'Yes. There are too many coincidences.'

'Yet nothing we can lay directly on Gutteridge's door,' said Detective Sergeant Scrivener.

'He wants something . . . Foxcroft, perhaps.'

'You didn't flash anything at Dc Nathan then, sir?' the other detective said quickly.

'I didn't see Detective Constable bloody Nathan. He must have been hiding in the hedge waiting for me.'

'And you just happened to be breaking your neck for a jimmy?' Again the cold staccato voice.

'If you live alone in the country you tend to ignore the little bylaws made to protect townees.'

'Living alone is probably the operative phrase, sir. In your circumstances it isn't wise to knock about with skinheads or handicapped kids. It's inviting gossip.'

'So where does it end?' Revilious said. 'You could apply that to the services, the priesthood, all-male clubs, male-voice choirs, football teams and so on and so on.'

'A billet full of squaddies is a bit different from a country house with two boys, a middle-aged man and an old man sitting down to fairy cakes,' the hostile voice said.

'Even if it were a homosexual rendezvous would that give Nathan the right to harass me?'

'No, sir, but it would lend weight to his claim that you were indecently exposing yourself.'

'My remark was hypothetical – not a confession.'

'Of course,' Scrivener smiled. 'But Nathan will deny turning the screw and in the end it'll be your word against his. Do you intend complaining to the Chief Constable, sir?'

'No – it's in your hands,' Revilious sighed. 'I've always believed for every corrupt policeman there are ten honest officers. All I want is that man kept away from me and Gutteridge warned off.'

'Nathan will be spoken to. But if Mr Gutteridge is as crafty and ruthless as you say he'll keep throwing punches after the bell. We can't give you police protection, sir. What we need is proof.'

'Could Nos help?'

'He could but he won't. His masculinity is about all he's got left. But don't worry,' the detective said cheerfully. 'Some day someone will slip up.'

'By then my otters may be dead.'

'We live in an imperfect world, Mr Revilious.'

'No, sergeant – we imperfect creatures live in a perfect world.'

'You know what I mean, sir,' the sergeant said. 'If I was educated I wouldln't be a jack.'

*   *   *

When he saw Skerry and Cariad together on the pond everything seemed worthwhile. The otters were a direct spiritual link with Eden before the fall. Looking out of the window he wished he were watching them through a child's eyes.

By moonlight the coombe was beautiful in a disturbing and artificial way, like the set of some mammoth production of *A Midsummer's Night's Dream*. He swept the hillside through the binoculars and saw the barn owls leave the linhay. They flew down to quarter Old Bethlehem. Ghost moths fluttering off the lawn sailed across his vision and Revilious lifted his binoculars. For a moment the bottom of the sky tilted and the stars blurred, then he had focused on the hilltop.

He knew the stranger would be waiting among the thorns. His heart lurched. In silhouette he could not be certain if it was

Gutteridge. His palms were sweating. Good! Good! – I'm not afraid, he thought. Sweat trickled into his eyes and he pawed at them as an extraordinary picture developed in his mind. A bearded man with a stag's head and antlers was struggling out of a bramble thicket. Under his arm was a calf which he released when he reached the sward. The cow walked up to the calf and licked it. Then she knelt before the man who had taken root and turned into a hawthorn tree.

He almost screwed the binoculars back into his face. The stranger had not moved. Revilious puffed out his cheeks and blew a sigh. Where were the dogs? Sweat leaked and dribbled, and passing a fingertip over the lenses he realized the figure was not interested in him. It was watching something else, willing something to happen. Revilious was afraid now. He felt sick and giddy and the life was leaving his limbs. The binoculars fell from his hands, struck the rug and bounced but before they could fall again he had blacked out.

Swishing across the field the otters paused and tested the night. Skerry trotted forward, wrinkled his muzzle and re-treated a couple of steps. Then danger hit his instincts and he yikkered. Cariad joined him and they turned and thumped through the gap in the blackthorn scrub and willows.

The alsations cleared the gate one after another and skidded on the wet grass. But the otters wriggled under the thorns and Shane, trying to bulldoze after them, received a spiked eye for his trouble. His yelps spurred Cariad and Skerry on to the water's edge. They plunged together and surfaced above the weir. Wading chest deep Buck saw them and barked but the darkness swallowed them. Sliding over the sluice the otters became part of the pond's silence. Buck splashed after them and the weight of the water pushed him down the weir. Behind him Shane was scrabbling up the chute to stand with his front feet on the sluice gate. At that moment someone parted the sallow branches on the far side of the pond and a shot was fired. The report of the twelve-bore slammed up the coombe.

Cadogan's lips were drawn back in a snarl of agony. The electric kettle was a carnivore and it held the sports master and pumped death into him. A tentacle had licked out of the swamp to burn the self-esteem and life out of the windbag.

Revilious stirred and sighed and smiled. The darkness was thinning. Someone was squeezing his shoulder, shaking him back to consciousness.

'Mr Revilious. Mr Revilious.'

Healey helped him to his feet and half carried him to the bed.

'Too much sun,' Revilious whispered.

'You look shattered.'

'I am shattered, Ted.'

He smiled wearily up into the young man's tanned and bearded face and added: 'Why are you here?'

'My wife thought she saw Gutteridge's dogs running loose in the lane up from Drang. She sent me out.'

'Your wife!'

'She worries about you, Mr Revilious. As far as she's concerned you're a – a –'

'A what, Ted?'

'A helpless gentleman who can't do ort for himself. Because her's so practical and takes things in her stride that sort of person puzzles her,' he blurted. 'Well I came over Old Bethlehem and crept round the house and to cut a long story short, shot one of Gutteridge's alsations. Least I think it's one of his.'

'Where is it?'

'Floating in tl e pond. It was after the otters.'

'Please go and phone the police, Ted.'

Gutteridge offered the simplest of explanations. He had been at his brother Colin's place and the dogs were let out for exercise and escaped from the garden.

'Chased off after a squirrel or something,' Detective Sergeant Scrivener said, pressing his glasses firmly onto the bridge of his nose. Then he smiled and they slid down again.

'You don't look surprised, Mr Revilious.'

'When you've found a badger nailed to your front door everything else has to be an anti-climax, sergeant.'

Encounters

The death of his dog Shane left Gutteridge unruffled but beneath the impassive mask he brooded about the incident. It was a real insult. One of Charlie Gutteridge's dogs had been shot by some yokel who had gone out of his way to help a gutless old Mary Ann! If Revilious had dropped him with a head butt on a street corner it couldn't have been worse. Things weren't going smoothly but he'd alter that. He would sort out something. But nothing violent, he thought, letting his left hand fall from the steering wheel onto his girlfriend's thigh. Old Bill would be looking for a violent caper. He ran a forefinger absently along the inside seam of the girl's tight-fitting jeans. All Revilious really cared about was his otters.

He turned on the radio. The windows of the Cortina were open wide but he was still sweating. When his companion lifted her hands to push back her hair there were dark, provocative sweat marks under the arms of her T-shirt. Hedges whizzed by and the pop music swelled loud then faded in a muzzy crackle of noise.

'I'd like to spend more time up in Birmingham, Charlie,' the girl yawned. 'This countryside is about as boring as going to church.'

Gutteridge ignored her.

Since sunrise the day had been unbearably hot and sticky. Flying ants were drifting about, settling on people, animals and food. They were largely males attending queens from local colonies scattered around Aishwell. On their nuptial flights the queens would be fertilized somewhere along the courtship trail and new ant dynasties would emerge from the eggs. It happened towards the end of every summer but the residents of Aishwell were surprised by the dense clouds of insects sweeping over their gardens and into their homes. Reg Yelland said he had never known such a plague.

Cats, dogs and humans vanished from the village streets and the afternoon was suddenly crawling with ants. They spilled into the Cortina Estate as Charlie and his girlfriend desperately tried to wind up the windows. Then they were in his eyes and nose and ears, and when Charlie opened his mouth to bawl obscenities he felt them crawling across his gums and tongue. Blindly he reached for the gear lever and fumbled on to set the windscreen wipers in motion. But as he braked he saw the cattle truck taking the bend far too fast. Spitting ants Charlie swung sharply into the lay-by, where the bus stopped, and the truck grazed his rear bumper.

'Shit,' he hissed, banging his fists on the dashboard.

He raked at his scalp, squashing the ants as he plucked them from strands of hair.

'Close the windows,' he added savagely.

The girl was sobbing but the ant lodged under an eyelid and the others wriggling out of her nostrils did not make her an object of sympathy. She tried to flick them away, uttering little squeals and grunts of disgust.

'There's a bloody jinx on you, Charlie. You want to get back to the Midlands before all this fresh air and bugs and stuff kill you.'

Something cold fluttered in Charlie's stomach, something new to him.

*   *   *

The brush with the alsations upset Cariad and one dawn she left the Aishbourne. The cubs moving inside her were a constant plea for solitude. Skerry trailed after her as she set her nose towards the Avon. Beneath the light of the new day she whimpered and hesitated, recalling the good holt at Brent Copse, remembering in her blood the water games.

A spinney of mounded beeches sat like a cloud on the hill-top. Now the sun was up and the long shadows of trees were pushing out across the fields. Dew flashed and winked from the grass where the otters had left their footprints. Skerry was reluctant to turn his back on the coombe but he no longer controlled his heart or his destiny.

So they came into the spinney and lay together on dry leaves under a mass of brambles.

The belling woke them. For a while they crouched hardly breathing, ears pricked and nostrils dilated. The noise struck the lower side of the spinney and burst around it. Then large animals were crashing about among the trees and a horn rattled its long, yelping cry. Skerry hissed and loosed a screech of fear and rage. Both otters broke cover together and hurtled down the field. All the marathon journeys and swimming had healed Cariad's injured hind leg and she moved only fractionally slower than her mate despite her condition. But the pack on the first cubbing meet of the season overtook them and surrounded them. The novice black and tan foxhounds padded up and down showing no desire to test the gameness of such ferocious animals. Before the bravest could get to close quarters the whips were doing their job and the huntsman was calling off the rioting pack.

'Otters,' the master smiled. 'A pair of otters on Primley Hill! Keep everyone back and let the plucky little devils go where they choose.'

'The Foxcroft otters, master?' said one of the whips.

'More than likely. They're heading for the Aishbourne.'

After this encounter the coombe and its comparative peacefulness was irresistible, and by the time the otters had reached Brent Copse Cariad had forgotten the alsation incident. She entered the water and sighed bubbles, feeling the cubs shift beneath her fur. Then she hung in the flow and the sunlight danced down through the leaves above her and sent shafts into the pool. Dog and bitch drifted to the shallows and kicked up tiny, noiseless explosions of silt. Here the living world faded for a while and the oneness was everything.

But it could not last. Cariad was heavy with cub and four nipples stood out of her belly fur. After a disturbed day he approached her and she flew at him screaming, and drove him off. Several times he tried to return but it was not to be and his cries piercing the night went unanswered. Revilious saw him alone on the island in the pond, up on his haunches, consumed by misery. Although half his heart bled for the dog otter the other half was glad for he knew Cariad was close to giving birth.

_____ Springing a trap _____

Revilious took Reg Yelland and the Healeys to dinner at the Horridge Inn. The steak meal was substantial if inauspicious and the wine disappointed, but his guests enjoyed the evening and brought their good humour to the bar. Mrs Healey had unstiffened sufficiently to giggle into her glass of Leibfraumilch. The conversation strayed from countryside matters, Gutteridge and Foxcroft to politics.

The Healeys were not political animals but Revilious, an uncommitted tory found echoes of his rather vague stance in Yelland's liberalism. Unpredictably the old man spoke against the Falklands campaign, insisting that the politicians should have sorted things out years ago. Listening to him Revilious thought the simple argument could be applied to all international crises if only human nature were different.

'The Venns of Leat Lane lost their boy, David, in that stupid bliddy cock-up,' Yelland growled, forgetting his antique courtesy. 'And I tell ee what – us should give Gibraltar back to the Spaniards before our youngsters are asked to spill their guts on another bit of foreign rock.'

'We were defending the people of the Falklands, Reg, not asserting imperial authority,' said Revilious. 'Galtieri was a fascist. Someone had to stop him.'

'What about the eighty odd wars that have been fought since 1945?' the old man barked. 'And no one tried to stop the Russians when they went into Afghanistan. Us didn wave any union jacks or send over the Ghurkas either when the Hungarian uprising was snookered or the Czechs got kicked in the teeth.'

The Wilkinsons joined them before going in to dine and Yelland calmed down enough to help the polite small talk along. At first Revilious welcomed cadences laundered by good breeding. Mrs Wilkinson wondered if the mild weather would continue and the old man said he could guarantee it.

'Sunny autumns make the winter seem so much shorter,' the woman smiled.

All of a sudden the evening had become very civilized and dull. Like so m ich of life, Revilious thought. What on earth was going on in the world? The otters shaded every area of his life. They had become symbols of wild animals' rights to freedom from persecution. But who was the stranger on the hill? What was Gutteridge? For God's sake, he cried from behind a smile of pretended interest, what is going on? What is happening to me? Again that faint, exciting thread of unease pursued him out to the car. Dusk was dimming a landscape of tawny fields and dark trees. The rooks climbing across the smoking gold horizon reminded him of the black birds in the last paintings of Van Gogh. 'Shadows we are and shadows we pursue'. He gripped the steering wheel so hard his knuckles gleamed. Please let me understand – life, my dying, the reason for it all.

The Healeys waved goodbye and the door closed. Two silhouettes merged behind the curtains. Revilious eased the Fiat over the bridge and passed a straggling line of runners on the hill.

'Rugby club training started last month,' Yelland said grinning. 'Mazed sods! Look at Wilf Moltram's pot! A couple of
miles of road work and back to the pub for a gallon of lager. No
wonder they never win a match.'

'Are you coming back for a scotch, Reg?'

'Wild horses couldn't keep me away. Let's make it a real
session – an all night job, and kip in the armchairs. I've got
nowhere to go, no special tomorrows.'

'I know what you mean.'

'You don't boy. It's called old age.'

Around ten o'clock The Plough was packed. Aishwell Rugby
Football Club was in full song and the tills were ringing out the
sort of music the landlord loved. Charlie Gutteridge held court
under the optics with Dan at his elbow and the landlady hovering attentively behind her Thursday night smile.

Charlie had just bought the biggest round of shorts anyone
could remember.

'Doubles,' Wharton crowed, dipping his nose into an inch of
Navy Neaters rum.

'It's Christmas,' Dan Gutteridge slurred. 'And Charlie's
Santa Claus.'

A quarter of an hour before closing time Alice and her friend
Doreen entered a crush of laughing, jostling men and Dan
collared them.

''Ere', Charlie beamed. 'What are you two darlings havin'?'

'Something strong and expensive,' said Alice.

'Better grab Charlie,' Dan giggled.

'I'd rather grab a handful of pig's afterbirth,' Alice smiled, the
high colour burning in her cheeks.

The gins were passed over the scrum of bawdy males and the
women stood facing each other like conspirators. Charlie
rubbed his cold left hand and lidded his eyes.

'Pump a double in there, squire,' he said and Dan took his
glass and lifted it for the landlord's attention.

Charlie elbowed a path through the winks and comments
and tapped Alice on the shoulder. If he was a bull elephant he'd
be trumpeting, she thought, grinning and swinging into the
attack.

'Where's lover boy?' Charlie asked. His cronies closed ranks behind him and the noise died as the other customers sensed the beginning of the baiting.

'Which one, Charlie? I got a waiting list like a telephone directory.'

'Randy Revilious. Ain't he just Jack the lad. Them AC-DC types get the best of both worlds.'

Dan snorted and nudged Wharton. Charlie slid a hand into his shirt front and teased the gold medallion out of his chest hair.

'I heard,' he said, 'that he watches while you and Kev do it.'

A few of the rugby players looked up to the ceiling and shook their heads in embarrassment.

'Unfortunately Kev don't fancy me. But he's more of a man than you are – in fact, everyone I've ever known is better between the sheets than you.'

She raised her voice. 'Charlie used to chase after me once and it was a bit of a novelty having a Brummie pick you up from work in a posh car. But the poor bloke is all mouth. When it came to the crunch he couldn't do it. He couldn't rise to the occasion. Poor little Charlie – and I mean little.'

She held out her little finger and derisively bent it downwards. There was a burst of laughter and Dan waited patiently for his brother to regain control. One of the leather jackets whooped and the jukebox remained silent and a flatulent wag broke wind. The skin had tightened on Charlie's cheekbones and his eyes were wide and full of venom. For the first time in his life he experienced panic. Slowly it dawned on him as Alice continued to mouth her contempt that the meeting was no accident. The bitch had set him up. His nostrils were full of her perfume and body smell, and he recalled couplings in the back of his car, steamed-up windows adding another dimension to sleaziness.

He laughed and said: 'How much is Revilious paying you to put on this performance?'

'Paul don't roll in the muck like you, Gutteridge. Is that why you keep knocking him? You grubby-minded, inadequate bum.'

'Shut your mouth, you stupid cow,' Dan hissed.

'Make me. You'd lick his backside for a handful of loose change,' Alice said, fixing him with her jeering eyes.

Dan Gutteridge shook a fist at her, baffled but needing a shove or another drink to send him headlong into violence.

He continued waving his fist like a child until a lorry driver from South Brent threatened to put him in intensive care. Several players also sided with Alice. Then the landlord bustled out from behind the bar and told her to drink up and leave. And she slowly tipped the contents of her glass onto Charlie's shoes and made a fine exit followed by a cheer of appreciation.

'Let's have another round of shorts,' Charlie grinned but the greyness showed under his tan and no gesture of bravado could salvage his dignity.

'Her don't go a lot on you, mate,' someone chortled.

'Win some, lose some,' Charlie said. 'But Revilious has got to be payin' her wages. She came across regularly as you lads know. And she was a film star.'

'Blue movies?' Wharton said.

'Very blue movies. Alice in Wonderland.'

'Leave off, Charlie,' his girlfriend said and she wriggled away from him, unsmiling.

Charlie stared past her from under his lashes and noted the number of backs turned on him. Only Wharton was laughing at Dan's crude jokes.

The following day three police officers called at his Rattlecombe Villa and drank canned Carlsberg on the lawn.

'He's straight,' Sergeant Scrivener asserted. The blond fizz climbed his glass, frothed, creamed and clotted.

'Phil had him going for a bit but the sod's harder than he looks.'

'You pulled Prowse?' Charlie said.

'Yes,' Nathan said. 'He thought we had him for conning Revilious out of a few hundred quid.'

'Revilious is likely to go to the Chief Constable if Phil keeps hounding him,' said Scrivener. 'So we will have to lay off until you come up with something concrete, Mr Gutteridge. If we catch him entertaining a load of choirboys in his bathroom or mincing down Totnes High Street in drag we'll feel his collar. But for the time being we are euchred. He's straight – and that is really bad news.'

Charlie folded his hands over his paunch. The cold little flutter went round his stomach until Dan arrived carrying a briefcase full of business problems.

All about dreams

Responding to the life kicking inside her Cariad roamed about preparing for the event. She lined the holt under the dead ash with sedges, moss, lichen and grass, and spent hours grooming herself. Whenever Skerry encroached on the home ground she showed him her teeth and screeched a warning to stay clear. Warily she emerged to spraint and hunt but loss of appetite reduced her night-time excursions.

Bones and scales of young salmon littered the drying-off places. Skerry sniffed them as he mooched about the old haunts trying to shrug off his loneliness. Then he would cry pitifully into the night, but the inevitable had overtaken him. Three kits were born under the ash roots where the river gently lapped and gurgled. They were blind little bundles of grey fur that squeaked and fought to draw milk from their mother's body. Cariad was painfully sensitive to the noises of the outside world; the clap of a bird's wings, the grunt of a badger, the scream of barn owls would set her on edge.

The pool below the island gave her all the food she wanted but she was not absent from the holt for long. The kits were everything and the flutter of their hearts, their sighing, the way they kicked out feebly against her in sleep filled her with mysterious joy. Running her tongue over them she was drugged with a heavy, possessive love and would curl up and close her eyes and inhale their fragrance.

Summer was nearly over and a rapid change in the weather hastened its decline. The last really hot day closed under a sun that wore a halo. Then cloud poured out of the west and rain fell steadily hour after hour. Fog and rain made successive dawns gloomy and although green returned to Foxcroft's lawn it had an unhealthy vividness soon to be studded with fungi.

Skerry was a wanderer again. He parted the spider-spin as he headed up the Aishbourne to Dartmoor. Starling flocks rushed over the country to descend on the hips and haws of the wayside. Thrushes and finches had also flocked and the restlessness of summer passing into autumn touched the otter. He no longer grieved for his mate but ran on taking whatever the world had to offer. From the source of the Aishbourne he climbed the boggy steeps of Miner's Hill and looked down upon a great reservoir. The first wave of departing swallows saw a slender black shape cutting through the water as they flew south.

Revilious was unwell and the disappearance of Skerry added to his seediness. His nose was running, and hot and cold flushes had him sweating one minute and shivering the next. The wind was chill and the fog made everything damp and claustrophobic. Yet he was watching the weir most mornings and listening for the contact call to carry above the roar. After dark if the night was moonlit he looked down on the pond hoping for a glimpse of dog or bitch but the water remained black and still. He had become even more introspective and his nerves were bad again. A knock at the door would make him jump and the slightest distress set him quivering.

Then there was a sunny spell and the coombe burst back to life. The collar doves crooned and courted, and the buzzards' skirl fell across the fields. He walked up the river and came noiselessly to the water's edge. Her seals were in the soft, rain-washed mud and he departed reassured.

Revilious lit a fire and waited for the red glow to break through the smoke. He must have sat hunched over the blaze for a long time. His knee joints cracked and he winced when he straightened his legs. Elgar's Cello Concerto was on Radio 3, and he listened deeply moved, recalling the last walking tour of Snowdonia. Jugs of good beer at Pen y Gwryd, laughter – always laughter, and a kind of brotherhood. He was crying. And she, the Wensley girl, had kissed him before the awful bedroom scene. A kiss can rescue you forever from trivia. The alcohol and the music nudged him into labyrinths of emotion. He dwelt on his misjudgment of Mrs Healey, on Alice's courage, Reg Yelland's stoicism and Kevin's nobility of spirit. Perhaps his pessimism had been unfounded. The monsters rose, mesmerized, bullied, terrorized and were brought down. There was triumph in the Lord's Prayer mumbled from small parish churches throughout England every Sunday. Revilious blew his nose and put away his handkerchief and poked the fire.

Reg Yelland saw smoke climbing from Foxcroft and smiled. The first fire since the spring, he thought. It went with age and slowing down. Dimpsey, too, had a woody flavour. The hateful mediterranean summer was going up in smoke and the barn owls were crying as they had done since he was a boy.

He hiked a little way along the Bullenford Road for a better view of the cider orchards. The crimson and yellow apples brought back memories of childhood. He rubbed his aching knee and jiggled his dentures with the tip of his tongue. Wood pigeons rattled out of the willows above the stream near Bowden's Pool and Yelland narrowed his eyes. Then a jay screeched and starlings lifted from Brent Copse. Yelland found a gap in the hedge and dropped into the field. He threaded through the apple trees and took the badger path upstream.

Wharton was crouching behind the rushes and the last light of day gleamed on his face.

'Wharton,' the old man rasped.

But he was lumbering like a deep sea diver through the ragwort and hogweed.

'Wharton.'

His arm was cocked and the fist clenched. The blow was telegraphed and Wharton palmed it aside and hit Yelland about the head with a flurry of blows. Then the old man landed a lucky right hook on the poacher's Adam's apple and had the pleasure of seeing him dance and claw at his throat, uttering a strange broken squeal of distress. Yelland laughed and the punch thrown viciously from blind rage and pain caught him on the cheekbone and sat him down.

'I'll kill you, Wharton,' he said groggily but as he climbed to his feet the poacher bolted.

'Bliddy coward,' Yelland bawled.

A search of the rushes produced a full petrol can.

'Now what was he about with that?' said Yelland, blinking in the kitchen light.

'Petrol burns on water, Reg,' said Revilious. 'What would happen to an otter caught by fire on the surface of the pool? And petrol would poison the water and burn an otter's eyes. But I think he was looking for the holt. Then he would have poured in the petrol from above and chucked in a lighted match.'

'The sod,' Yelland whispered.

'Yes – the sod.'

'Tidn no use phoning the law,' the old man said taking the tumbler of scotch and tipping it into his swollen face. 'Wharton will deny it and the petrol can don't prove a thing. But at least I shifted un. Dang me! – if he idn a prapper ornament. Twenty years ago I would've planted un in the soil.'

'The police will have to be told, Reg. He's made a terrible mess of your face.'

'Don't waste your time, boy – half the CID round here are like that with Charlie Gutteridge.' He folded middle finger over forefinger. 'They go to his parties and wherever Charlie boozes after hours they're tucked away in the corner sipping free ale. I'll have a chat with Steve Wotton down Aishford. OK, he's only a beat bobby but he's honest. Maybe he can whisper in an important ear.'

'And you'll move into Foxcroft for a day or two, Reg. I don't want you on the road after dark.'

'This has got out of hand, Paul. I reckon your mate Charlie has gone off his head. Tidn the otters he's after. It's you.'

'But I'm not running. I won't shift unless Gutteridge burns me out.'

'He's capable of anything, boy. He's riding the devil piggyback to hell.'

'The trouble is men like him are never content to make that journey alone.'

Alice descended on them just as Yelland was beginning an account of his colourful early life on the farm. She was told of Wharton's latest escapade and her comments were coarse and appropriate. Translated into polite English Gutteridge was a castrated, illegitimate monster of dubious morality and diseased stock. The old man laughed until the tears ran over his bruises.

'And that Wharton,' she hissed, 'beating up a pensioner!'

'He idn no snob,' Reg sang, giving her one of his broadest grins.

'What you boys need is friends who can handle themselves. Ted Healey's useful but he's just one bloke.'

'I don't want a full scale war Alice,' Revilious said mildly.

He sat by the fire watching the animals appear and vanish behind the flames. Reg Yelland slept with head on one side, mouth open, breathing hoarsely and mumbling snatches of a drunken monologue. It was strange eavesdropping on another person's dreams. But it was all about dreams. The Christian God might be down on his uppers but the need for larger-than-life superbeings remained. Cadogan had worshipped the Australian batsman Donald Bradman. Thousands followed Elvis Presley, the good-looking lead singers of pop groups or television and soccer stars. Always the search for excellence in others, the craving for the charismatic. Christ's love and humility were no longer enough. The masses wanted new gods in the macho mould, unencumbered by morality, to condone the uncertainty of the age. Even dark evil gods bearing gifts. Christ offered something too personal, something to be explored in silence.

Reg Yelland slept on. Revilious eased the glass from the old man's fingers. Then he stretched and yawned and caught a whiff of Alice's cologne. The room had become stuffy. He opened the door and the owls called from a sky so bright and full of stars it took his breath away. The coombe amplified those thin double-notes, distorting them into a kind of primitive music concrète. Revilious let the roar of the weir sluice his mind. Beyond the garden wall where the blackness reared up and stood against the sky in the silhouettes of trees he sensed an alert presence. The hair was stiffening on his neck.

The barn owls continued to scream but instead of adding to his agitation the cries were comforting and the night no longer crouched around him. He fetched the binoculars and opened a bedroom window above the lawn. It was a compulsive act. His knees had turned to mush before he had brought Horse Wrangler into focus.

The stranger remained perfectly still, like a megalith, Revilious thought. His eyes were watering and he lowered the glasses for a moment. When he pointed them again at the hilltop the figure had gone but the feeling of darkness within darkness persisted. The hall light threw a long, white rectangle onto the lawn and where it ended and night waited the stranger stood with bowed head.

Revilious sailed weightlessly downstairs and tried to enter the drawingroom to wake Yelland. He got as far as the door and peered in and shouted. No sound came from his mouth. The flames stood yellow and unmoving, and the clock on the mantelpiece was silent. Revilious was drawn gently to the front door and out into the garden. The stranger stepped forward but the barn owl glided out of the shadows and screamed. Then the figure was a trembling pillar of moonlight and Revilious was on his knees, pressing his face into the wet grass. The scream rang through him as he came back to the drawingroom, pieces of grass falling from his forehead and mud clinging to his trousers.

'I thought I saw someone on the lawn.'

'Who?' Yelland said. He blearily pushed a log into the fire and turned, puzzled.

'It was too dark to tell. But I'm sure it was a friend.'

The old man yawned and nodded. 'Sometimes I think I see things – people, old mates, my mother. Maybe I do. At times I think I'm sleepwalking, going backwards. There's nothing up front anymore, nothing.'

But I'm not old, Revilious wanted to say. I'm not sleepwalking. Then the pain burst along his collarbone and shoulder and he smiled.

Stubble fires

His resolution strengthened as the evenings drew in and the stubble fires crept across the hills of the South Hams. Even without frost the horsechestnut leaves were yellowing and Revilious was out in the coombe with the binoculars ready to glass anything interesting. The sight of young badgers playing in the entrance of their sett helped him regard his predicament philosophically. The voice inside him no longer brayed 'I'm dying', and the thud of falling apples conjured up a vision of another springtime waiting to explode from the ground at his feet. The worms ate the husk but the seed was indestructible.

So the stubble fires burnt along the edge of darkness, and the starling flocks billowed, contracted and crumbled onto the smoke-shaded fields.

The otter bitch left evidence of her presence on the upper reaches of his river; the sedges of the drying-off places were flat and bleached with constant use, and the sprainting posts displayed fresh droppings. But Skerry had gone and the long dusks of autumn played on Revilious's sorrow. He searched the reed mace by the pond but found only mink scats and fish bones. The pike parading its strength under the surface brought to mind summer nights full of otter activity, and he could not check the tears.

Towards the end of September hot sunlight opened the bush roses along the borders and peacock butterflies brought the

summer briefly alive again in Revilious's garden. He left Yelland beside the pond plotting the pike's downfall and walked to
Aishwell with the intention of attending the Harvest Festival
service. Once through the lych gate his enthusiasm died and he
stood awhile at Bob Maunder's grave where Yelland had placed
a bunch of chrysanthemums. Soon the last of the children had
finished trooping into church and Revilious came and sat on
the bench under the old lime tree. Over the rooftops daws
lifted and fell, and a heron beat slowly through the haze
towards the Aishbourne. Revilious tilted his face to the sun,
half-expecting a miraculous cure. Then the organ picked out
the music of the great autumn hymn which never sounded
hackneyed, and the congregation went at it with gusto.

> We plough the fields and scatter the good seed on the land
> But it is fed and watered by God's almighty hand . . .

The strong Devon accent added something touching to the
hymn's majesty.
Revilious shook his head and smiled. Harvest Home, Harvest
Supper – the ancient pagan rites would not relinquish their
hold on folk imagination.
   'We mustn't let the apples go to waste, Reg,' he said. 'I'd like
them gathered and made into cider.'
   'What about the otters? If you bring in half the female
population of Aishwell to pick 'em up you'll get noise.'
   'Oh we can overcome that, Reg! Keep the ladies out of the
lower fields. And there will be children eager to earn a few
bob.'
   'Ted could bring his tractor and trailer, I s'pose. It might be
feasible if the work force was supervised.'
   'Just the job for a retired farm foreman.'
   'I don't want no wages, Paul. It'd be fun.'
   'And you'll organize things?'
   'Like I used to,' he said quietly.
   'Some things don't change, Reg.'
   'Maybe not,' he murmured without conviction, rubbing his
leg.
   Throughout the week village women were harvesting the
cider apples in the coombe. Yelland made sure they worked
quietly even when they were joined by their children after
school. Revilious was content to remain a peripheral figure and

distance seemed to be expected of him. It was part of his status as landowner-employer.

They shook the trees and picked up the Fox's whelps, Bloody Butchers, Slack-ma-Girdles and Sheeps' Noses in plastic buckets which were then emptied into bags. The full bags stood against the trees and Healey collected them and carried them in his trailer to the gate on the Bullenford road. Sunlight smoked through the branches and the wasps gathered on sacking stained by the dark oozings of the fruit. All Revilious had to do was patrol the Aishbourne and keep the children away from the water.

The work was done and for a while the coombe was strangely dead. He sat on his waterproof waiting for the stranger to rise amongst the hawthorns. But apart from flocks of birds and a solitary brown hare the hilltop remained deserted. Rain returned on the westerly wind, walling in the coombe and swelling the Aishbourne so that it split into field corners and ran khaki and full past the house.

The holt was situated well above the flood level but the grumble and rush of water pouring down off Dartmoor excited Cariad and she thought of Skerry and the games they had played together. Then driven by some unfathomable instinct she deserted her den in Brent Copse and hauled her brood one by one to another holt on Orchard Island under Lower Bowcombe. Here the chamber was concealed by thick blackthorn and willow scrub, and there were three entrances.

The kits' eyes were open and their coats were rougher and a deep chocolate brown with ivory coloured throats and chests. They were still suckling and showed no interest in the outside world. Pressing against their mother they luxuriated in her body heat and took life from her. Once or twice while Cariad hunted Bowcombe Pool, Skerry called to her and she answered with some of the old eagerness.

The dog otter had returned from his wanderings. He had spent several nights killing coarse fish on Slapton Ley before taking to the sea and swimming up the Dart to Hay Creek. Now he was eager to have his mate again but although she played the water games Cariad would not allow him to enter the holt. He slept alone on a couch of bracken, between two rocks at the other end of the island.

The Friesian bull

The rain had stopped and a watery sun was heightening the gold of the maple leaves along the drive. Revilious put on his wellingtons and went to check the pond. The pike glided across the shadows breaking the film of light which raindrops shaken off the surrounding trees had scratched and pitted. He glanced up. The willows were rocking. Pieces of blurred bronze-tinted green were breaking free and dissolving in the sky. A series of random thoughts escaped with a rapidity that attends nervous breakdown. The child hurried out of the news-reel, arms raised, dark sunken eyes staring from under the peaked cap and the Star of David phosphorescent on the front of his grubby overcoat. Warsaw was fragmenting, falling. Where is my human dignity? the old man whispered. The crematorium was sited in a beautiful park. Respectable people with respectable blood were feeding the ducks. Slowly a puff of smoke uncurled from the crematorium chimney and the guard looked down from the watch tower and lit a cigarette. But the child reached up unconcerned and pulled the handle of the fruit machine and the man without a face was slashing un-acceptable sentences out of a book. His razor opened little windows of nothingness in the pages. Full of remorse Cadogan sank to his knees and the hare sniffed his tears. Hare, honey-bee, cat and wolfhound. Why the need to shapeshift unless to deceive or by adopting a more sympathetic form, catch an opponent?

The magpies' harsh complaint rattled through his head and the two birds hung like a pair of crucifixes from the branch. A leaf spiralled down and settled on the young woman's shoulder. 'Where is the boy?' she said. Her burgundy hair swung and loose tresses veiled her breasts. 'The boy.' But the pike broke surface and she smiled and shapeshifted into an otter. Now the bright knife-blade glare of the pond forced Revilious to look away. The oaks along the edge of Big Wood stepped out of shadow and sunlight breathed over them. Rooks peeled from the top branches and floated away. Their cawing nudged the landscape into clarity.

Revilious trod the badger path under the trees. The wood was alive with a myriad small rustlings and the patter of falling leaves. Then the louder noise of undergrowth crackling and breaking sent the goose pimples over his scalp. A dark creature breasted the gloom and moved off through the brambles. Revilious saw the broad sweep of antlers and the back that was human not stag. He ran crouching until the trees parted, and tottered into the orchard. Astonishingly his breathing was normal. Up the hillside where bracken filled the gaps between the apple trees a cock pheasant crowed.

Kevin Piper had a bad cold and after visiting him at the farm Revilious strolled up Horse Wrangler Hill. From the top he could trace the passage of the wintering flocks of birds – the immense clouds of starlings and small flocks of foreign thrushes and wood pigeons. A biblical vision of the world before the Fall emerged from the mist. But Ceridwen the shapeshifter wasn't the Mother of All Living. He had a vivid memory of reading *The Mabinogian* by the gas fire in his room at Cavendish Towers. The heroes, bards, Kings and giants of the long lost Celtic Avalon were given the run of his imagination. Only lip service had been done to Jehovah. Yet outside the eleven stories Cernunnos was defeated by the early Christian missionaries. Cernunnos the horned god, protector of sick and injured animals, had been branded as Satan and driven into the hills of the west. Poor Cernunnos, Mrs Revilious had said, smiling down at Paul. It was her book and she had written her name on the title page.

'Mother,' Revilious whispered.

He gripped the hawthorn twigs and the tree dragged at his spirit as water tugs a dousing stick.

'Mother of All Living.'

Under the grass dead hunters lay and Horse Wrangler Hill was a great uterine dome housing those who had known birth and death. The choking sensation nudged him to the edge of panic but quickly abated leaving him trembling on the summit with rain darkening the distances. The unhappiness of his childhood churned up the stomach pains. Was it necessary for the past to keep taking reprisals? It was like an old wound demanding respect by menaces so that one moved carefully and uncomfortably about the world.

'*Dulce et decorum est pro patria mori*' said the voice, Major Shackle's voice. Revilious let go of the hawthorn twigs and the wind washed over the hill, bending the trees, making them vibrate.

*   *   *

Gutteridge spent most of the morning on the telephone. The recession had ignored his business interests. The simple-minded were still losing money on the horses and the new poor somehow managed to slot cassettes into their hired videos. And children could raise the cash to keep the gaming machines busy.

He put the pocket computer away and glanced out of the window at the weather. The shower was sprinkling its remaining drops on the lawn and a rainbow arched and faded. His girlfriend Val had left him shortly after breakfast. Maybe, he thought, I pushed her too hard considering her talents between the sheets. You didn't get flesh of that quality from the supermarket. Maybe he'd salvage Sandra. Yes, he'd phone his mother-in-law around teatime and soft soap the old bitch. He checked his watch then called to cancel the golf match arranged for mid-afternoon. Councillor Brassley was already in his pocket and required no further sweetening this side of Christmas.

Charlie flicked through the holiday brochure. North Africa or Majorca? he mused. The wind gusted hard and beech leaves were dancing above the garden. Buck lifted his ears and yawned a whine of boredom. Charlie reached for the leashes and both animals dragged themselves across the carpet on their bellies in anticipation of the walk.

'You soft old fellas,' he grinned.

The Cortina Estate sizzled over a road plastered with leaves. Dan had taken the Jag to London and the BMW was at the garage. Charlie sniffed. The old Ford suited his style. He called it the 'cowboy motor' and behind the wheel he was just one of the boys. One of the boys who could afford to grab three weeks in the sun any time he chose.

Majorca or Morocco? A touch of the topless bathing therapy, nubile young Scands, plenty of plonk and fancy grub and mucho bronzo! He grinned into the driving mirror thinking of the difference a tan would make.

The countryside meant very little to him. He was wary of junctions, hidden gateways and lanes which might release animals or vehicles into his path. Charlie was only conscious of those forces affecting him physically for he had no spiritual life. The country was a gymnasium where he could work up a beer thirst hunting or fishing and playing rugby.

Lateral bars of light and shade created a hypnotic effect on the lane but another cloud bank was gathering and rain dropped its curtain. Charlie pulled in and braked and waited for the shower to pass. Then he rubbed at the condensation on the windscreen and lit a cigar. The sky was blue from Horse Wrangler Hill to Dartmoor. Further off more clouds were assembling. Charlie got out and opened the back door for the alsations. There was no need for leashes. If he walked them twenty yards up the lane they could take the public footpath to Bullenford and back. They pranced and pirouetted on stiff, quivering legs.

'Come here,' Charlie said, snapping his fingers but they turned together to flatten under the gate and gallop across a field of heifers. The cattle craned their necks and lowered their heads. The gate was padlocked and barbed wire had been wrapped around the top bar.

'Laddie, Buck,' he called and pursed his lips to whistle.

Pushing through the massed bodies of his paramours the Friesian bull confronted the dogs and pawed the turf, beating the steady rhythm of his rage. Charlie experienced at that moment another loss. A part of himself was ripped out and despatched into darkness. The bull charged, swinging his horns from side to side, exhibiting remarkable speed and balance. Buck tried to dodge but was impaled and hung squirming and yelping on the side of the bull's face. Charlie roared the dog's name as if the sound of his voice could exorcise the horror.

Laddie escaped and crawled whimpering to his master's feet. And the bull gored Buck, his small eyes overflowing with malevolence, tossing the dog time after time and trampling the carcass and nailing it to the ground. The blood of the dog was the colour of the ploughed hillside above the pasture. Gulls speckled the dark, congealed blood of the dead cornfield which the metal had laid bare ready for new life.

'Buck,' Charlie cried.

The bull trotted up to the gate and glared at him. Behind the blood-flecked eyes human hatred stood stark and unashamed.

'No,' Charlie roared. 'No.'

He bundled Laddie into the back of the Estate and gunned the engine. Swerving to the right and left repeatedly the car shot off and the dream of advancing countryside possessed Charlie again. He glanced behind him. Laddie lay whimpering on the floor but Buck had really gone and Laddie was wet, dirty and very frightened.

It did not end there. Alone Charlie Gutteridge brought his brandy to the window unwilling to accept the dream death of his dog. Rain dribbling down the glass had become the burst entrails of the moon. He flung open the windows and the owl sat and stared at him from the sun dial. Charlie's teeth were chattering. The owl's gaze forced him to close the windows and pull the curtains. Then the phone rang but it was someone dialling a wrong number. A couple of days later he flew to Morocco.

Interrogation

The clocks had been put back an hour and the shorter days at the end of October were crisp and sunny with dense early morning mist and some frost. The trees of Foxcroft were suddenly very beautiful, especially the sycamores which stood among the oaks. When Revilious took his daily stroll up and down the coombe the treetops were usually full of starlings. At the edge of the wood the rooks gorged acorns and barn owls winged in to seize the small creatures that fed by night. The faint screech of the birds added to Revilious's enjoyment of the fireside before he switched on the stereo. Had he over-rated Gutteridge? Knowing his enemy was abroad made life easier. What if he had come to his senses? Even a person like him would have his limits. Then what? No, Revilious sighed, I can't see him waving the white flag. He has to slog on or lose face.

'"Vanity of vanities; all is vanity,"' Yelland who had had the Bible knocked into him as a child was emphatically pessimistic. '"As a dog returneth to his vomit, so a fool returneth to his folly,"' the old man asserted. 'Charlie may be absent in body but he's present in malice. Check your mail for letter bombs, Paul.'

Cruising home from the Horridge Inn one night Revilious was stopped by a panda car and breathalized. He had only sunk a half pint so the test proved negative, but the disturbing aspect of the affair was the sight of Dc Nathan in the passenger seat. Two evenings later he was pulled up again and told to blow into the bag. The crystals did not turn green.

'I'm damned if they'll stop me going out for the occasional drink,' he told Yelland. 'I'll walk to The Plough and damn the bikers and the police.'

Yelland kept his thoughts to himself.

The atmosphere at the pub was far from convivial. Revilious went alone on a windy night and had three or four stiff whiskies before the glares and comments became too much. Once outside he panicked and instead of taking the road back to Foxcroft he hurried through the top of the village and walked the open fields, keeping close to the hedges. Presently he heard the roar and snarl of motorbikes and saw headlights flash and swing in the lanes. The riders raced up and down the Bullenford road, massing every so often at the entrance to Foxcroft's drive.

'Oh Christ,' Revilious whispered. He crossed the road as quickly as possible and crawled through the hedge into Top Field a little before a pack of bikers came round the bend. The numbing pain in the upper part of his left arm nearly made him cry out but eventually he saw the drawingroom light and was soon unbuttoning his raincoat in the hall.

So, he thought, coming to the fireside, it's a siege situation. Very well, Mr Gutteridge, let's see if you can winkle me out. It was gratifying to discover he had a stubborn streak but Cavendish Towers had probably provided that.

Hallowe'en and Bonfire Night did not produce the disturbances he and Yelland expected. Gutteridge seemed to have settled in Morocco. It was a puzzling state of affairs but the stealth of autumn varnishing the coombe in browns and golds then stripping it could not be ignored. Revilious was happy although the season carried within its beauty nuances of sadness. Then again, the decay of a landscape – the unleafing and filleting of a place was thrilling to experience. Those dusks closing round the house and the virginia creeper's wine red leaves alive with roosting sparrows brewed their own magic. And Reg Yelland helped. The old man loved to sweep the dead leaves into bonfires and lean on his rake watching the smoke climb from the garden. Striding up the coombe Revilious would glance over his shoulder and see the smoke flattening to a blue haze as it drifted away through the oaks.

The river ran clear once more and Kevin Piper hidden among the bracken in the orchard saw dog and bitch playing in Bowcombe Pool. Their heads poked from the tinfoil sheen and their cries carried a long way. They caught trout but when the dog chivvied his mate and tried to manoeuvre her into the shallows her moan of irritation became a deep, querulous growl. The larger otter backed off wearing that look of baffled embarrassment Kevin had seen on a farm tom's face when it was rebuffed by a she.

Skerry ranged along the Aishbourne checking to see if other males had entered his territory. The river was heavy and the swimming was all life to the otter. He nosed through the sluice and flowed over it and dog-paddled across the pond to the island. Then he spent a whole dusk tidying his kennel. The pond was full of fish and the hunting was good and easy but the pike avoided him and lay hidden in a mat of duckweed.

'He's back on the pond,' said Yelland, kicking off his muddy wellingtons at the door.

'I know, Reg,' Revilious smiled. 'Do you think we've done it?'

'Ask Skerry and Cariad.'

'And Gutteridge?'

Yelland's tongue rattled his dentures and he shrugged. 'Charlie might have changed targets and is aiming at the house, the car, you, me. The bugger's bound to be a bit desperate. Not much has gone right for un.'

Gutteridge came back from North Africa with a new girlfriend whose resemblance to Miss Sweden ended when she opened her mouth. She sounded like a Birmingham barmaid with adenoid trouble. Her 'charms' as Charlie called them were paraded before the enthusiastic rugby club rams at The Plough and her new master was running again in the popularity stakes. But on Saturday evening after a massive home defeat the pub atmosphere was Juliet's tomb and Gutteridge's ineptitude on the wing was discussed unsympathetically.

Soddin' hillbillies, he thought gazing out from the fuzz of his eyelashes. And he had considered giving them new changing rooms! The girl Stephanie gabbled away in his ear and the rugby club chairman and secretary were trying to win back ground the loudmouths had lost. That kind of grovelling amused Charlie. It established a peck order which the young rams would be forced to join when marriage, mortgage and credit repayments ate into their beer money and freedom. Before long the entire committee gathered round him while the foundations of the changing rooms were dug in his bank balance.

'You must be bloody mad,' Dan said when he and his brother were alone in the urinal. 'I wouldn't give a penny to them wankers.'

'I'm not giving them a penny,' Charlie smiled.

'You said – '

'I said, I promised, but I'm not putting my hand in my pocket for a bunch of gormless bloody farmboys. It's a giggle. Words. That's all those wallies have got to splash about. Words.'

'Charlie,' Dan chuckled, 'you are a twenty-four carat gold-plated bastard.'

Drinking after hours was part of the Gutteridge brothers' pub ritual. The Saturday night marathons of dirty joke telling, spoof and raids on the optics were an assault course geared to the size of a man's wallet and resistance to alcohol.

Charlie drank methodically, pacing himself, observing the rapid disintegration of his cronies. Darkness was defeated with the help of sacrifices and for Charlie this was an important victory. Being alone at night was a death. When I die, he told his brothers, I'm going to be cremated. I don't want to be alone in the ground while all the fun is going on above me. Burial was like that – the earth opened a small brown mouth and swallowed you. It was bloody obscene, you down there full of worms and life blasting on like you had never existed.

Then, as he drove home, the unbelievable happened. He was overtaken by a panda car and moments later was swaying in the road clutching a bag of green crystals. Charlie made one mistake after another. He offered money to Pc Wotton and cursed the policeman when he cautioned him, and finally tried to run off. Wotton brought him down hard in the mud and snapped on the handcuffs.

Pupating from nightmare Charlie stared from his hangover at the cell ceiling. Someone was shaking him. He was given back his shoe laces and belt and taken to the lavatory and on to the interview room. His solicitor met him at the door.

'What the hell is this?' Charlie demanded. 'OK – I had a few wets and I got caught – so why the bother?'

Two plain clothes men were waiting to enlighten him.

'Do you know a Ronald Lewis Wharton of 7a Hartley Road, Aishford?' one of them said.

'I've seen him around.'

'Have you had any contact with him during the last day or so?'

'Why?'

'Have you?'

'He said good evenin' sometimes in The Plough.'

'Nothing else?'

'He isn't my type,' Charlie quipped, but coldness was hollowing his guts. The detectives were not local. They were soberly dressed and soft spoken. The taller of the pair was wearing a Remembrance Day poppy in his buttonhole. His name was Madden and he was an Inspector.

'Wharton was caught at Woodburn Barton Farm last night,' he said and Charlie belched. Nothing registered on the faces before him.

'Wharton was tampering with a storage tank full of diesel.'

The skin tightened on Charlie's cheekbones.

'If he had broken the lock and turned on the tap thousands of gallons of diesel would have poured into the Aishbourne.'

'So?' Gutteridge said.

'Wharton claims you put him up to it. You paid him to deliberately pollute the river.'

'Now why would I do that?'

'To get at a certain Paul Revilious of Foxcroft.'

'Do I have to tolerate this crap?' Charlie asked his solicitor.

A document was produced and the solicitor placed a forefinger to his lips.

'There are other claims,' Madden continued.

'But is there any proof?' Charlie said.

'Wharton maintains you paid him to put nets in the Aishbourne with the intention of catching otters. He also swears you hired him to burn out the animals with petrol.'

'A load of bollocks.'

'This statement refers to another occasion when you paid him to go out and shoot otters. But the most serious allegation is that you approached him and offered him money to give Revilious, quote, "physical aggravation".'

'Alleged, claimed, maintains – are you charging me?'

'Not at the moment.'

'Then I'm free to go.'

'Not too far, sir. We'll probably want to have another chat fairly soon. Oh, and while I think of it,' the Inspector said, straightening his tie, 'Eric Prowse and David Widger are in custody.'

'What are you running? – a hostel for dossers?'

'Let's go home, Charles,' said the solicitor.

'But no trips to North Africa,' the policeman said and Charlie's lids descended and the eyeballs flickered.

'Can they do this to me, Roger?' he asked his solicitor from the security of the car.

'It's the tip of the iceberg, Charles,' the portly little man sighed.

'Madden was at pains to tell me three local detectives have been suspended. He gave me their names. Nathan, Sergeant Scrivener and Bates. Mean anything?'

Charlie shook his head. 'Who copped Wharton?'

'A chap called Healey.'

Charlie's eyelashes lifted a centimetre and the eyeballs were shifting again under their blue-veined lids.

How had it come about? he asked himself. The Brummie Venus half-filled two glasses and splashed in generous amounts of angostura. Revilious was actually winning and the old fairy hadn't broken into a sweat. How had he recruited blokes like Healey and that lunatic Trevisick? Not that it mattered. Just a bit more shit to sweep under the mat, Charlie thought. And the filth wouldn't be looking for something spectacularly out of order from Gutteridge Enterprises, not now. Being pulled by Old Bill had set the adrenalin pumping and Charlie enjoyed the sensation. Even if he came out second best it would only cost him a few bob.

Sipping the pink gin he gazed across the lounge. But if Wharton tied him in with anything ugly like polluting rivers he'd be as welcome locally as a fart in a crowded lift. Above the Cornish stone fireplace hung a huge reproduction of Constable's 'Cornfield'. Sandra had said it was real art. Charlie sniffed. Stephanie was a masterpiece. She bulged and curved provocatively like one of those inflatable rubber dolls perverts bought from sex shops. Charlie let the alcohol rime his taste buds. Then he made a clicking sound and Laddie attentively hauled himself from under the settee and stiffened his haunches and yawned.

'Animals bring me out in spots,' Stephanie said.

'Beauty spots,' Charlie purred, laying warm, moist palms on her breasts.

_____ Iachimo's business _____

A week of cloudless skies produced the calmest end to a day Revilious had ever known. Trees stood absolutely still and gradually there was a deepening of tones except on the western horizon which retained its glow long after dark. Leaves broke free and collar doves flew over the garden on creaking wings. Then the far side of the coombe surrendered its detail and mist rose off the river. At first faintly but soon with the brilliance of diamonds, stars crowded the places birds had deserted a few hours earlier. Darkness prompted him to look up and wait for the moon to rise and complete the serenity.

He recalled his first evenings at Foxcroft, his hopes and resolutions and the soul searching. Nature was never enough because it was always viewed from the human condition. Human ugliness always intruded. The horror generated by man rumbled along the margins of history mocking the achievements of the heart and spirit civilizations claim to hold dear. What good is all the culture, he thought, all the soul-life if

the bombs are exploding. Can you have genuine soul-life between the missile silos of Russia and America? Or was art the
only light strong enough to burn on in the abyss?

Then the moon came up and he was overcome by an intense
sadness. Somewhere under those stars political prisoners were
immured within despair. Human beings were dying awful
deaths, tyranny was flourishing and sanity, charity and compassion were refugees. Only when you sifted through the
statistics and looked closely at individual lives could the horror
and pity of it all click into focus. The face of the grieving mother,
the widow too ill with misery to shed tears, the moan of the
terrified child. The sorrow was relentless. Yet he conceded on a
gush of self-hatred that he expected others to act and clean up
the mess. Like everyone else he was looking for the Messiah.
'They', 'Someone' – never 'me'. Opt out and whisper from the
sidelines. Closing his eyes he saw Mozart with less than a year
to live writing begging letters to friends, pleading for tiny sums
of money. Then he thought of the otters who had no vanity and
did not seek acclaim. They were an unconscious celebration of
the living world Man had forsaken. They saw it, heard it,
smelled, breathed and touched it, but did not question it or try to
alter it. Left alone the earth fed its children.

'Do you know what,' Alice said. 'You look like Robert Donat
in that old movie Goodbye Mr Chips.'

'The old Mr Chips, I presume,' Revilious smiled.

'No – when he was up the mountain with Greer Garson.
You've put on weight, Paul.'

'He eats well,' said Kevin Piper.

'Maybe I should start jogging,' Revilious said.

'Or just cut down on the booze,' Yelland observed, but he
leant over and refilled his friend's wine glass.

'To be honest,' said Alice, 'I'd rather have a port and lemon.'

She had cooked the Remembrance Sunday lunch and was
pleased with herself. The slices of beef were thick, lean and
succulent, and the Yorkshire puddings little works of art. The
dinner service and shabby elegance of Foxcroft's diningroom
provided the flourishes necessary to such a meal.

After the caramel they retired to the drawingroom and found
the fire halfway up the chimney. Outside it had begun to drizzle
and the gloom accentuated the cosiness of the hearth. They
sipped brandy and gossiped.

'It's all so lovely and posh,' Alice giggled, gazing round and throwing out her arms. 'Here,' she added, dropping her voice. 'Ted Healey's missus is expectin'. Dunno when he finds time to lift a leg over her. He's out and about like a fox.'

'I'm glad he is or Wharton would have polluted the river from here to Hay Creek,' said Revilious.

'Wharton's one of they blokes who should've been smothered at birth,' Yelland growled.

'Captain Courtenay shares your opinion,' Revilious said. 'I received a letter from him yesterday deploring Wharton's behaviour and recommending a horse whipping for friend Gutteridge. The Aishwell grapevine is pretty effective.'

'Folk whisper in other folk's ears occasionally,' Yelland admitted.

'This time Gutteridge had committed social suicide,' Revilious said. 'But I can't help feeling a little sorry for Wharton and the other blockheads. Iachimo is about his business.'

'Yakkermo can do what he likes,' Yelland said. 'The day horse manure like Wharton, Prowse, Widger and Wayne bloody Steer win my sympathy eggs will grow beards.'

'Paul is suggesting there are degrees of wickedness, Reg,' Kevin smiled.

'Bad buggers and evil buggers,' said Alice. 'Weak buggers and Charlie.'

'I'm praying the press won't get hold of this,' Revilious said. 'We don't want that mob stampeding around Foxcroft.'

'All this over two small wild animals,' Alice said angrily.

'It's not a unique situation,' Kevin said. 'Think of the seal culling, whale hunts, persecution of the golden eagle, osprey and badger, I bet you'll find scores of tales of human heroism and dedication.'

'Sorry, boy – but you're wrong,' said Yelland. 'This is different. Otters have nothing to do with it. Gutteridge idn all there. Old Bob Maunder had un taped and Paul knows how to handle him.'

When the guests had departed, Yelland hobbled up to the bath pretending his knee was 'rheumaticky'. The old man loved hot water and would wallow in it for hours. Yet towards the middle of the evening his age showed and by the time the owls came screeching across the river to quarter the garden he was asleep. Revilious opened the window and the clamour of the weir rushed in on a cool draught of night. I've nothing to offer, he thought. Nothing. I think too much and can't act. Too many thoughts sucking me down into inertia.

He awoke shivering. The bedclothes were in a heap on the floor and the bedside lamp was on. He had nodded off and the paperback lay crumpled under his armpit. Revilious shrugged into his dressing gown and padded to the window. It was dark but the rain had stopped and the greyness creeping across the bottom of the sky hinted at the approach of dawn.

He dressed unhurriedly and went downstairs to make coffee. The pleasant reek of wood smoke hung over the lower part of the house and made his eyes water. He brought the mug to the door and swigged hot Nescafe. Silver and pink suffused the grey and as the clouds began to break up the first smudges of blue materialized. A thrush started to sing but abandoned the idea halfway through its refrain.

The breath caught in Revilious's throat. From the swirl of nausea he heard his own frantic gasping. Then the mug slipped out of his fist and was falling until the click froze the moment and the mug never reached the ground. It was immobilized like everything else in the coombe – the river that had stopped flowing, the hare paralyzed at the centre of its leap, the starling flock like shrapnel holes in the sky. A page from a child's picture book, Revilious thought. But I am a child. Dear Christ, not the little Jewish boy marching with upraised arms! No, some nameless child who belonged on another page. He closed the book and reopened it at random. 'The Wicca weren't wicked. They were wise – the whisperers that spoke to horses. Then the Christian missionaries in love with death and the after-life drove them into the hills and coombes of the South West, calling them witches, and telling the people to shun them.' With the Wicca went the old gods and goddesses – Cernunnos, Ceridwen, the horse goddess Epona, Bran, Arianhod, – all banished to the green secret places. They lurked in the overgrown cider orchards and goyals of Devon, and the mountain valleys of Wales. Kestrel-hued Devon full of birdsong, streamsong, song of the trees; and at dawn and dusk the animal-headed fraternity keeping faith with the old religion, dancing to the rhythms of the seasons.

Ancient realities stared through the dream of modern life waiting to step out and occupy the landscape and the people's consciousness. But something was missing. Something vital.

The mug struck the terrace and shattered, and the sounds and smells of morning flooded back. He was leaning against the wall and the pain was receding from his chest. The thrush took up its song once more and completed it. Revilious crouched and gathered the fragments of broken crockery. Then he went down to the weir and saw a creature coming up the race under the final arm. At first he thought it was an otter but the movements were too jerky and it turned out to be a mink.

Sunlight brushed the crown of Horse Wrangler Hill and Revilious's throat was suddenly dry. He hastened indoors and looked down on the pond. It was a mirror full of sky but his instinct had not betrayed him. Cariad swam out from behind the island followed by her three cubs. The one bringing up the rear seemed to dislike the water and was squeaking loudly. Cariad turned, dipped her head, submerged and surfaced beside the cub. Her chirrup brought the others to her muzzle.

A dark, streamlined shape trailing bubbles passed beneath her and the bitch dived to join her mate. Together they wove the underwater patterns which were an expression of their love of life. Bodies entwined they sported with effortless grace below the facsimile of the oak trees. But the cubs cried for their mother and she abandoned the dog and came to them through a flurry of bubbles. Skerry did not pursue her. He was content to tread water as she fussed over the young. When they hauled out and rolled he hunted eels by the sluice.

Cariad had moved to the island near the house. Sometimes the family lay in a large holt under the willow scrub, brambles and a tangle of fallen blackthorn. Good weather encouraged the animals to sleep on Skerry's bachelor couch. Now the bitch otter rubbed herself against the willow roots and shook the last drops of water from her guard hairs before relaxing to groom her fur until the spikiness vanished. Afterwards the cubs were free to burrow into their mother and form a circle of warmth.

Skerry called to his mate and receiving no answer left the pond and vanished over the weir. Revilious shut his eyes on the joy which was also a recipe for anxiety.

'Nearly there,' he whispered.

He had opened the door of the Ark but a perilous world lay waiting for the young otters beyond Foxcroft. Man had placed his booby traps all over the Garden of Eden, unaware that he was the ultimate victim.

Revilious was eating lunch and failed to hear the car draw up. Inspector Madden introduced himself and his colleague, and they questioned him about his dealings with Nathan, Scrivener and Bates before turning to Gutteridge's campaign of intimidation and menace.

_____ The green robe _____

Revilious scuffed through drifts of oak leaves and the silence closed around him heavy with the spirit of things long gone. Mother of All Living. The pale green shadow of winter wheat lay on some of the hillsides and Kevin Piper going about his solitary business might have been mistaken for one of those Celtic gods shuffling across the land crippled by heartbreak. Then the bubbling song of the starlings rang from all the trees in Big Wood and the din of the flocks coming home to roost blurred to a deafening scream. In another place the cruise missiles had arrived on the Starlifters and the women demonstrating outside the compounds were also screaming.

The constant movement of birds fascinated Revilious. Dark, tightly-packed flocks hastened into the coombes and covered the treetops only to mass again and vanish. He walked the Aishbourne from the estuary to its well-head searching for some clue to the enigma of his own existence. But nature offered only life, and the deaths of creatures were like leaves drifting away on the river. Many great English poets had proposed pantheism yet the river was the only metaphor Revilious needed. It was not a question of *cogito, ergo sum*. It was: I am, therefore I will be. Never in nature was there decay and death without rebirth. So dying had to be just about the most exciting journey anyone could take.

When night fell and the coombe was lit by moon and frost the owls perched on the guttering above the virginia creeper that was rapidly losing its leaves, and spoke to each other. Cariad hunted fish for her cubs. Every once in a while she broke surface with an eel squirming in her jaws and the young swam to meet her, hungry for the sweet flesh. Skerry was permitted to share the sport but he did not carry prey to the cubs. If they swam near him he was gentle yet displayed no paternal instinct and sought only the closeness of their mother. A little later the migrating redwings came crying across the stars to drop exhausted into the trees, and the otters like the man, looked up. The thrushes had flown from the high latitudes to join the fieldfares on kinder countryside than Siberia could offer. It is a privilege, Revilious thought, to be here now in the company of these birds and animals. There was holiness present although it was clothed in darkness. The owls were silent and the weir hushed. All around him the night was stiff with cold.

'Kev's on one of they anti-nuclear demonstrations,' Reg Yelland frowned.

'You don't seem to approve,' said Revilious.

'Tis sheer bliddy exhibitionism.'

'Kevin isn't an exhibitionist. He's one of the most level-headed young men I know.'

'Then why is he mixing with that lot?'

'Maybe he feels deeply about it – about the threat to the future and the possible extinction of life on this planet.'

'You sound like you'm on their side, boy.'

Revilious shook his head sadly. 'No Reg, as usual I'm on the fence. In fact, I've been here so long the crease of my backside runs horizontally.'

Yelland chuckled.

The window was waiting. Looking out over the trees he saw the moon edge up. But the otters did not appear. He had a drink, got into his Solway and went out. Stars flashed and throbbed over Horse Wrangler Hill but Revilious's mind was elsewhere. You grew accustomed to people making decisions for you, and in the end they did your thinking. Then comes the apocalyptic moment. He had gone to Reg Yelland's place one evening to collect the old man and take him for a drink. The television was on, flashing from one glimpse of horror to the next. Rocket fire, Beirut burning, tall blocks of flats buckling at the knees and collapsing, smoke and dust billowing up. Such chaos – the fires, sirens wailing, children shrieking, the planes making their strikes. Such pain and lamentation but Reg chattered on about his garden and troublesome moles as he buttoned himself into his gabardine. No wonder the old deities ran away and hid! Ceridwen, otter woman, brown hare, hawk, owl and fox. In dying she purchased life, soul-shifted, and her living was a game of chess with thirty-two queens. Take this one and that one and there's always one left rendered helpless by the lack of an adversary. She would stand immobile until a new game was set up. Revilious smiled. He was glad the figure had missed its entrance.

The dog fox barked once, twice, three times then repeated the sequence over and over until in the sudden fall of silence the vixen screamed. From these verbal exchanges he supposed their courtship flourished. It was the language of those shadowy beings seen by the very young, the old and the sick when sensibility nudges intellect to one side and the wonder of the world pounces.

Revilious returned to the house and the phone rang. Gutteridge had been drinking.

'Listen,' he whispered. 'I'm going to give you real aggravation.'

'Why?' Revilious said.

'Aggravation. Physical aggravation.'

'You sound desperate.'

'Oh you patronizing bastard,' the voice crooned. 'I can't wait to put the boot in.'

'But it won't be one of your size tens, will it?'

'Right in until the shit and blood squirt out your ears.'

Revilious was shaking but could not drop the receiver. Gutteridge wanted that.

'Have you got the message? Aggravation.'

'I take it as a compliment that you hate me,' Revilious said.

'In the end when they're wiring up your jaw and stuffing your lungs back in your ribcage all you'll want to do is scream.'

There was a click and the phone went dead.

Three times that night it rang and the frosty whisper breathed threats and obscenities in Revilious's ear. Eventually he called Constable Wotton and took the receiver off the hook.

About mid-morning of the next day Inspector Madden and a detective constable were on his doorstep. He seated them in the drawingroom and needed no encouragement to talk about his miserable night.

'I've spoken to Gutteridge, sir,' said Madden. 'He denies making the calls. He says if there were someone on your phone it must have been a nut impersonating him.'

'That's ridiculous! Why would anyone impersonate him to get at me?'

Madden shrugged. 'It wouldn't seem so straightforward in court. But I don't think you'll get another call.'

'Do you believe me, Inspector?'

'Yes, Mr Revilious. I believe Gutteridge is guilty of threatening behaviour amongst other things. He's giving you a rough time, isn't he sir?'

'He's trying to,' said Revilious. 'The quicker you put him behind bars the better.'

'It won't be that simple,' Madden said. 'He's rich and even if we nail him he'll bring a gang of smart-ass lawyers down from the Midlands.'

'And get away with it all?'

'Get off lightly, perhaps – unless, of course, he becomes directly involved.'

'Which he won't. The phone calls are the closest he'll stray to actual participation,' said Revilious.

'Have you any idea why he's pushing it even though we're in the middle of an investigation which could dump him in very serious trouble? You haven't crossed him have you sir? – before you came to Foxcroft, I mean.'

'No, Inspector. I've done nothing. You'll be more skilled than I am at unravelling the irrational.'

'Don't you believe it, sir,' Madden smiled.

Something was missing. The sun filtered through one of those mists which proclaim a fine, fresh day and the hill was hardening in the sky. Now behind the tracery of hawthorn branches he saw the dark green robe and the wine-coloured hair but the stranger's head was lowered. On an impulse he fetched Yelland and gave him the binoculars.

'The top of Horse Wrangler, Reg. Tell me what you see.'

'Trees, grass, a hare, sky.' Yelland murmured. 'What am I supposed to see?'

The binoculars were passed back and Revilious eagerly glassed the thorns. The figure had vanished and the hare sat up on its haunches.

'A bird, Reg. I saw a bird, one I couldn't identify.'

'Probably a tawny owl,' said the old man. 'People see 'em by day and get confused because they'm usually out and about after dark.'

Revilious set off alone to the hilltop and searched the grass for footprints but there were none. The day was marvellously bright, and mist rose from valleys right across the South Hams. The hills stood out like islands. Flocks of birds passed to and fro on mysterious errands and he turned and looked into the coombe. The last shreds of mist floated away and the river ran silver among the dark skeletons of trees.

The stranger stood deep in the water at Forders, her green robe spreading about her and her lovely wine red hair falling to her waist. She was young and beautiful but her face had a hardness about it and her eyes had never held a glimmer of pity. While he watched she sank below the surface and for a while her robe was visible floating like a mass of green duckweed. Then even the dark blood stain of her hair was gone and the final swirl was smoothed quickly away by the river.

Masks and animal heads

Breakfast over Revilious walked round the garden and discovered three snowdrops in the grass at the bottom of the lawn. He asked Yelland if it were normal and the old man said it was. A missel thrush sang from the drystone wall. The rain of the previous day had turned to sleet but the showers were dying out.

Revilious had some letters to post and chose to go alone over the field to Aishwell. Coming down the hill past the church he was aware of being followed and glancing back saw the leather jackets free-wheeling astride their yellow Suzuki trail bikes. They rode straight at him but swerved when collision seemed inevitable and swept on to turn into the square.

There were other bikers lined up outside the pub, sitting aggressively on their machines. No one spoke or moved until he had passed and rounded the corner. Then the engines were pumped into life and their noise pulsed between the hills, rising and falling in a menacing growl. Revilious entered the post office and bought the stamps. Behind the mesh the old lady stared dispassionately out of her myopia. The jam-jar bottom lenses of her spectacles presented him with a pair of enormous unblinking eyes. As the envelopes clattered into the letterbox silence returned.

He stalked home and slammed on a record, glad Yelland was visiting Kevin Piper and the house was empty. Beethoven's Fifth echoed his defiance and also set him giggling. He was hopeless when it came to heroic stances. Inexplicably his mind went back to his student days in Dublin. He had read Yeats's *Easter 1916* under a lamp in the autumn rain, shielding the book of verse with his hand. And Trailer's girlfriend thought the tears were just dribbles of rain. There were so many beautiful marble angels peeping over the cemetery walls all the way to Dun Loaghaire. The Irish knew how to celebrate death in style. A Celtic facility! God – but he'd been happy and he was happy now under the anger.

Revilious switched off the stereo and the cawing of rooks carried through the house. Yet moving about the room he felt again that sense of incompleteness. It was tempting to regard it as a simple need for love and companionship and turn to Alice.

'Vile macho,' he smiled.

He'd taken Jane Wensley to see a Bardot movie at a cinema in Bristol but it hadn't helped the romance. Why were athletic people generally so good looking? Trailer played rugby and was fast over the 440 and half-mile. He had perfect teeth and the physique of Tarzan. Trailer made Jane pregnant and paid through the nose for the abortion. Good looking people often led such messy lives.

Upstairs he wondered if his private audience with the otters was a sort of confessional . The cubs were hunting the margins of the pond in the furrow left by their mother. The sun was down but the western sky still held some of its gold. What was missing? What? He dug his nails into his palms.

'A roebuck came out of Hazard Copse this morning,' Kevin said. 'And I can't remember seeing so many magpies in the coombe. Seven in one tree, Paul!

'Bloody pests,' Yelland said.

'I like crows,' Revilious said absently.

'They'm a bit better than gulls,' the old man conceded.

'Why are we at war with nature, Reg?' Revilious asked.

'There idn a lot of room on the planet, boy. We'm competing.'

Nearly seventy years in the twentieth century, Revilious thought, and he still thinks like a medieval peasant. How could the differences be bridged? Revilious was light-headed. Ready for the chop, he chuckled to himself. A couple of large whiskies before the gallows.

Alice phoned and asked, quite out of character, if it were convenient for her to come over. He had a bath, washed his hair and clipped his moustache. Above the plum-coloured haze the dog star gleamed and then the white owls were screeching and the deafening chorus of the starlings rang through Big Wood. Trees melted into dusk and the owls continued calling to each other in a language as old as the river. A great golden-red moon came up and Revilious remarked on its beauty. Alice and Kevin had opened an ordnance survey map and Yelland was in the kitchen waiting for the kettle to boil. The clock ticked, the logs shifted, flames leapt and died and leapt again. But something was missing. He sighed and snapped his fingers. Alice glanced up and smiled. The wine red hair swung through the mist like the sun and dissolved.

The motor bikes roared. Revilious went outside and saw headlights flashing against the far hillside. Then the din ceased and the lights went out.

'Noisy devils,' said Alice.

'National Service would knock some sense into 'em,' Yelland grunted. 'They'm a bliddy menace.'

'If the tea's in the pot, Reg, I'll take a stroll down to the weir while it brews,' Revilious said, unwilling to surrender to small talk.

Stooping under the apple boughs he brought a spider's web away on his head. The gossamer clung to his face and he beat at it with a little shudder of revulsion. The pulsing of the weir rose from the darkness. Raising his eyes he saw a beam of light shoot across Westerland and the snarl of a trail-bike kicking into life came as no surprise. Slowly back and forth over the field went the machine, challenging me, he thought. And how would an otter with cubs react to all that noise?

He forded the river and blundered through Ley Brake into Old Bethlehem. Yelland called after him, from the dream of the house and the remoteness of the future. Revilious began to run until the hedge brought him up sharply. Clouds covered the moon. The gate was somewhere to his right but a gap in the hazels let him through. Less than thirty yards away the trail-bike was belching noise.

He came slithering and stumbling up the field until he was level with the machine. It turned slowly and stopped, holding him in the headlight glare. Revilious raised a fist but the gesture seemed comically impotent.

Without warning an explosion of light and noise erupted from the darkness and he was trapped in a ring of machines which the riders were revving up to an ear-splitting roar. Revilious pressed his hands to his ears. Nose to tail now the trail-bikes circled him and the final piece of the jigsaw slotted home.

The shock of excitement left no room for other emotions. From the thunder of hooves came the grunt and scream of the ponies and the shouts of their riders. They had lit a bonfire on Horse Wrangler Hill and figures were dancing around it to the drums. But he was the one, honoured above all others beneath the plaited manes and swords of bronze, the masks and animal heads. Catching the torch light the swords whirled and sang in the warriors' fists. Something hard caught his hip and he staggered and dropped to his knees. A blade flashed and opened his forehead. Blood welled and dripped from his nose and chin. Into the earth crowed the voice he had once owned. The Covenant. Smell of soil and grass and blood. Yes, yes it had to be, for the hunters were no longer sleeping under the grass on the hill and he was no longer a man.

He sprawled on his back and the moon shone once more.

The faces were savage but not cruel. Blind with tears he waited and the roaring tribe urged him on to the dark cavern where he would plead their cause. The field moved beneath his shoulder blades and he stared up into the bewildered eyes of the horses. Warrior faces daubed with vertical streaks of black and white to borrow the fierceness of the badger boar. Fox mask, wolf, antlers of red deer stag strapped to the head thrown back in ecstasy. Blood trickled through his hair into the grass. The riders had dismounted and were gathering around him, naked as in war and chanting. His nostrils caught their body smell. Then the blades descended and his chest was full of pain. Light expanded, flickered and faded and he followed his blood down into darkness.

'He's dead,' the leather jacket gasped. 'For Christ's sake! – you killed him.'

They cut their engines and the hush held the bleak whisper of the wind.

'I only gave him a knock with my knee,' Wayne Steer said. 'Then the tip of my handlebar caught his head. Twadn enough to kill a dog. It was an accident.'

Yelland and Alice pushed through the crowd of youths and bent over the body.

'Bastards,' the old man cried. 'Bastards.'

'It was just a joke,' someone said. 'We were going to buzz him for a bit then shoot off down the river.'

'A joke.' Yelland passed his hands across his face and swallowed.

'And Gutteridge put you lot up to this?' Alice said. She stared fiercely about her and repeated the question. Then she lurched forward and brought the back of her hand across Steer's face.

'Well – big man?' she hissed.

He hung his head but the knuckles gleamed white on the hands clenching the crash helmet to his chest.

'Gutteridge gave us a tenner each to ride over Foxcroft and take the piss out of – out of,' the boy's voice broke. 'I didn mean to kill un. God's honour, Alice – I didn mean to.'

'We were supposed to make a lot of noise,' said another voice. 'Use the coombe as a scramble course.'

'And the otters would go,' Alice whispered. 'Anyway, the police will be here in a minute and you can yap to them.'

'Nothing was meant to happen to the bloke.'

'Cover him up,' Yelland said. 'I idn going to have him lyin' there staring at the sky like that.'

He knelt beside Revilious. Across the dead man's forehead was a graze that ended in a small cut. The lifeless eyes stared past him and as Yelland stretched out a hand to close the lids he began to sob.

In the island holt the she cub stirred and whimpered but Cariad laid her muzzle on the cub's neck and drew her tongue over the small ears. Much later Skerry returned from Hay Creek and played alone in the weir that was full of the broken moon. His whistling was clear and poignant and coming into the garden for a breath of fresh air Yelland stood listening and remembering while the tears flowed.

Events took them over. The police and the doctor arrived and a little square was fenced off on Westerland. The bikers were removed for questioning and Yelland could hear voices rasping over the radios of the police cars that gleamed beside the house with their doors open. The aftermath of tragedy had its own inevitability as if the events leading up to it were a dress rehearsal.

The media people descended on Foxcroft and the papers were full of accounts which were more imaginative than accurate. But gradually the story of Paul Revilious's attempt to provide breeding space for a couple of wild otters emerged, and the interest of the nation was focused on the Devon coombe. Dismayed by the flood of sightseers Kevin persuaded Morgan to go on television and beg the public to stay away. Local support mustered by Healey and Trevisick made sure no one got onto the estate but for a while Foxcroft was under seige.

Then the rain came murmuring incessantly from an Atlantic sea mist and the trouble at the nuclear missile bases shifted attention elsewhere. Wayne Steer was relieved to learn Revilious had died of heart failure but he stayed out of the village on the day of the funeral.

It was a quiet intimate occasion. The rain sodden gloom pressed down and a scattering of black figures stood under their umbrellas among the headstones and tombs. And when it was over Revilious's friends gathered round the table in the drawingroom for the reading of the will.

Alice received the Fiat and a large sum of money, and Ted Healey was presented with Drang and five thousand pounds. The legacy left to Reg Yelland was half-expected because Revilious had dropped a few hints. But the old man had forgotten their chat about a world cruise. Bertish sprang it on him. Arrangements had been made for him 'to do his Ulysses thing'.

'His words,' Yelland said softly, and he broke down.

Everyone who had helped the Foxcroft project was remembered – Morgan, Copeland, Trevisick and of course, Kevin Piper. The young man inherited the estate and all its problems but Yelland knew Revilious's dream had been passed on to a kindred spirit.

Bertish incanted the various bequests to trusts and other worthy causes. The scrawny little solicitor in his navy-blue suit and highly polished black shoes smelled strongly of shaving soap and cough sweets. He was too clean, too well turned-out for Yelland's palate. As soon as he had gone Alice opened a window and breathed a sigh of relief.

'I didn't know Paul had a heart condition,' said Kevin. 'It was killing him but he never spoke about it.'

'Never said a word,' Yelland whispered. 'We had to wait for the bloody post mortem to put us in the picture.'

'Oddly enough there are no tablets,' Kevin continued. 'I looked everywhere.'

'Meaning?' said Alice.

'Perhaps he didn't care too much about himself or what happened to him.'

Yelland nodded. 'Bob Maunder wanted to die. But Bob had lost something and had to go and find it.'

'I think Paul just came to terms with things,' Alice said briskly. 'He didn want us making a fuss. Pills couldn't cure him, so –' she lifted her shoulders and let them drop.

At last the rain was pushed away by an east wind. Stars shone once more over the coombe. They blazed from the otter's eyes and twinkled in the pond and Reg Yelland carried his grief down to the fireside. On the mantelpiece stood a framed photograph of a youth wearing a duffel coat and college scarf. Had Revilious ever been that young? What was a human life when you took a backward glance at it? The photo of your dog could set your heart aching. Yelland saw his mother and father shopping in the Home & Colonial. Always serious if they were spending money. What else? Something left over from schooldays, a bit of fun, a bit of love, a little joy, lots of hard work, then old age – on the shelf. The disc jockeys and teenagers made sure of that. The bloody youngsters stole the world from under your feet.

The telephone bell fetched him to the hall.

'Who is it?' he growled.

'A friend, Reggie.'

'Who?'

'The war is still on. Why not leg it while you can still walk? Have you tried walkin' without kneecaps? I know someone who blows off naughty old boys' kneecaps with a shotgun.'

'You mazed bugger,' Yelland said hoarsely.

'Move out of Foxcroft or I'll put you in a wheelchair.'

'Bliddy try, boy – bliddy try.'

'How's your mate Paul, Reggie?'

'You – you –' the old man choked. The receiver slipped out of his hand and clattered to the floor.

'Reginald,' the voice said. 'The war isn't over.'

'But why?' Kevin said, frowning into the fire. They had eaten supper and pulled the armchairs up against the hearth. Spots of golden light twinkled on his glasses.

'Inspector Madden came round while you were up the farm,' Yelland said. 'They can't pin very much on Gutteridge. That ornament Wayne Steer assumed Charlie paid them to ride all over Foxcroft. In actual fact a bloke he'd never seen before approached un in The Plough and set things up. A bloke with a Birmingham accent.'

'It doesn't answer my question, Reg. Why is the war still on? It can't be for the sake of his damned holiday village scheme.'

'I'll ask Charlie,' Yelland said simply. 'He'll be in the pub. He always is on Friday nights. The sods still drink with him.'

The walk along the glistening lane did little to sweeten his temper. He was an old man, lonely and tired, pushing though darkness and trying to puzzle it all out.

'Bloody old,' he grated. 'Something you'll never be, Paul.'

The barn owl swung over him, spread its wings and flopped clumsily down onto the gate. Yelland glared at the bird and plodded on. Then he stopped and cried: 'This is my bit of the world, Gutteridge. You won't run me off it.'

His wife would have said the cider was talking. All sorts of things talk through you, he thought. That was Paul's theory. But he was a little drunk and too sick and weary to go anywhere except Foxcroft. He retraced his steps and the owl gazed thoughtfully after him.

'You were quick,' Kevin smiled.

'I'm knackered, son,' the old man groaned. 'This business has really done me in.'

'Go on your cruise. We may not have a world to cruise around tomorrow. Have a rest.'

'Maybe when we've seen off the bugger I'll seriously consider it. I'd like to drink Paul's health under the Statue of Liberty.'

But the Gutteridges gave The Plough a miss that Friday night and Mike Trevisick drank morosely by himself. His violent intentions would have to be shelved until he met Charlie or Dan some dark night, preferably in a lonely place. Clearing away the glasses the landlord saw blood in the postman's eyes which reminded him of the eyes of Piper's Friesian bull.

*   *   *

Charlie Gutteridge took on the police with something resembling enthusiasm. Wharton might prove a problem but Nos and Widger could be leaned on and the biker incident would never be laid at his doorstep. He was not distressed by his current unpopularity. Once he had Foxcroft he'd work on a new image. Allow the hunt onto the estate, he thought. And the rugby club could have the changing rooms after all. Charlie's appreciation of human frailty surprised even himself. He needed good publicity and a few of his bent journalist friends would see to that.

Running the Ronson automatic over his chin he wondered what sort of money was required to tempt Wharton to perjure himself. Nathan was OK. His bosses were nailing him for taking back-handers off anyone who could afford it. The landlord of The Plough and other publicans specializing in after hours trade were paying him wages. Nathan was going to get sacked and five hundred quid under the table would brighten his redundancy.

Charlie's reflection grinned back at him from the shaving mirror. It was a giggle. Then he remembered he was up before the Bench on Tuesday. He could kiss his driving licence goodbye but the barrister was confident they would screw the other charges. Emotional stress! Christ! Emotional stress brought about by his wife leaving him.

'Did you pack the talc?' he asked watching Stephanie sling the holdall in the back of the Cortina.

'Talc, body spray, jockstrap – the lot,' she said, climbing in beside him. 'And I cleaned your boots.'

'You're like mother.'

'After what you did last night I hope not. Hark at old Laddie. He hates being left behind. God – don't he howl!'

Charlie laughed and gunned the engine. His left hand had gone dead. He rubbed the scar and thought of the otter and the sound its teeth had made crunching through his flesh and bone.

Aishwell were playing away to Bovey Tracey. Charlie had been looking forward to the game all week. The second most important thing in life was being 'one of the boys'. Being one of the boys and hoisting yourself up the social ladder. As soon as he was lord of the manor he'd spread some bread around, throw a few parties, make dicks like Captain Courtenay bend or move over. Then Alice Larkin came to mind and the colour burnt in his face. He'd stitch her up. That dyke was high on the list.

Dan and a team mate were waiting by Totnes police station.

'George says Garry Westaway's out,' Dan yawned.

'How come?' said Charlie.

'He was pissed last night and got picked up by the law,' said George. 'If you go clubbing in Torbay and try to drive home along the pavement at three o'clock you're asking for trouble. Garry got it.'

'Who's fly half?'

'Young David Hayman. The one with the beer gut and slippery fingers.'

'Jesus,' Charlie breathed.

The sunshine and hazy blue sky were conspiring to construct the sort of Saturday he felt he deserved. When Foxcroft was his he'd go out before breakfast and blast a brace of pheasants. Or an otter. His eyelids descended. Give it both barrels and dump it on Revilious's grave for that sour-gutted old dosser Yelland to find. Colin wouldn't approve. Him and Karen cared about animals.

His upper lip curled and he took the Cortina off the motorway at the roundabout and turned left onto the Bovey Straights. The two miles of fast country road cut directly through birch scrub and the expanding industrial estate to the town on the edge of Dartmoor. Charlie put his foot down and shot past a Volvo. Dan smiled. The needle on the speedometer touched 75 and the steering wheel was juddering in Charlie's fists. Immediately ahead a couple of cars jockeyed to overtake a large van. There was a series of clicks in Charlie's brain like a computer setting something irrevocably in motion. He accelerated and swung out. The road was clear and the Cortina was doing as it was told but the van driver was also in a hurry. Now Stephanie could read the words printed on the side of the vehicle. 'Morena Van Hire, Brixham'.

Then the van swerved hard to the right and Charlie jerked the wheel and did not brake. His reactions were brilliant but the van was skidding and slewing broadside in his path. For Charlie free will and time had been eradicated. Like a kamikaze pilot he sat transfixed, aware of impending doom yet remaining detached from it, knowing it could not be happening to him. Dying only happened to other people.

Striking the low mound of the verge the Cortina became airborne and turned over in mid-flight before smashing into the trees and disintegrating.

An upside down world, Charlie thought, gazing placidly through the fog. A numb white silence engulfed him, like the white satin lining a coffin. A white coffin, obscenely perfumed. I'm alive, he screamed and the undertakers bent over him. Something dark descended on his face. Don't close the lid, he screamed. I'm alive. Alive. The scream corkscrewed out of numbness and the lid came down silently to seal him within a capsule of deeper silence where his brain buzzed like a trapped wasp.

'He must have been doing eighty,' the woman said. She sat on the bonnet of her Volvo and closed her hands gratefully around the plastic cup of coffee the policeman had given her.

'But he could have got away with it if the van hadn't pulled out and skidded.'

'The van driver's still in a state of shock,' the traffic policeman said. 'He's really groggy. I've never seen a bloke shake like that.'

'Was it a blow-out?'

'No – a bird, a magpie. He had the wipers going to clean some muck off his windscreen when this magpie slams into it and gets the feathers of one of its wings stuck under the wiper right in front of him. He watched the bird, not the road and was suddenly all over the place.'

'How awful,' she whispered. 'I didn't go up to the car because I knew no one could have survived. It looked like it had been blown up.'

'The three passengers were killed outright but the driver was conscious when they cut him free. There was talcum powder everywhere. He was covered in it.'

'And he's alive! My God, he's lucky!'

'I wouldn't say that, ma'am. His back is so badly broken he'll be paralyzed for life from the neck down if the trip to Torbay Hospital doesn't kill him.'

With blue light flashing and siren starting to wail the ambulance did a three-point turn and roared off up the Straights. The draught of its passing set a handful of black and white feathers dancing along the road. Then another ambulance was catterwauling and the Entonox steered Charlie gently through trauma.

Dimpsey

The pond was empty. One evening Cariad led the cubs from the coombe to hunt quiet reaches of the River Avon. Skerry was forgotten and the old holt sites abandoned for her blood was wise and she was playing the survival game. Soon the shadows of the Foxcroft summer faded from her knowing and she was part of what was to be.

The autumn salmon run up the Dart to the spawning beds had finished but Skerry continued to catch feeble cock fish. He ranged from the East to the West Dart and the River Swincombe, and was seen only by crows and buzzards. The high wilderness gave back echoes of his excitement and the water-life had never been sweeter. But sometimes as he curled into sleep under the bracken he felt the tug of the old, quiet place where the hunting had been rich.

At dimpsey the brown hare was on Horse Wrangler Hill with dew beading its whiskers and some of the evening's serenity in its eyes. Sitting beneath the hawthorns it gazed down upon the coombe. Smoke climbed from the chimney of Foxcroft and a light shone in an upstairs room. Then the winter moths were dancing and the foxes began to bark.

Reg Yelland leaned over the parapet of Woodburn Bridge and saw a swirl with a tail glide out from under the arch below and undulate upstream. Beyond the pig shelters at the bend of the river Skerry surfaced but did not whistle.

The old man smiled and the river ran away to a silence full of the past.